I0678503

Gray Skies, Concrete Dreams

By Milo Denison

Copyright © 2023 Milo Denison

Updated 2025

All rights reserved

Fervorfish Publishing

1420 NW Gilman Blvd. Ste. 2351

Issaquah, WA 98027

ISBN:

978-1-7324479-3-6

This book is a work of fiction, and, except in the case of historical fact, any resemblance to an actual person living or dead, is purely coincidental.

All rights reserved. No part of this publication may be reproduced, distributed or transmitted in any form or by any means, including photocopying, recording, or other electronic or mechanical methods, without the prior written permission of the publisher, except in the case of brief quotations embodied in critical reviews and certain other noncommercial uses permitted by copyright law.

1

When Kai messaged me about meeting him tonight, saying he was 'out with the girls,' this is not what I had in mind. I find myself sitting on the floor of a small studio apartment in an outdated building on First Hill, sipping a warm Coors Light and waiting on some new friend of his to finish deciding what shirt to wear. Despite the variety of options hanging in the closet, he can't seem to make up his mind. The room has a mattress on the floor, covered in clothing that I expect will be pushed to the carpet rather than hung back in the closet. Dirty dishes litter the space and a TV is placed on a small stand with a PlayStation 3 plugged into it. I was ready to leave as soon as I arrived.

Kai leans back in a small wooden chair, the room's lone piece of furniture. It creaks, resentful, under the weight of his muscular body, which is impressive, considering almost every night he is out at some party or club. Yet, most everyday he manages to be up early in the morning for a visit to the gym before work, giving him the look of an Asian MMA fighter without the telltale sign of cauliflower ears. However, the only time I know of him getting into an actual fight was once in high school, and it didn't last long. As soon as the other kid got kicked in the nuts, the fight was over.

"That burgundy shirt definitely suits you," Kai offers as Percy tries on a tight short-sleeved button-up shirt, prepping himself as if he were about to compete on Dancing with the Stars. "But of course, you look stunning in anything, darling," he continues.

"And my ass doesn't look too big?" Percy, the guy who seems to care more about his wardrobe than his living environment, asks.

He turns around after giving the front of the shirt a French tuck. Kai whistles in response.

I roll my eyes.

"Where's the bathroom?" I ask, having lost interest in the show.

"Down at the end of the hall," Percy points.

Leaving his room back through the corridor, I'm hit with the musty smell of mold radiating up from the worn red carpet underneath my feet that greeted us when we arrived. At some point in history, this must have been an elegant building. Crown molding still lines the edge of the walls and ceiling, the contours virtually hidden by multiple generations of paint. The lobby entrance has some of the woodwork still in place, around what was once the check-in desk of the former hotel turned into run-down apartments.

Stepping into the bathroom apparently shared by everyone on this floor, the air is heavy and warm from a recent shower, reminding me of my college dorm. The open window doesn't seem to be doing much to improve the ventilation. I turn and lock the door behind me before taking out one of the spliffs I stashed in my pack of cigarettes, light it, then take a deep drag and exhale out the window.

I don't have much knowledge about antiques, but it occurs to me, as I'm pissing into it, that this toilet could be worth some money for an antique dealer.

Percy had better be ready when I get back.

The first stop is a small bar called Triage. The decor is black with black accents, and the place is lightly populated with a crowd of guys who most likely frown at any woman who makes the mistake of entering *their* space. We meet up with another one of Kai's friends, who orders a round of Jäger shots for us all, which I follow up with a Jack and Coke for myself. The bartender knows how to pour a drink – ice, mostly whiskey, and a dash of Coke for color. Kai's friend – 'Mr. Shots,' as I've decided to call him in my head – is short and stocky, like a bulldog. And I'm pretty sure I've met him before, but since he doesn't say anything, neither do I.

After finishing our drinks, our little group strolls a few blocks to a nearby dance club. The music bounces from inside, beckoning people from the street. We enter the club and pass the dance floor with a dozen or so dancers. Plenty of space for more to join as the night continues. To the left we climb a set of stairs to an upper level, to a table where two totally fuckable Asian women are seated as if ordered from an exotic catalog.

"Hey giiiirl!" Kai announces as we walk up.

The girls stand in unison, and he gives the first a big hug.

"Mira, girl, let's check you out," he continues while having her spin. "OMG, you look gorgeous in that dress!"

The spinning one is wearing a tight black off-the-shoulder short dress, with heels so long I'm impressed she can walk. The other is also dolled up in a way that says she must have spent an hour or more preparing herself before leaving her house. She is wearing tight red leather pants and a white blouse top. Her black hair is brushed straight past her shoulders with not a single strand out of place. She is possibly slightly taller than the first. It's hard to tell since she is also wearing heels. Kai goes around the group doing introductions. They are introduced as Mira and Anna, but they could easily have been introduced as generic high-maintenance party girl in a dress, and generic high-maintenance party girl in leather. High maintenance isn't really my type, but of course I'm always willing to make an exception. If one of them were to give the word, I'd gladly toss her over my shoulder and take her home for some proper grunting to satisfy the caveman within me.

We all sit down and order a round of drinks. Annoyingly, I'm stuck sitting between Percy and Mr. Shots, who keeps trying to engage me in conversation with questions like, "How straight are you?" and "How do you know you won't like it if you don't try it?" All of which he does after buying another round of shots for the table.

The dance music is blaring so that he must lean close to ask these questions. He's annoying, but honestly, I take it as a bit of a compliment.

"Look dude, I've been so drunk I could barely walk, and never did I think to myself, 'Hmm, I'd like to suck a dick.' However, no matter how sober or drunk I am, I would happily bury my face between the thighs of either of those girls," I say, referring to the two girls on the opposite side of the table.

He scrunches his face at the idea of going down on a girl. "Eww."

"But hey, if you want to keep buying me drinks thinking that it's going to loosen my butthole, go for it. I don't mind drinking for free."

He is clearly offended, turning his attention towards the other side of the table where Kai and the girls are chatting. Predictably, their conversation is not worth paying any attention to, something about Britney Spears' father.

"I'm going to get another drink," I say, to get away from Mr. Shots, and since it doesn't look like he will be buying me any more drinks.

The bar is crowded but I squeeze to the counter to order another Jack and Coke, then move towards the edge of the dance floor.

Blinking a few times to clear up my vision, with the shots and whiskey working their magic, I scan the dance floor for any potential opportunities. Next to me is a douchebag in a pink sleeveless muscle shirt, with sunglasses propped up on the top of his gelled hair, bobbing his head to the music, wafts of the cologne he bathed in excreting from him. He is probably thinking he has better chances with women here than at a straight club. He looks over at me and nods, as if I'm like him. I turn away, so he knows to piss off. We are not alike.

It is not long before we all find ourselves on the dance floor. I'm attempting to get as close as I can to Mira, or perhaps it's Anna. I forget which is which at this point. Trying to lose myself in the beat of the music on the dance floor, I edge closer, attempting to sway my hips in sync with hers.

"So, how do you know Kai?" I lean in and ask, not really caring about the answer, using the question as an excuse to move closer.

"He was the MC at my fashion show. I'm a designer. What about you? Are you his fag stag?"

"Actually, we've known each other since high school. However, since I just met you, you must be his latest *fag hag*?" I reply. "They come and go with him."

She shoots me a glare before pivoting to dance alongside her friend and the others who are nearby.

"What, you can dish it but can't take it?"

Whether she heard me or not is irrelevant; I'm not that desperate. Plus, this place sucks anyway. The girls are snotty bitches, and truthfully, even if I hook up with one, she'll probably just lay there like a boring pillow princess – not worth the effort. I walk away, then grab my coat to head outside for a smoke.

A short line has formed in front of the club. The women are shivering in their high heels that they will later complain about wearing, and the guys are looking forward to a drink and the possibility that those heels will end up on their bedroom floor. At least the straight guys are. I turn in the opposite direction and stand to the side before lighting up.

"Can I get one of those?" asks some guy who could be a homeless bum, starving artist, or maybe a bit of both. He can see me tapping a cigarette out of my pack and since it's not empty, I can't pretend that I'm almost out to avoid giving him one of my precious cancer sticks. I tap one out, then hold the pack in his direction for him to grab it.

"Thanks."

He takes it, then motions for a lighter. After lighting mine, I pass it in his direction. He does the same before handing it back.

"How's your night going so far?" he asks.

Christ, now he wants to have a conversation.

"Not bad. You?" I respond.

"Just trying to survive, man."

This is the part where he asks me for money, or something, I assume.

"Well, keep on surviving buddy," I say as I head towards a taxi.

Did this girl start talking to me or did I start talking to her? We are standing next to the bar at the Lava Lounge with people continually pushing past to get the bartenders' attention. There is a bottle of beer in my hand which I take a long swig from while trying to hear what she is saying over the noise, something about what it is like being a yoga instructor. Looking down, she has the trim body of someone who takes care of herself, and her straight blond hair frames her soft face with a narrow nose nicely. I smile and nod along as she continues speaking. She pauses and looks at me expectantly. I realize she asked me a question, but I was too busy eye fucking her to hear it.

"I'm sorry, what?" I ask.

I should see if she wants to get out of here. Head back to my place … or hers if she prefers.

Some meathead squeezes between us at the bar, before she can respond. I try to ignore him, assuming he is attempting to get the bartenders' attention.

"Hey, I'm Rick," he says.

He holds his hand out towards me as I realize he is talking to me. Instinctively, I reach out to shake his hand and he does the power squeeze to establish what a badass he is.

"Good for you," I reply while dislodging my hand from his grasp.

"This is Lisa. She's my best bud's girlfriend. How do you two know each other?" Rick continues.

Oh, I see.

"Dude, relax, we're just talking."

He leans in closer. "He's not here, but I am." There is a little spit coming out of his mouth as he speaks.

I'm not sure if it is intentional or because he is that drunk, but being so close, it is impossible to avoid the little droplets landing on my face with the rotted smell of his breath.

"Yeah, I get it. But say it, don't spray it," I reply while holding my hand between our faces.

"Fuck you dude."

He smacks my hand down.

I tense my left hand, which is clutching my beer, I pull it back instinctively, getting ready to swing it at his thick skull.

"Hey," I hear a man's voice from the opposite side of the bar. "Take a breath, guys."

It's the bartender, which gives me pause as I realize smashing a bottle over this guy's skull wouldn't do much.

"It's all good," I say.

Then turning to walk away, I give a wink to the girl who has been standing there doing nothing. I'm not in the mood for this jackass, or to explain to him that I'm pretty sure she started talking to me while I was at the bar. It's a bit of a blur at this point. I've been pounding beers ever since the taxi dropped me off.

"You can't take that outside," the bouncer tells me, referring to the bottle in my hand.

I down it quickly and set it on a table next to the door with a collection of empties and partial empties left by other patrons on their way out.

The chill in the air is a nice contrast to the condensed heat trapped inside.

I look at my phone to see if there's a response to the text I sent earlier to an ex, wondering if she is up and interested in some late-night company. There's no response. It's probably for the best, as that usually ends up in an argument. Although, it would have been nice to get laid tonight.

After walking for a few minutes to clear my head and taking a long piss next to a garbage bin, I flag down a cab.

"Pike and Boren," I tell the guy, knowing my car is somewhere around there.

Heading north on I-5, it dawns on me that I should not be driving right now. Setting the cruise control to maintain a steady speed, I crack open the window for fresh air and concentrate on keeping an equal distance between the lines. Passing a car pulled over on the side of the road with a police cruiser's flashing lights illuminating the area, I take breath.

Better you than me, buddy.

Someone once told me that a penny in your mouth will trick a breathalyzer, so I take a penny out of the ashtray and start sucking on it. Yep, it tastes like copper. I wonder where this penny has been over its life. At the thought of that, I spit it back into my hand and replace it in the ashtray as my stomach curls a bit. A cigarette is probably the better option if I get pulled over. At least the cop won't smell the alcohol on me.

Thankfully, I arrive home without any issues. Walking in the door, impressed with myself for making it, I stumble a bit while kicking my shoes off and head straight for the bedroom to collapse on the bed. Unfortunately, the bed doesn't want to stay still – the room wobbles around me. Needing some stability, I pull the comforter and pillow with me onto the nice solid floor. It feels better but sleep is still out of my reach, so mostly I lay looking up to the black of the ceiling waiting for unconsciousness to arrive.

2

As the hours tick past, waiting for the workday to conclude, in what feels like endless weeks, months, years of one lost memory, like bits and pieces of moments I know should count for something, but only count as a reminder of one day leading to the next, I sit and stare and wait. Coldplay calmly drifts out of the little speakers I have attached to my laptop, indifferent to the events unfolding on the screen in front of me.

My office is a standard 10x12 foot office, along a row of similar shaped spaces occupied by mostly tech-savvy young and middle-aged proud-to-be-called-geeks. I sit behind a gray desk with its lightly stained wooden trim. A white dry-erase board is attached to the wall on my left with the remnants of a workflow diagram drawn in black dry-erase marker. The opposite wall has an empty shelf that stands six feet high. This shelf collects dust in places that others fill with project management books, instructional manuals, pictures of children and pets, or electronic devices that are too cool to throw away, yet too yesterday to be of any use.

I'm doing what I regularly do around this time of the day. After all the emails have been sent, and the meetings attended, I'm online waiting for the next player to bet, fold, or check. I'm waiting for a player sitting at a virtual table with other virtual players. People who might be seated in an office just like mine across the country, around the world, or perhaps on the other side of the street. Others who occasionally look over their shoulders so that someone doesn't sneak up behind them to witness what they are doing during company hours. All of us living under made-up names and avatars, counting down time the same way, waiting for the day to end. Players who are already thinking about that after-work drink, what traffic will be like, or who will get kicked off this week's *Survivor*.

I look to the corner of my laptop screen to check the time. It's 3:32 pm. Only about an hour to go until I can justifiably shut off the computer, close the door, and head out with the rest of the herd to fight for position during tonight's rush home. The player before me raises and with a poor hand, I fold. I click on Office Communicator to check on my manager's status. It's red, which usually means the person is in a meeting or busy, or at least has their calendar blocked off to look busy. What I care about is that he is still in the office. There is no rule around work hours, but it wouldn't surprise me if he were to swing by my office after the meeting with some "action item" to complete by the end of the day.

Everything always seems to be needed by "EOD" in corporate speak.

The next hand is dealt, and it looks to be as unimpressive as the last. I haven't been doing all that well today. It is one of those days where the cards just have not been coming up, or when they do, one of the other players still manages to get the better hand. I look to see who is on Facebook, selecting the chat to see my friends' list pull up. Quickly scanning, I read the names of people whom I haven't spoken to in years. People that found me on Facebook and friended me, mostly old friends from high school, acquaintances who I've met at some point in my life and barely remember, or friends of friends who are just upping their online status by attempting to have more friends than anyone else. No one is showing as available who would be worth chatting with. I look down at the corner of my computer. It's 3:38.

Blip the laptop notifies me with a noise and icon that a new email has arrived. Clicking on the pop-up, the email opens in a window that I minimize to continue watching the poker game. It is from my manager:

Matt,

Can you update slide 3 of the attached PowerPoint time tube with a new launch date of the 14th, and move the other dates back a week in accordance? Please send it to me by EOD.

Also, set up a 30-minute meeting later this week with Kerry and Dave to review.

Cheers,

I let out a quiet moan at reading the word 'cheers'. We have a small office in London, and they tend to sign every email with cheers. Now, it seems the drones on this side of the world are using it as well, as if saying cheers makes them hipper and cooler, like those fancy Brits. Or maybe by saying cheers at the end, it lessens the impact of being told to do work that the sender could just as easily do themselves. *How exciting, I have work for you, happy day – Cheers!*

I know instantly which presentation he is talking about. It is one I put together a few days ago with a release schedule for the software update we are conducting. I look through the folders on my laptop for the one that matches the name of his attachment and open it, then jump over to more important things, such as the online poker game I have running in the background. I sigh at being dealt another weak hand of 7 and 4 off suit. As the presentation opens, I keep one eye on the game. At the flop, a 7 is showing, and the players before me have checked. Seeing a potential opportunity with a middle pair, I place a cautious bet, careful not to risk too much on a poor hand. As I revise the timeline with the new dates, switching back and forth between the windows, I watch most everyone else fold except for two players. Both players call my bet without raising. With a king showing, it's possible one of them might have a higher pair or the other king, however since it is the highest card and neither has raised, I assume they are waiting for a needed card.

I complete the revisions to the presentation as the river card drops. Nothing much is showing. No potential straights or flushes. My guess is the best either of the other players has is a better pair than mine, maybe three of a kind or two pair, but I doubt it based on the way they have been wagering. Feeling good about finally winning one, I decide to play it as if I hit it on that last card and over bet the pot to bluff them out. As I type "updated" in an email and hit send, the other two players fold, winning me a modest pot. I look up with a slight grin on my face. A petite blond girl in tight blue jeans saunters past the door. She is most likely on her way to a meeting or leaving one, as it seems to be how most people spend their workdays with this company. She's cute, I think to myself, having never seen her before and wondering what group she works with in our small company. Maybe she's new.

"Hey Matt, coffee break?" Jeff startles me, leaning his head around my door.

"Umm, I don't know," I respond. "I just won a hand in poker and I have to set up a meeting for Chris."

"Whatever bro, you know you are going to lose anyway. The meeting can wait, let's go have a ciggy."

I notice his thin blondish hair reveals the receding hairline that will force him to go bald or invest in transplants in a few years, which contradicts the boyish expression on his face.

"All right," I say, exiting the game. "We walking or driving?"

"I can drive. I don't feel like walking today."

The Starbucks is only a few blocks away from the office, but with the warmth of summer having faded away months ago to the typical cold and dreary Seattle winter, a two-block walk can be an unpleasant experience. Of course, driving in downtown Seattle and finding a parking spot can also be a somewhat miserable experience.

"So, what's the meeting about?" Jeff asks as we walk to the elevator.

"I don't know. The release date has moved back a week, just like I said it would. So, probably to talk about that."

"Wasn't that the purpose of the three o'clock? I was just in a meeting with Chris and he told us about the change of dates," he says.

In the elevator, I press the button for the basement garage.

"Sounds like you know more than me," I say.

"I've been sitting on the process updates for weeks, just waiting on *your* release to happen so that I can post them."

"Yes, *my* release. As if I have any say in it," I reply. "You know, if they had listened to me in the first place, the schedule wouldn't constantly be getting pushed back. I told both Chris and Kerry that the dev team wasn't going to be done in time."

"Kerry wasn't there. Apparently too preoccupied to grace us plebs with her presence."

"Think she'll remember me this time?" I joke, referring to a previous meeting with her when she wasn't even aware that I work for her, asking who I was and why I was there.

"Probably not," Jeff responds as we exit the elevator. "Why are you setting up that meeting, anyway? Chris said he was going to do it."

19

"If he did, that would involve using Outlook, which would involve learning how to actually set up his own meetings," I say with a sarcastic grin, opening the door to Jeff's Volvo. "Clearly 'project manager' translates to 'personal assistant' or personal 'bitch' in his eyes. He views waterfall project management not as a linear flow of phases, but a cascading set of tasks, and of course that cascade of work flows downhill. Hence, to me."

The drive is a short one from the office to the coffee shop. Walking probably takes the same amount of time, considering the extra steps required to get through the security gate in the garage and then finding a parking spot. Today, we luck into parking right in front of the Starbucks.

"Hey, guys!" Jessie the perky barista yells out as we enter.

"Hey," we reply in unison.

Jessie is an adorable little thing, probably just over five feet tall with shoulder-length dark brown hair, dark eyes, beautiful white teeth on display when she smiles, and a body that I would enjoy playing with, tucked behind the green coffee-covered apron she wears each day. She always seems to be in a good mood and knows how to work her customers for tips – or, at least, how to work Jeff and myself for tip money, because we always make a display of slipping a bill or two in the jar. Which overall works out well for us, since when her manager isn't around, she occasionally doesn't charge us for our drinks.

"Usual?" she asks, grabbing the cups.

"Yep.," Jeff says.

"No," I quickly cut in before she starts making my drink. "Can I just get a tall Mocha today?"

"Sure thing. Looking for something sweet today?" she asks with a wink, referring to my usual double tall latte.

"No, just changing it up, throwing a little excitement into my day," I say, waving my hands back and forth to demonstrate fake enthusiasm.

She smiles with that delightful big smile surrounded by sumptuous red lips and begins making the drinks, as the guy working the register rings up our orders.

"Can I bum a smoke?" Jeff asks while we walk around to the alley near the side of the building with coffees in hand.

Reaching into my jacket pocket, I pull out a pack of American Spirits and give it a sharp smack to knock a cigarette out for myself, then hand the pack towards Jeff to take one. After lighting my cigarette, I hand the little plastic lighter to him while inhaling a nice long drag. I hold it for a few extra seconds and exhale as my shoulders relax. I let the taste of smoke and nicotine linger in my mouth along with the rich mocha and coffee flavor. A splash of Baileys would go nicely. My thoughts then turn towards Jessie's tits, wondering what they would taste like with a nice cool shot of Baileys poured over them, my tongue lapping it all up.

"Hey fucker, give me my lighter back," I say, noticing Jeff pocketing my little lighter.

"Oh, whoops." He smirks.

"Do you think if I asked Jessie out, she would say yes? I mean, she totally flirts with me every time I'm there."

"She flirts with all the guys while they are there. That's how she makes her tips, bro."

"Yeah, maybe. But I think she might be into me."

"If you say so. You want me to talk to her for you? I could talk you up a bit, be your wingman."

I laugh. "Thanks, I don't need a wingman. As we established the other night, your wingman skills need work. But, yeah, maybe next time, just be like 'that Matt is such a good guy,' or something like that," I say.

"It wasn't my fault, bro. I told you someone bumped me."

"Well, the awkward attempt at wiping the drink off didn't really work. It turns out women don't like to have drinks poured on them and then be groped by some dude."

"I offered to buy her another drink," he says with a smile.

I shake my head.

Back in the office the nine-to-four crowd has cleared out, and, not wanting to show too much enthusiasm for setting up meetings on behalf of others, I decide to call it a day, shut down the laptop, and head home. Off to the mad dash of hurry up, stop, slow down, speed up, change lanes, slow down, and stop again – a process that begins as soon as I leave the parking lot onto the crowded downtown streets of Seattle.

After reaching a slightly consistent speed on I-5, I reach into the middle console in my car and pull out the little wooden case that contains a fake cigarette and my stash. I remove the fake cigarette and insert it into the end of the wooden case, packing the already ground pot into the tip. With one hand on the wheel, I use the other to further tamp it in, quickly checking to make sure there is enough inside. Satisfied, I place it between my lips and light the end. To the casual observer, I look like any other smoker lighting a cigarette as they drive down the road. For me, it's pure relaxation. I inhale, the familiar flavor as it floats across my taste buds, then fills my lungs, where I hold it for a moment before exhaling slowly through the cracked window. Lynyrd Skynyrd's

"Simple Man" is playing on the iPod plugged into the car stereo. I turn up the volume.

Looking down at the speedometer, which is bouncing between 10 and 15 miles per hour, I speed up for a second then slow down, attempting to shift as little as possible. A heavy sigh leaves my body as I look at the road ahead; all lanes are jammed with afternoon commuters. This little black Mini Cooper of mine, with its slick-looking white bonnet stripes, will not be weaving through traffic today. A manual transmission is one of the joys of having such a sporty nimble car when there is not much traffic, but one of the pains when there is.

Rolling down the window, I tap the little metal cylinder on the rearview mirror, dumping the burned remains into the wind. After giving it a quick check to be sure it is cleared, I roll the window back up, leaving a two-inch crack for air. Out comes the little wooden box, and in goes the cigarette pipe, packing in one more hit: one more for the drive, and one more for the *simple man who is unsatisfied*.

3

Most people would view coming home from a long day at work and finding a cute brunette sitting on their front porch as a good thing. However, in this case, it only elicits a desire to smash my head on the steering wheel.

She looks up and gives me a slight wave and a smile. In response, I give her a brief nod before pressing the button to open the garage door and pulling my car inside. Killing the engine, I sit in the car for a moment, taking a few deep breaths. I brace myself and head inside, through the house, and open the front door. She looks good, with her light brown hair cascading around a face that I have kissed more times than I can count. Her form-fitting blue jeans stir up a mix of emotions that I have no interest in revisiting.

"Yes?" I say with a tone of annoyance.

"Can I come in?"

"I don't think that's a good idea."

"I left a couple of things here that I'd like back," she says.

"Really? Because you've had plenty of time to get anything left here. In fact, I specifically said, 'is there anything at my place you want?' And you very clearly responded with 'no.'"

"No, I didn't."

"Um, yes you did. In fact, I could probably find the text to get the exact words you used."

"Well, I was mad, and I'm not mad anymore. Besides, I really did forget that I left my winter jacket here. I didn't need it until recently."

"Fine, wait here," I tell her, pointing to the same spot she is standing and making it clear I have no intention of allowing her to follow me into the house.

Checking the closet next to the entrance, there is a blue winter jacket hanging; it's the one she was wearing when we first met. I grab it and open the front door, handing her the coat, then close it without saying a word. This is followed by a soft knock.

"Come on! I'm not in the mood for this shit. I had a long fucking day at work, I'm tired, I'm hungry and I'm not interested," I say, opening the door again.

"Can't we just talk?"

"No, we can't just talk. I don't want to hear any of your bullshit lies, excuses, stories, or anything else you have to say on any subject."

"Can't we at least pretend to be friends? We could order some food."

"No. No, we can't. I don't want to be friends with you. I, in fact, don't want to have anything to do with you," I say, fully aware of what would happen if I let her in.

"Excuse me for just wanting to have a conversation with you."

She is starting to look as if she is going to cry. Why the fuck do women always have to start crying?

"Fine. What?" I say, still standing at the door, ready to slam it in her face at the first chance I get.

"Can I come in?"

I sigh. "Fine."

I walk away from the door and sit in a chair opposite the sofa, making sure she will have to sit across rather than next to me.

We stare at each other, waiting.

"So …"

"I don't know, I just wanted to see how you were doing."

"Doing just fine, thanks."

She sits and stares at me. "Well, I guess that's it."

She stands to leave, and I don't move.

"Okay. Goodbye."

I give her a wave, she exits, I exhale deeply and head to the kitchen. I reach for a whiskey glass in the cupboard, add a handful of ice, and fill in the rest with Makers Mark. The alcohol burns as I take a long drink, enjoying the relaxation it brings as it works its way down my throat. I then pull out a single

California Kitchen pizza from the freezer, turn the oven on and remove the food from the box. Life sucks sometimes, so I take another sip before sticking the pizza in the oven.

It doesn't seem like it was that long ago when she walked into the coffee shop. I looked up when the door opened, bringing with it an icy breeze, and she entered. The place was pretty busy with all the tables taken, and I was sitting at one of the larger ones by myself reading *The Stranger*. Despite spending the previous night out with friends, I was feeling reasonably decent for a Sunday morning, enjoying a large latte and Asiago cheese bagel. She looked around, scanning for an available seat, then came over to where I was sitting.

"Do you mind if I sit here?" she asked.

I motioned for her to sit. "No, go for it."

She placed her bag on a chair between us and removed the thick blue coat with a fur-trimmed hood that covered her upper body. It was clear even before she removed the coat that she had an attractive figure. The first thing my eyes were drawn to were her perky tits filling out the contours of her form-fitting white cashmere sweater. She paired it with a navy skirt that grazed her knees, stockings, and brown UGG boots. Her long chestnut-brown hair fell loose, looking as if it had only a brief encounter with a brush that morning. Strands rebelliously jutted out in all directions as if a touch of static electricity lingered in the air. The clear smooth skin on her face shone, with a slender aristocratic nose.

After setting her stuff down, she went to get a coffee. Suddenly a bit self-conscious about my disheveled appearance, I brushed my hand through my hair to style it a bit.

She returned to the table with her coffee and a pastry and taking a seat across from me. She opened her laptop, while I continued to read the latest letter in the Strange Love advice column. The writer was looking for advice from Dan about what to do because his wife's diminished sex drive was leaving him unfulfilled, and if it was appropriate to go outside of the relationship.

Listening to the steady click-click-click of her typing, mixed with the generic background noise of people talking and the sound of the coffee machines steam wand, my eyes would occasionally drift upward, drawn to the young woman seated across from me, her attention wholly absorbed by the laptop screen before her.

What the hell, I thought. "So … What are you working on?" I asked.

She looked up. "Just getting some work done."

"Working on a Sunday. That sucks."

"I don't really mind it. Besides, it helps me get a start on the week, preventing me from having to work late."

"Oh, what do you do?" I continued.

"I work in a lab."

"Oh, that sounds interesting."

"It's not as exciting as it sounds," she said with a small smile, the laptop screen casting a soft glow on her face.

"Okay then. I'm Matt, by the way."

"I'm Jennifer," she introduced herself with a smile.

I gestured towards her nearly empty mug. "Can I get you another cup of coffee?"

"Maybe next time," she grinned.

Taking that as a positive response, I asked, "What do you like to do for fun?"

She gently closed the laptop screen and slid it aside.

"Hmm, well, I like to go hiking."

"Oh, me too," I lied. "Where do you like to go?"

We chatted a bit more before I asked her out for that following week. She accepted, and as they say, the rest is history. As to whether that historic record turned out to be a good one or not, for me, it's a history filled with poor choices and anguish.

After sitting in front of the TV, flipping through channels and working my way through one glass of Maker's after another, I give in and grab my phone, sending a message I know I shouldn't.

Want to come over for a drink?

It's not long before she responds.

okay

The words *total dumbass* run through my head, as I pour myself another drink, check that the door is unlocked, and dim the lights before settling in to wait.

After about 30 minutes, she finally arrives. In the meantime, I've been working my way through the bottle of Maker's. I hit the button on the remote, turning the TV off and the receiver on. It switches to the iPod I have plugged into the docking station. Opening the door, I stand back as she enters. We don't speak, as she stands before me and I begin kissing her. It's a familiar feeling, but tonight it feels even better than usual. Leading her into the living room, we continue our passionate embrace. It feels good. It feels too good, as I grab her and lay her down on the sofa.

Al Green is ironically singing "Let's Stay Together," as we quickly undress each other.

She tastes slightly of wine, which doesn't bother me tonight. In fact, knowing she's a little buzzed mixed with my own state of intoxication heightens the intensity of the moment.

It doesn't take long to remove each other's clothing as she straddles me. My right hand is pulling the back of her hair, as my left squeezes her nipple. I'm doing both harder than I normally would, her vocal cues informing me that she is enjoying it as much as I am.

She rolls off of me, kneeling, legs spread, inviting me to take her from behind. I position myself between her thighs, one foot on the floor and one on the sofa, as I thrust into her. The intensity builds as I pound harder and harder to the sounds of her moans climbing to orgasm. Our bodies move together in perfect synchronization, as only two lovers fluent in each other's desire can. Her moans crescendo as we reach climax together. Collapsing into the sofa, exhausted and satisfied, my flaccid cock slides out of her. We lie naked catching our breath. Satisfied for a few moments, until the uncomfortable feelings begin to creep in. I get up and grab my underwear, t-shirt, and pants, followed up with a sip from my now diluted bourbon.

"Well, thanks," I say uncomfortably, hoping that she's not planning on spending the night.

"Um sure," she responds while getting up and beginning to put her clothes back on as well.

I sit at the end of the sofa and watch her while turning the music back to the television. An episode of *Bones* is on, showing the team gathered around a body on the lab table.

After getting dressed, she goes to the bathroom, followed up by a trip to the kitchen for a drink of water.

"I have wine or Maker's if you want."

"No, I have to work in the morning," she responds in a way that implies she will be leaving.

She walks over to where I'm sitting and gives me a nice long kiss that I think implies she wants me to ask her to stay. Either that or it implies she wants to give me a nice long kiss before leaving. Since she says nothing, I'm going with the latter choice.

I walk her to the door and give her another kiss. "We should do that again sometime," I add, not knowing what else to say, and regret expressing the thought as soon as the words come out of my mouth.

"Yeah, okay," she responds before I close the door behind her.

The activity has worn some of the alcohol out of me. Knowing I shouldn't have any more to drink as the morning will be hell, I pour myself another half-glass. Then I step out onto the balcony to smoke a cigarette and think that I should probably take a shower and wash off the smell of sex and regret. Although, I don't really feel guilty. She came over here first, and she could have said no when I texted her. So, fuck her. I refuse to feel like I'm using her when she used me just as much. As long as the bitch doesn't think I'm interested in getting back together with her.

4

There are mornings when I open my eyes and all I want is to pull the pillow over my face and ignore the world outside. This is one of those mornings. My brain is pounding the inside of my skull, like an alien baby trying to escape. My lungs hurt, and I feel like someone shoved me into a burlap bag, buried me under a pile of coal for a month, then tossed me into a rusty dryer for a few hours. The shower doesn't help, and the poorly made hazelnut latte I pick up from the scantily clad bikini barista at the drive-through near my house does nothing to improve my mood.

Our Wednesday morning team meeting usually doesn't bother me; today, however, I have no interest whatsoever in engaging with my co-workers. The thought of calling in sick briefly crosses my mind, but I decide against it. I resign myself to suffering through the day. I figure a couple of aspirin, a better cup of coffee, and maybe a pastry will alleviate the hangover.

I arrive at the conference room early, thanks to lighter-than-usual traffic, with a fresh cup of coffee in hand and sit far from the door with my back to the wall. The smell of the ham and cheese Hot Pocket I microwaved fills the air of the small space, making me feel slightly better already. Unfortunately, as soon as I take a bite, I immediately regret it, burning the roof of my mouth with the scorching hot cheese.

"Fuck!" I yelp, quickly taking a sip of my coffee to soothe the pain.

As I wait for the Hot Pocket to cool, the rest of my team begins to arrive with the usual good morning greetings. All I can think about is my churning stomach, and the headache that is getting worse by the minute.

I glance at the clock, wondering just how late Chris will be today. It turns out he is only about seven minutes behind schedule, a minor delay in the world of Christopher Brenman the oh-so-busy manager. Everyone gives him the usual acknowledgments of our understanding that it is not a problem. Which of course it is. Given that Chris typically makes his entrance at least ten minutes into most meetings, always looking as if he just sprinted from an incredibly important engagement in his supposedly jam-packed schedule. Even though he is well dressed in slacks and an ironed shirt, I can see the bags under his eyes. He was probably up late emailing and doing whatever it is he does to convince himself of his importance. His laptop is in one hand, and predictably, he also has a coffee cup in the other, with text on the side reading, 'first coffee, then work'.

"Did you guys see the story about that lady who was attacked by those pit bulls," Joline starts saying. "That's why people shouldn't be allowed to own dogs like that. My dogs might bark a lot, but they aren't able to hurt anyone."

The thing with Joline is, it's not just her weight that makes her unattractive. Even if she were to shed a significant number of pounds, her facial proportions would still be off. Her mouth is too small for her face, regardless of her puffed-out cheeks, and her eyes could use some dark sunglasses to hide the bags beneath them.

Most meetings usually involve Joline telling us some story about her dogs, such as the one she is telling now. If not the dogs, it would most likely be a story about her kids, as it seems those are the only things in her life. Chris should, of course, put an end to it. But he doesn't. Looking on the bright side, at least she didn't roll in today with food to shovel into her pug-like face.

"Well, Joline, I think it's less about the breed and more about how responsible owners handle their dogs," I say, with a tone of irritation.

"Really?" Joline replies, her eyebrows raised. "Because I've heard so many stories about pit bulls attacking people. It's just not safe," she adds a shake of her head.

Before I have a chance to reply, Chris speaks up. "Let's focus on today's agenda, shall we? We have a lot to cover," he says with a forced smile, effectively ending the dog discussion. Something he should have done when she first brought it up.

"Fine with me," I say.

I turn back to my Hot Pocket, which has cooled to the point of being edible, and my laptop screen to clean out this morning's emails.

"Yeah, actually I have a call at ten I need to be on," Frank, one of the other PMs on the team, adds. "So, I'll need to leave a bit early."

He is wearing a t-shirt, a size too small, with the phrase 'I paused my game for this?' on the front. It makes his long skinny arms look stretched like Reed Richards in Fantastic Four. I picture his arm snaking over the table and backhanding Joline and Chris in quick succession.

When it gets to the list of new features for the next release, I look up. I watch halfheartedly as Chris goes through the spreadsheet projected on the wall. Joline interrupts with a question about how one of the features will work, demonstrating her lack of comprehension, and Chris turns to me, most likely because he doesn't understand it either. I attempt to break down how an algorithm works, but you can only dumb down something so much. She pretends to understand or simply gives up; I'm fine with either as long as she shuts up.

"Do you have a minute?" Chris asks me, as we are leaving the room.

"Sure," I say.

"Great. Let's go to my office," he says it in a way that reminds me of being sent to the principal in school.

I follow him to his office, where he ushers me in, then closes the door behind us. He has a selection of books on the shelf about project management, people management, and different coding technologies developed over the years. It's a topic that I doubt he has any expertise in. His desk has an everlasting pile of papers on it, with a mismatched disorderly way about them. There's a notepad he takes with him to meetings, even though he also carries a laptop with OneNote on it he could use. He has different PowerPoint presentations that he has printed and, for some reason, hasn't placed into recycling.

"How are things going?" he asks, as he sits behind his desk, sliding his laptop into the docking station, and I sit in the chair across from him.

"Nothing exciting," I hunch my shoulders. "Just waiting on the release at this point." Assuming that's what he is asking about.

"How are things at home?" he asks, leaning back in his chair. "You seem unhappy lately. Unfocused."

"Excuse me?"

"You didn't say much during the meeting. And when you did speak you looked annoyed, arguing about dogs and talking down to Joline."

"Um … okay."

"Well?" He asks with a smile on his face, but not the kind that says he is happy or interested in being open and helpful.

"I'm not really sure what you're asking?" I respond, too tired and hungover for whatever discussion he is trying to have.

"Are you happy here at Electronix? And is there anything I can do?"

"Um, no."

"The door is closed; you can be honest with me. Open communication is a key priority with me, you know that."

He sounds like he must have just read some book on management communication. *If your employee looks like he has a hangover, open a line of dialog with him.*

"Do you want me to be honest, or do you want me to give you the PC response?"

"You can be honest with me. Anytime"

"Ok then," I say, knowing full well that I should shut my mouth, yet too tired and irritated to stop myself from speaking. "No, I don't feel challenged here, at least not in a good way. The only challenge I have is keeping my mouth closed when someone like Joline opens her yap in a meeting asking dumb questions that she should already know the answer to. The job we do basically involves each release being designed around providing an excuse for customers to purchase the latest version of our product just so we can make more money. Very little of which trickles down to me. And, it seems like we have a complete lapse in conversations between engineering and our team. So, when we do finally release something, it won't work and we have to go into fix-it mode. This could easily be avoided by hiring competent people and listening to those people instead of arbitrary policies put into place by people I've never met."

There is a bit of silence before he responds.

"Done?"

"Yep."

He leans forward, with a slight creak coming from his chair, placing both hands together on his desk,

"Well, if you are not happy here, maybe you should consider looking for work elsewhere."

"It's a job. I'm not supposed to be happy. It's called *work* for a reason. You think some guy working on an assembly line is happy every time he clocks in, doing the same monotonous task day after day?"

"I understand," he responds, but I can tell he's offended at my blatant honesty. "You know if you are unhappy, it comes across in your work, and reflects badly on all of us."

Oh, so that's what this is about. He's worried about how *he* looks.

"I'm really not that unhappy," I say, in an attempt to backtrack a little. "I'm just tired that's all and could probably use a little vacation. Plus, I might be coming down with something."

"Well, maybe once we ship, you can take some time off," he says, knowing full well I'm bullshitting him.

I smile and nod my head in agreement, not really wanting to talk to him anymore, hoping to leave the room as soon as possible.

"Nonetheless," he continues, "until that happens, it's crucial that you begin considering how your attitude is perceived by others.

"Okay, I will."

He looks pleased with himself, having successfully followed the steps outlined in *How to Manage your Employees.*

"Also, I need you to do one more thing for me," he says.

Just as I thought I was about to leave.

"The reporting team ran a report of active AdMatics accounts using the same activation code. Can you merge that with another report of user accounts for me?"

"So basically, you want me to combine two spreadsheets into one?" I ask, annoyed at such a mundane task.

"Yes, I'll email them to you. All you need to do is use the v-lookup by account IDs so we can match each email address with its corresponding account." He says as if talking to a child.

"Yeah, I know how to do a v-lookup," I reply, struggling to keep my frustration in check. "What, I don't get is why you want me to do it, and why can't the reporting team do it? Isn't that their job?"

"They have a team meeting today, and this is time sensitive," he states with that same forced smile.

Time sensitive – this issue we have had since day one is now suddenly time sensitive.

I suppress the urge to leap over the desk and smash his face into it.

"Okay," I respond.

He turns to his laptop screen, letting me know I can leave now that he has established his dominance over me.

Before heading to my office, I swing by Jeff's to see if he wants to take a cigarette break. His door is closed. Looking through the floor to ceiling window next to it, it looks like he is on a call. I knock and put two fingers to my lips in the internationally recognized gesture for 'smoke break', but he shakes his head, motioning to the phone, so I have to smoke alone.

Outside, as usual, I move to the side of the building, keeping a good distance from the main entrance. A middle-aged woman walking with a child, loudly exclaims, "You see that man. He's doing something filthy. He's a bad, bad man! Don't grow up to be like him."

The child looks confused, as the first thought that comes to me is blurted out. "Yeah kid. Better to suck a dick than a cig. Right mom!"

"Asshole," she yells back as she pulls the child along faster.

"Great parenting lady!" I yell, not sure she can hear me at this point.

A few other people walking past are giving me the stink eye, so I stomp out the cigarette, leaving the butt on the sidewalk, and go inside.

Back in my office, after picking up a couple of aspirin and a fresh cup of coffee, there is an email from Chris with the spreadsheets he wants me to compile for him. I decide to save it for later. Instead, I browse a few job posting websites. Unfortunately, none of the available jobs look any good – one of the joys of living in the middle of the great recession, where no one is hiring, and even when they do, the listed salaries are much lower than what I currently make. Thanks George Bush. I give up and move on to browsing the news on CNET.

After CNET, I rotate through some of my usual blogs and online newsgroups. There is an article about one of Electronix Systemz's software products. Technically, it is not one of my projects, so I don't care too much. My involvement usually means attending a couple of meetings a week, making a few statements during those meeting, and not much else. The product is in beta status, yet the article has to do with the product going into a wider release. Which I was not aware we were doing. Nice of the company to keep us in the loop.

Not long after, Chris sends me the same article, requesting that I forward it to a larger distribution group we collaborate with, seemingly unable to manage it himself. With little thought and still recovering from the remnants of my hangover, I add a brief note before sending it along as requested, "FYI – AdMatics is going out of beta."

It doesn't take long before my screen is inundated with email notifications popping up. Office monkeys trying to outdo each other in demonstrating how on top of things they are. Reading the first reply, I discover that AdMatics is not actually off beta, rather, it's just that the beta release is being opened up to a larger audience.

I shake my head in disgust, partially at myself for not paying attention to what I was typing, and partially at the responses. People don't bother just responding to me personally; they have to correct my statement by replying to everyone in the email distribution.

To put off sending Chris an angry email blaming him for having me forward the email, I walk to the break room for a soda, only to encounter some douche-bag co-worker passing me in the hallway, saying, "Matt, AdMatics is going out of beta," then laughing at his little joke as he keeps walking.

I feel the urge to stop him, flip him around, and give him a solid knee to the balls, watching as his 40-something, gray-haired ass falls to the floor as I kick him, while he curls himself up into the fetal position. I would have lived well in the old west, where disputes were settled with fists and alcohol was used to quench a thirst. Instead, I insert my money into the vending machine and make my selection, then walk back to my office, drop off the Coke, and retrieve my coat for another cigarette outside.

Rain starts to fall as I take one last drag before dropping it to the ground and crushing it under my foot, avoiding eye contact with the people walking past. I turn and walk back to the building with my head low in a useless attempt to protect my face from the wind blowing cold rain into it. If I were a dog, I could shake my head to remove the wet from my hair. But then again, if I were a dog, I'd be at home curled up and soundly sleeping on my owner's recently vacated bed, instead of finding myself wet, hungover, and dreading the elevator ride back to my desk.

5

Friday night at the end of a week filled with an endless parade of soul-sucking meetings, unnecessary action items, and being forced to chug the Kool-Aid. Another week in a string of never-ending weeks, amplified by the constant rain and darkness that greets me each morning when I wake up, and is waiting for me when I leave the office each day. All I want is to go home, where a slice of leftover pizza and a cold microbrew awaits me in the fridge. Yet, here I am, at The Garage on Capitol Hill to shoot some pool.

Walking in, Jeff and I see Kai, who has already scoped out a spot near one of the tables. He is wearing a pastel button-up shirt that is tucked in tightly with short sleeves that look as if they are cutting off the circulation to his biceps.

"There you are," he says with an exaggerated tone of offense.

"Dude, I texted you like ten minutes ago."

"No." He pulls out his phone to show me the message. "It's been almost an hour."

"Oh, sorry, I guess it took us longer than I thought to get out of the office."

He rolls his eyes. "Ummm, hmmm."

"What do you want to drink?" Jeff asks me.

"A whisky and Coke."

"Would you like me to get you something? he asks Kai.

"No, thanks," Kai replies while holding up a near full pint of beer.

Jeff heads off to grab a couple of drinks, while Kai hands over a cue, offering for me to break.

"I can't believe how different this place is," I say after making what amounted to a terrible break, not sinking anything. "Did they always have the windows overhead? It must have been a good five or six years since the last time I was here."

"I think they have," Kai responds.

He moves to take his shot in an unsteady way that tells me he is already drunker than I will be all night. Yet he is still not as drunk as he will most likely end up before stumbling home or to the bedroom of some random hookup before the night is out.

The bar is in a large old brick building on Capitol Hill, in what used to be an actual automotive garage. The back wall has a garage door, as well as the front, where there is some seating that appears to have been liberated from an airport auction. The place has that industrial old Seattle aesthetic, with its exposed brick walls, the exposed ceiling above, and the old skylight windows at the peak.

The place used to be a bit of a dive with pool tables by the hour and cheap booze. But times have changed. Now it's become more of a place for hipsters to hang out. The hourly rate for the tables has increased, along with the drink prices. At least it has maintained some of its dingy feel, with the low lighting and tables. The speakers fill the room with the annoyingly overplayed song "Low" by Flo Rida and T-Pain.

Jeff returns from the bar and hands me a whiskey and Coke. "What did you get?" I ask, noticing what I assume is a vodka and 7-up for himself.

"A Gin and Tonic?"

"Really, I thought only old people drank those."

"I like G and Ts."

"If you say so, grandpa."

"The reason why you don't like them," he replies, holding his head high, "is because you lack exposure to quality gin. When Evelyn and I went to London, we went to a quaint cocktail bar that had an extensive array of Gins. Once you've had good gin, you will develop a taste for it. You just lack the palate."

"Oh, isn't that quaint?" I mock with a British accent. "All I need to do is develop a sophisticated palate such as yours."

He shakes his head with a smile, then takes a sip from his fancy cocktail, followed by a smack of his lips. Even though Jeff is a few years younger than me, his tired lanky frame and receding hair is a reminder that we are not getting any younger and the future is no friend.

"I find it interesting that for a lot of people in England, Gin and Tonic is as acceptable as traditional tea. During our time there, we would sometimes have a Gin and Tonic with lunch, followed by the usual afternoon tea, complete with little sandwiches and pastries. And we might have another G and T with dinner, or supper, as they would say. You know, gin was originally developed for medicinal purposes as a remedy for illnesses like upset stomach and diarrhea …"

Around this point, all I can do is shake my head and roll my eyes as my attention shifts to a small group who arrive and walk past our table with no acknowledgment of our presence. However, one of the girls catches my attention. One that I have an extremely fond memory of.

The other girl with her has a similar vibe of confidence. Both look as if they strolled off the pages of a fashion magazine. The odd one out is the guy. He clashes with the high-class appearance of the women with his slicked-back, pony-tailed, dirty brown hair and an aura of sleaze that clings to him like the cheap cologne I have no doubt he is wearing.

"Matt, your turn," Kai interrupts.

I take a long pull from my glass, go for the five, miss, and go back to remembering the night the two of us met.

Kai and some of his friends had rented a room at the Alexis Hotel in downtown Seattle for New Year's. I was going solo and could hear the music before I knocked on the door. It was still early, but I wouldn't have been surprised if at some point in the night we found ourselves on the receiving end of a noise complaint. Even with it being New Years in downtown Seattle.

I knocked and was surprised that someone could hear it. I didn't recognize the guy who answered the door. He was wearing oversized cardboard cutout glasses in the design of 2008, with eyeholes cut into the 0s.

He cocked his head to the side while he scoped me out from top to bottom and then back up again with an approving expression. I was looking good that night, with black slacks and a dark purple button-up shirt, and a sleek black velvet jacket.

I raised the bottle of vodka in my hand, making it clear I was an invited guest, and he opened the door all the way to let me in. The room was well lit and already half-full of people. Most hotel rooms are not much for space, just enough square footage for a few guests on vacation in need of a place to sleep for the night. This must have cost the guys a bit to rent for a new year celebration. The room felt more like a small apartment.

There was a loveseat with two people conversing, while most others were standing, engaged in various conversations. A song I didn't recognize was playing, with a beat that seemed to compel involuntary movements in some of the attendees. The bed had been removed, allowing for extra space for the partiers. To the right was a long, low dresser that had been repurposed into a table for snacks and drinks. A large 'Happy New Year' banner was taped to the far wall, possibly covering up a picture that normally hung on the wall. There were also a few streamers strung up in celebration.

Taking the bottle of vodka to the table, I made myself a vodka and Sprite with one of the red plastic cups that were being provided for drinks. The ice was a bit low in the little cooler sitting next to the table.

"We've ordered some more ice from room service," some guys said to me.

I nodded my head in response.

There was a large door that led to a balcony where I could see a few people congregating. Taking my drink, I went in search of a face I might know. The view from the balcony wasn't much to look at, hung over an alley with a brick building on the other side. However, the cool night air carried a hint of salty sea breeze from the nearby Puget Sound. Without that building, it might have been possible to see the water, but set up as it was, the only thing possible to view was any individuals walking along the streets below. The room shared the balcony with the one next door. The door to that room was open as well, with other partygoers inside.

"Hey," I nodded to a guy I vaguely recognized. He nodded in return with the look of someone trying to figure out if he knew me or not. He was talking to some other guy that I didn't know. I went into the next room, looking for the one person I was actually friends with.

The room was a bit smaller than the other, the bed also removed to make space for the partygoers. There were about a dozen or so people inside.

"Hey, Kai."

"Heeey. Oh, I like this jacket," he said after giving me a hug and rubbing the velvet jacket.

"Thanks."

He was wearing a tight black short-sleeved button-up shirt. The shirt had the top three buttons undone with a gold chain hanging.

"This is my friend Mathew," he said, introducing me to the guy he was talking to. "And this is Andrew, my darling co-host for the evening."

Andrew was a relatively short and skinny Asian, wearing a nice black suit jacket, with a perfectly pressed white shirt and black tie. By the way Kai introduced him, it wouldn't have surprised me if Kai was looking to hook up with the guy at some point in the night. Something in the way he looked at him as he stated his name, with a bit more ooze on it than his usual voice.

"Are you ready for the new year?" Kai asked me, after doing the introductions.

"Yeah, I guess," I said, with little enthusiasm.

I took a large drink from the plastic cup, looking forward to the buzz to kick in. Through the corner of my eye, I took note of someone casually entering the room dressed like a nineteen-twenties flapper. The thin material of her long black skirt flowed behind her as if she was walking into a soft breeze. The fabric had ruffles around the bottom, which hung just above her ankles, displayed a pair of dark brown cowboy boots underneath. Her top was a black blouse that clung to her figure, accentuating the gentle curve of her body, and the short sleeves framing her slender arms. She stood with the poise of a ballerina. She had olive skin and dark eyes; if I had been a teenager, I would have popped a boner simply from looking at her.

She walked over to a girl who handed her a red plastic cup and flashed a radiant smile before taking a long drink. Her teeth were straight and white, her lips full and red.

"Who's that?" I asked Kai while nodding in her direction.

"Thomas?" he said referring to the guy standing near her.

"No, the brunette in the cowboy boots."

He hunched his shoulders with an unknowing expression, and looked to Andrew who said, "She's a friend of Thomas's but I can't recall her name."

"I love those boots! Want me to introduce you?" Kai added.

I shook my head, feeling the need for another cup of liquid courage first. Maybe it was because there weren't many attractive women at the party, or the way her group of friends seemed drawn to her, as she confidently held their attention even when she wasn't speaking. First things first, and that was a refill of my empty Vodka 7. Wouldn't want to come off as too eager, after all.

I spent the evening wandering back and forth between the two rooms, talking to random people, some I didn't know, some I did, and others simply because they were standing next to me at the time. I had burned through half a pack of American Spirits with the rest of the pack having been handed out to people asking me for one when they saw me smoking. The vodka bottle also seemed to disappear quickly, adding to the haze of the evening. In the blur of booze and tobacco, I hadn't noticed it was getting close to midnight. It wasn't until Andrew started handing out plastic champagne flutes that I realized the hour was approaching. I hadn't really given much thought about kissing someone at midnight. Yes, it's a tradition, but so is consuming excessive quantities of alcohol, and I was doing pretty well with my plastic cup of liquid fun that evening.

Suddenly, like a ghost manifesting out of thin air, her eyes were half-closed in the haze of a good buzz recognizable to any proper drinker. People were beginning the countdown; she wrapped her arms around me and pulled me in for a tight, passionate kiss. Her tongue slipped into my mouth with an urgency that mirrored our mutual intoxication. I could taste the alcohol on her and didn't care, as I was sure she could taste it on me in a shared vice that brought us together. I wrapped my arms around her and forgot all about what I had been doing prior to her, enjoying the softness of her breasts against my body and the heat burning between the two of us.

We continued to kiss passionately, only breaking once for her to tell me, "I'm a lesbian but I also like to fuck."

I liked this girl. The countdown was happening around us as her hand slid between my legs.

Kai abruptly interrupted at some point, tearing me away from this muse to suggest that we should go to the bar across the street. Why did I follow him? To this day, there is no satisfactory answer I could provide, considering I probably could have taken the girl into the bathroom and fucked her on the counter and licked the alcohol-infused sweat from her tits. Or taken her home and spent the rest of the night pleasuring each other.

"You want to go with?" I asked her

"No, I'll stay here," she replied.

At the bar I was standing with another Vodka 7 in my hand, while Kai was talking to some friends of his, wondering to myself what the hell I was doing there instead of back in the room with the lesbian who also likes dick.

Among the group that had migrated with us, there was one young woman who stood out. She had an attractive geeky quality that set her apart from the others, with large-framed glasses that rested on a petite nose. Her long brown hair fell gracefully around her face, framing it perfectly. A straight fringe adorned her forehead, evidence that she was the kind of woman who took pride in caring for herself.

My attempts to strike up a conversation with her were being interfered with by some guy who felt a need to dominate the conversation, uttering a constant stream of nonsense, preventing anyone else from speaking. He was a bit taller than me with a stick figure frame, His tight black jeans seemed to elongate his legs, giving him a cartoonish Mickey Mouse appearance.

"Have you ever read anything by Kurt Vonnegut?" he asked us. We collectively shook our heads, at which point he told us we should. He continued regaling us with his vast knowledge of Vonnegut's life during "the war." Once he reached the limit of knowledge on that literary great, he moved on to Salinger.

Who the fuck was this guy trying to impress? I thought.

I rolled my eyes not-so-subtly towards the girl, hoping my exaggerated expression would encourage her to slip away with me from the obnoxious ass-hat dominating the conversation. Whether she noticed or not I couldn't say, as there was no apparent reaction from her.

"I imagine there is a lot of Salinger in Holden Caulfield," he went on.

I looked the guy over. He had a long thin nose, narrow face, and spoke in a tone that indicated he should be wearing a beret with a red scarf around his neck.

"Did you get the shit kicked out of you a lot when you were a kid?" I said, looking directly at him.

There was a pause, as the little group turned to me.

"What?" he asked.

"Know-it-all, who feels the need to impress others with how much he knows about everything, the kind of kid who in school would randomly get stuff thrown at him while walking down the hallways."

"What the fuck is your problem," he said, while squaring off to me.

I had already sized him up and felt confident that I could take him. A quick punch to his fragile nose or the gut would probably drop him to the ground. Of course, I was also well inebriated and barely standing at that point, so it's also possible that one of the girls could have given me a quick shove and I would have ended up on the ground as well.

"Oh, I'm sorry. Were you the only one allowed to talk?" I turned to Kai, "I'm heading back to the room." I looked to the douchebag. "Feel free to follow me outside if you want to talk some more."

I finished my drink with one long swig, fighting a bit of brain freeze from the cold ice, then set the empty glass on the table with a grin as he stared at me with a blank look, unsure of how to respond. While swaggering out of the bar, basking in the glow of self-satisfaction, I realized I hadn't paid my tab and was forced to return to the bar counter. I ignored the judging looks, fully aware of the silence and glares as they watched me perform the task of settling my tab and collecting my card before leaving once again.

Back at the room, there were still plenty of people at the party, except for the girl. She probably left with someone else. I made another drink and went to the bathroom with the other pot smokers to get as baked as possible before taking a long lonely taxi ride home, where, instead of spending the night playing with a gorgeous woman, I lay staring at the ceiling of a spinning room fighting the urge to vomit.

As the night wears on, my interest in pool has dipped and been replaced with alcohol fueled desire to see if she remembers me. I'm encouraged when she looks in my direction, a slight smile on her lips. Was it recognition, or just her response to some guy checking her out? Looking as she does, it must happen often. The time and haze of intoxication has blurred the lines of memory, and this, this could just be someone with a chance resemblance to that someone I only knew for a few moments one night.

"Hey, Kai. Is that the girl that I made out with at your New Year party last year?"

He looks. "Oh absolutely! The one who was with Thomas."

"Cool. Do you think she remembers me?"

"Of course she does!"

Without hesitation, he moves over to their group like a child with no attention span and says something. She hugs him, as does the other girl. He shakes the hand of the guy. The four of them begin talking as if they had been together all night. Jeff and I don't move. Instead, we order another round of drinks from the waitress, and re-rack for another game. Over the sounds of the bar chatter, punctuated by the sharp smack of pool balls hitting each other, I tell the story of that New Year to Jeff, all while my eyes keep moving in her direction.

We don't make it through the game before I say, "Hey, let's close out this table and go join them?"

We turn in our balls, pay the bill for the table, and head over to the group.

Jeff stands, looking nervous, probably not having actually engaged an attractive woman in a conversation in years, and Kai is chatting up the greaser guy.

"Hey!" I say.

"I was wondering if you remembered me," she responds right away with no nervous signs of her own.

"Really?" I smile. "I was wondering the same thing about you."

We move over towards one of the small tables at the side. Sitting across from me, she turns slightly to cross her legs, showing off the toned calves under her skirt.

"I was so drunk that night," she tells me. "I can't believe I did that."

"Hey, I didn't mind at all."

"You probably think I'm a total slut though."

You are correct, but in a good slutty way. In the slutty confident way that makes me imagine your body up against mine and the taste of your skin under my tongue.

"No, not really ... well, I think of you as someone who is confident, who knows what she wants, doesn't mind going after it ... and I take it as a compliment that I was that person."

That works, and she relaxes a little, or is it me who relaxes a bit? I take a long drink from my glass and look for the waitress to get another. I still wonder if she ended up going home with someone else that night, but I'm not so drunk as to actually ask her.

"I'm Matt, by the way."

"Sophie."

Before I have a chance to say anything else, Jeff walks over and in his typical, yet unintentional way, interrupts the conversation.

"Even if I were single, she's not my type," he states, pointing to the blond about ten feet away.

"What?" Sophie asks the same question I'm thinking.

"I was talking to her, just talking being nice while Matt here puts the moves on you, and she's like, 'I'm not going to sleep with you. Just so you know.' Seriously, do you not see my ring?" He holds his hand up to demonstrate the ring finger. "You know just because a guy talks to a girl, she assumes he's trying to have sex with her, like we can't just have a normal conversation."

I look over at the girl who is completely oblivious to Jeff's rant about her. She is now engaged in a conversation with the others.

"Oh, don't worry about her, she's probably just tired from work. Rachelle is really a sweet girl," Sophie responds.

Personally, I find that hard to believe. She looks like the kind of girl who has spent her life getting what she wants based on her appearance, using her beauty – something she spends hours in the morning perfecting – as a currency; the kind of girl who assumes every guy wants to have sex with her because she goes out of her way to look like someone guys would want to have sex with, yet being offended when they attempt it. But I'm not going to argue the point on Jeff's behalf. It is entirely possible that he did say something to offend her.

Jeff changes the subject for all of us although not necessarily for the better. "Well, I'm glad he's finally talking to you anyway. He's been staring at you all night."

"This is my friend, Jeff, by the way," I say.

"Sophie," she responds with a slight smile directed towards me.

"Tell us about yourself." Jeff says. Not waiting for a response, he continues, "We work for Electronix Systemz. My buddy here is responsible for releasing all our products."

"Oh," she says with a slight nod.

There is something about her that makes me want to wrap her in my arms and hold her close, to lean over and kiss her deeply, savoring the intoxicating flavor of her lips. I want to inhale the scent of her perfume, her skin, her shampoo, as we melt into each other.

She nods as Jeff keeps talking, in a way that shows she is placating his chatter, yet she looks over at me, raises her eyebrows and smiles, with an awareness of my thoughts.

Under the table, I pull out my iPhone and begin typing a message.

dude! You're cramping my style.

With the noise from the music, I don't hear his phone beep from my message, and he does not appear to hear it either as he keeps talking about the software our company makes to help me impress her.

Jeff continues, "We both were brought on board at the same time, and were in the same new hire introduction classes, bonding over those cheesy 'this is the best company ever' orientation videos they showed us," he chuckles. "We don't report to the same manager. I handle content management and Matt does releases."

"This is a fancy way of saying he updates our company's online how-to content and spends the rest of his time watching YouTube videos," I interrupt.

A server arrives with another round of drinks, including a round of tequila shots that Kai ordered. The others join us. We all toast, then shoot them back with the scrunched faces and gag sounds that always seem to accompany shots of tequila.

Why do we do this to ourselves with tequila? It is not like anyone has ever ended a story about tequila shots with, "… and I had so much fun." No, the story usually ends with, "… and that is why I hate tequila," or "… that's why I don't drink tequila anymore," or "… that's how I ended up with this butterfly tattoo on my back."

It dawns on me that I am extremely inebriated at the moment and no longer interested in the conversations happening around me. A new pleasure in life has presented itself: watching Sophie drink. She brings the glass up to her lips, looks down, slowly tilts the drink back, purses her lips as if to kiss it, then slowly sips at it. Sometimes her eyes look up to me with a slight curve of joy in the corner of her mouth. She seems to drink at a slower pace than everyone else, even though quantity-wise she is keeping up.

I gesture to Jeff, putting two fingers to my lips. He nods in agreement.

"Going to have a smoke. You want to join?"

Sophie shakes her head. "I don't smoke. Thanks"

Outside the fresh air works its magic on my blurry eyes.

"How are things going with the hottie?" Jeff asks me after adding flame to tobacco.

"Good, I think. Except for you keep cock blocking me."

"What? How am I cock blocking you? I was just talking you up to her earlier."

"Umm, you keep interrupting, for one."

"Just trying to help a brother out. I can't get any myself so I have to live vicariously through you, you know."

"Okay," I say realizing I'm being a bit of a dick. "Thanks, I guess."

"Actually, I think I might take off after this." He gestures to his cigarette. "The wife is probably wondering where I'm at."

"Are you good to drive?"

"Yeah, I'm fine. I switched to water about an hour ago."

I mentally question his statement as I don't recall him drinking any water, but he seems fine. We go back inside where he pays his tab and I head back to the table after picking up another whiskey and Coke.

6

Opening my eyes, it takes a few seconds to realize where I am. The girl I want to be with, whose bed I want to wake up in, is not the girl I am lying next to. Could I quietly sneak out? Should I? Or should I continue to lie here with my dry cotton mouth tasting of alcohol and cigarettes, my throbbing head, and the panic at wanting to leave and not being able to do so?

It's stifling hot in this room and even though I'm completely nude, my body is covered in stale sweat, the pores oozing with last night's memories. The room is full of light, shining through the beige curtains that I've woken up to again and again in the past. On this occasion, they are casting a defused regret upon me. Mixed with the sweltering morning rays of sun edging past the curtains, is the radiator attached to the wall, drying the air of any moisture. Slowly, my body snakes toward the edge of the bed, trying as hard as possible not to move the thick comforter we are both under. She is lying next to me with her mouth half-open, breathing heavily with a slight snore, informing me of her sound sleep. I remember taking my pants and shirt off in the room and dropping them onto the floor next to the bed, and I think most of the rest of my clothing is in the living room near the door.

I keep inching my way out of the bed, but the loud breathing stops, and it is clear she is waking up, so I give up on trying to be quiet and slide all the way off the mattress, quickly picking up my pants and underwear and dress with my back to the bed.

"You leaving?" she murmurs.

"Yeah, I've got stuff to do today."

"Sure you do."

"Well, Jennifer, if you can use me for an occasional booty call, it's only fair that I get to occasionally use you for one as well."

I turn around to look at her. My pants are on by now. She is leaning up on one arm, and I'm trying to decide if I should give her a kiss or not. I really don't want to. For one I can taste each breath as it passes through the hole in my face. And secondly, I'm disgusted with myself for having texted her last night and coming over.

"Okay," she says.

She follows me, climbing out of the bed. Watching her naked body slide into the panties she has picked up off the floor does give me a slight urge to take them back off her. She then reaches for a bathrobe that hangs on the back of the closet door.

"Why?" she asks.

"Why what?"

"You don't mind calling me up in the middle of the night. You don't seem to mind it when I call you, yet you don't want to be in a relationship with me. You just want to use me for sex."

I let out an obvious sigh before saying, "I'm not in the mood for this. And let's be honest, you are the one who messaged me for the same reason last weekend. So, it's only fair that I do the same. If you are not okay with that, then fine. We just need to agree no more booty calls."

She follows me into the living room, where my shoes and jacket are waiting. The only thought in my head is getting out the door and home to enjoy a long piss and a large glass of ice water.

"I'm just asking a simple question of why you don't mind having sex with me, but don't want to be in a relationship? You owe me that much."

"First of all, I don't owe you shit, you fucking nutcase. You lie and create conflict for no apparent reason—

"No, I don't, you're the one who gets mad all the time."

"Really? How about the time you told me that your ex-boyfriend had been in a gang and was in jail after shooting someone."

"That was a joke."

"No, that was not a joke! You were serious and the only reason you later said it was a joke was

71

because I brought it up to Leah and she didn't know what I was talking about, and to cover yourself from that lie you created another by lying and saying you had been joking. You have the emotions of an insecure 15-year-old who has to lie to be liked—"

"Coming from the guy who smokes pot literally every day!"

"And you never let me finish sentences before getting mad and interrupting me."

"Fine, go on."

"I have nothing more to say."

"Fuck you!" she yells after the door has been closed.

Turning the key, the Mini's engine comes to life. Rolling down the window, lighting a cigarette I inhale a deep, soothing drag, allowing the crisp embrace of the morning air and tobacco to calm the anxiety gnawing at my nerves.

As I make my way north on I-5, which is relatively void of traffic this morning, the sky is clear and the morning sun is shining bright; I think back to last night. It was only around 11:00 when Sophie and her friends had to leave. It's a bit fuzzy why they had to go so early, but at least I managed to get Sophie's number before she left. Maybe they had a party or something. Kai had been messaging with someone he wanted to meet, not interested in joining him and not ready to head home alone, I texted Jennifer. From the Garage it was a short drive to her place where she was waiting and ready to go. She's such a mental case. At times amazing at others bat-shit-crazy – like someone with multiple personalities. One minute, she could be the most caring and loving person, and the next, an emotionally unstable and insecure child.

7

Driving in to work, I think maybe it would be a good idea to pull out the one-hitter and medicate myself to operational tolerance. The ibuprofen I took this morning doesn't seem to be doing much. Normally, the one hitter is reserved for after-work use only out of fear that I might get drawn into something during the day that requires my full attention. Luckily, my morning today is empty, and in all reality, I can do my job on autopilot, just like this drive. The real question is, will that leave me enough for the commute home? And which is more important: unwinding after work or before? I reach over at one of the traffic slowdowns and pull the pipe out of the little central cubby between the seats. Packing it, I take a hit, roll down the window, and exhale, feeling good about the decision.

As always, I find myself weaving through the same congested traffic, destined for my usual parking spot. Forward for a minute or two, shift down, slow, stop, speed up, third gear, not fast enough for third gear, then back down to second. Take another hit. Repeat.□

Exiting the damp and dim parking garage, I step into the elevator, which carries me to the third floor, where drab light-brown carpeting and white walls guide me to my office.

Placing my laptop into the docking station, I press the power button; the screen begins to glow as the startup process begins. Then I amble toward the break room for today's first of many cups of coffee. Alongside the coffee, I retrieve a couple more ibuprofen from the medicine kit attached to the wall. The first cup of coffee is like the first cigarette of the day or that initial sip from a frosty cold beer. It always tastes better than anything to come after it – a wakeup call for the taste buds.

The break room isn't really a room; it's more like a break area in the center of the building on our floor. There is a long counter against a wall that has the coffee machine, cups, and other appropriate accessories. At the end of the counter is a fridge that is mostly full of plastic containers brought in for people's lunches and left over to be cleaned out by the janitors after time turns the food into rancid birthing colonies of mold. There is also an island counter separating the kitchen portion of the break area from the seating area. The counter it is empty, with some stools next to it so that people can sit and eat if they want. The seating area has a black leather sofa, and four matching armchairs arranged in an oval around a wooden coffee table with stains from coffee and other cups that have been placed on it over the years.

As I set the coffee cup under the Starbucks-branded coffee machine and press the button, waiting for it to brew, I stand back and enjoy a rare moment of tranquility in the building. The gentle hum of the coffee maker working its magic is the only sound, as the strong bold scent of ground beans is added to the air.

Most of my coworkers have yet to arrive. Only a few having fought their way through the traffic congestion into the office, or after having dropped the kids off at school. In this city, doing this work, and with the traffic jammed bumper to bumper as it always is, it is rare to see many people in before 9 in the morning. Most prefer to come in later and to work in the evening.

Arriving back at my desk, coffee in one hand, granola bar from the vending machine in the other, the computer has come to life, with today's set of emails waiting for me. Emails having been sent by various people throughout the night from their Blackberry, iPhone, or laptop. Whatever it is they have to say that could not wait until the next day, because if they don't send the email, they will forget it. Mostly, I suspect they send it to prove how dedicated to the company they are. I find most of my inbox of unread messages to be from people letting me know that AdMatics is not out of Beta. Those are all promptly deleted. Next up is a bunch from Chris, who must have a miserable home life and not be particularly fond of his wife. Otherwise, he might spend a little less time on his laptop and a bit more time with her, or with his new child. I don't know at what point a baby moves from newborn to annoying, but it still must be in that phase of cute and lovable. Another one of his advice books, I'd imagine. *If you can't sleep, use the time wisely and be productive.*

It was not that long ago they had the kid. He took some time off for paternity leave around six months ago. That was an exceptional month spent watching Netflix and YouTube videos, playing Words with Friends, online poker, and not having to deal with his email spam. A month during which, without him, somehow, the job still managed to get done.

Before I read the list of "super important e-mails" I open my Outlook calendar and type in the names of the people that need to be invited to a meeting I forgot to setup last week. I start by looking for a time that everyone is available – tomorrow or the next day? No. It looks like the meeting will not be until next week. I type a quick summary of the purpose and send out the invite, knowing full well what will happen next. Chris will see the invite, then message me asking to move it earlier in the week, oblivious to the reason that I set it up for the date and time I did. At which point I will have to explain the reason for the date, along with offering to set it up late in the evening if he wants it this week. He won't want that, and will eventually give in on the meeting time for the following week after a lot of back and forth that will all happen in email or Communicator, because even though his office is right around the corner from mine, he is way too busy to swing by and speak in person. I, of course, could just walk to his office but don't want to.

While waiting for the inevitable response from the man in charge of my life, I go through the rest of my inbox, deleting most of the emails based on the subject line. The rest, I skim over the text before deciding to delete them. Of course, there are a few relevant ones, that are filed away in case I need them to reference at some later point. Only two require a response. The first was from someone looking for the new release dates sent Saturday afternoon. I quickly respond with the new date and attach a copy of the updated project roadmap PowerPoint. The second email is a meeting invite which I accept without really paying attention to the purpose beyond the subject.

I've now been in the office for about 30 minutes, and most of what I need to do today is done. I take a sip of my coffee, then pull out Saturday's lottery ticket from my wallet, open a browser window and type "Washington State Lotto" and wait for the page to load. After scanning the numbers, I crumple up the ticket before tossing it into the trash can near the office door. I want a cigarette, a joint, and a drink, in that order. At least I can get one out of those three. After checking Communicator to see if Jeff is in yet (he's not), I hit control-alt-delete to lock my computer, grab my thick jacket, and walk down the wide staircase in the center of the building to the glass lobby doors. The oversized glass entrance door is surrounded by even larger glass windows, allowing a preview of the cold and low contrast scene outside as the thick gray clouds overhead mute what little color there is in the city.

Zipping the jacket up to maintain my body heat as the cold wakes me, I pull my pack of cigarettes out of the pocket, smack one out of the pack and flip it into my mouth. Outside on the downtown streets of Seattle, morning commuters walk past like a colony of penguins, marching from one place to the next, heads tucked down, lost in their thoughts.

I move away from the entrance of the building, so as not to offend anyone with the smell of the smoke. Yes, it's a dirty, nasty habit, and maybe one day I'll quit, only that day won't be today or any day soon. My history with the cancer stick began back in junior high, back when it was easier to get convenience stores to sell cigarettes to kids, and when it was easier to get adults to buy them for you. That moved into smoking in college to release stress and relax, to the real world of smoking because it's just what I do, who I am, and the provided excuse to take a break and leave my desk for a few minutes. Standing in front of the building, attempting to not make eye contact with each passerby, so the person can't attempt to bum a smoke, or give me the stink eye, I quickly finish the cigarette before heading back inside.

After I've been sitting at my desk for about 10 minutes, munching on a granola bar and sipping on my coffee with The Huffington Post open on my screen, I close the tab and open a requirements document that needs to be finished this week, determined to make some progress.

"Smoke break!" Jeff says, standing in my office doorway.

"Nice shirt," I say, raising on eyebrow. He's wearing a blue shirt with little flower patterns all over it.

"The wife bought it for me."

"That's new? It looks like you stole it from a 1970s Vietnamese refugee."

"I like it. Come on, cigarette break?"

"I just got back. It's not my fault you are a slacker who just now arrived to work. Plus, it's cold outside."

"Come ooon, don't be a baby. You know you want another one. Yummy, yummy, yummy, smokey, smokey, smoke."

I look at my computer screen as if something interesting might magically appear and motivate me to remain at my desk.

"Fine," I moan.

It's not long before we are huddled into the narrow alley next to the building. The overhang from our office and the one next door is barely keeping the haze of rain off of us.

"So, guess who I have a meeting with today?" I say after we've lit our cigarettes.

"Who?"

"Heather."

"Oh yeah."

"Yeah. And it's just her and me in a dimly lit conference room. First, I'm going to go through the new feature set with her, followed up by her thanking me as she locks the door, bends over the table and demands that I do her from behind."

He laughs. "Of course."

Heather is married, and a really nice person. However, that has never stopped us from making inappropriate comments about her in nearly every conversation we have involving her.

"Well, while you're busy with all that," he tells me. "I'll be busy surfing my way to the end of the internet."

"Still nothing to do?"

"Nope, my job is basically dependent on your job. I have nothing to do except watch Netflix and read blogs."

"Rough life. Do you think people at large software companies sit around as much as we do?"

"I know they do, bro. My neighbor works for Microsoft and he is always talking about how he is always sooo busy."

"Just like we talk about how busy we are?"

"Precisely, the busier one appears, the less one is actually doing."

"True that," I reply. "They must be super busy to buy those fancy houses out in the Quah." This is a reference to the town of Issaquah where a large concentration of highly paid tech employees live. "When are you going to apply?"

"My wife keeps bugging me too."

"Tell her to get a job there, then."

"She's trying, man."

"Haha, sucka! She'll drag you with her."

"Yeah, I know, but least I'll get access to the company store. Which might be nice. And getting to

Redmond from my house is way less hassle than getting here."

"Oh, come on, you mean the free copy of Picaresque you get here isn't enough," I say, referring to the Photoshop rip-off our company sells.

We begin to walk inside, ignoring the looks of some girl who is expressing her offence at the two smokers that just dropped cigarette butts on the cement.

"It's not like working there would differ all that much compared to this place."

"True, one large soulless corporation isn't that different from another." I pause as we wait for the elevator. "Personally, I'll just wait for someone to buy us. And if I'm lucky I'll get laid-off with a nice severance check."

"It was pretty nice when I was laid off from AT&T," he boasts. "That's when we bought the Volvo. The timing was perfect. A three-month severance package, coupled with securing a new job in under a month's time."

"And a sweet ride it is," I say as we get off the elevator and begin to walk toward our offices.

"Hey Bro, don't be jealous just because I can fit your car in the back of mine."

"Later," I respond, heading back to my office, thinking maybe I'll work on that godforsaken requirement document.

But upon returning to my desk, I stare at the document like I've been doing all morning, and I wonder if anyone would notice if I fell asleep, taking a nice little nap before my meeting. Locking the door and closing the blinds sounds like it could work. But Communicator would show me as inactive, so instead of napping I join a poker room to stay *active* and look busy.

8

I arrive at the restaurant a little early for my date with Sophie. It's not raining, so I light up a cigarette on the corner while watching cars circling the block in search of parking.

Knee High Stocking plays itself up as a hip speakeasy-styled bar and restaurant. It's in this nondescript building with no signs outside, windows dressed in curtains like they have something to hide. I hope she can find it, and more crucially, that she won't flake out on me. We've tried planning a night out for weeks and can never seem to arrange a good time. I was beginning to think she was just having fun stringing me along. But tonight, she claimed to be available, so let's see if this date actually happens.

It isn't long after I finish the cigarette and flick the butt into the road that I see her walking down the street in my direction. She's wearing a long black skirt or dress with frills at the bottom sticking out from under an overcoat. Instead of heels, she has sneakers on. As she closes in, I see they're blue Vans. I smile.

"Hi."

"Shall we go in?" I ask.

"Sure."

We walk over to the entrance and I press the buzzer. It only takes a few seconds for the hostess to open the door.

"Hi, I had a reservation for two under Reynolds."

She looks at her list for my name, then guides us to our table. The restaurant is a narrow single-story building on the corner of two intersecting streets. Tables are snugly arranged next to each other, forming a single row on each side of the slender building. The faint sound of jazz music plays in the background, mixed with the soft chatter of other diners. Behind a compact bar counter which displays a variety of liquors, a bartender with a neatly curled mustache is mixing cocktails.

We take our seats at a small two-person table on the left side of the restaurant. Sophie removes her coat to reveal a dark burgundy blouse. It looks to be made of silk and has long sleeves with ruffles on the cuffs and neck, in a similar style to her long skirt.

The waitress hands us the menus and says, "The bartender is doing a special drink tonight called The Red Robin, a martini with whiskey, grenadine, lemon, and a dash of bitters."

We both order the recommended drink while we review the menu.

"So …" I say.

"So …" she responds.

"Did you find the place okay?" I ask.

"Yeah, I looked it up on Yelp."

"Cool, cool." I nod my head, not really knowing what else to talk about.

Luckily, it's not long before the server returns with our drinks and takes our food order. The cocktail hits the spot, the burn of the whisky blending nicely with a touch of sweetness and a hint of sour. It won't be long before I order another one.

"What do you do again? Your friend made it sound important," she inquires, breaking the silence. "I'm a project manager. And no, it's not important work. He just likes to make it sound like it is. Electronix Systemz is a small software company with a stupid name. We have a few different products we sell. Essentially, my job is to manage changes in release versions from one product to the next. So, when someone decides a button should be blue instead of green, I help make that happen."

She nods, obviously not finding it that interesting, yet for some reason, I keep talking.

"And um, I take all the change requests and compile them and run meetings with people about them. And stuff like that."

"It doesn't sound like you care for it all that much."

Not wanting to go into the *I hate my job* speech, I change the subject. "How about you? What do you do?"

"Well," she pauses, "I'm an accountant and do the books for a property management company."

"Like Century 21?"

"No, they don't sell property, they manage properties and own a few businesses. Most people don't realize that most businesses don't own the buildings they are in; they lease them. That's what we do. But we also own a few businesses ourselves, like Dolls. We own both the building and the business.

"The strip club?" I ask.

"Yes."

"Do you also dance there?" I ask in a teasing tone.

"Actually, I do," she responds.

"Oh! Interesting."

"Do you have an issue with that?" she asks, raising an eyebrow.

"No, not at all," I say, while imagining the body she has under that dress up on a dance floor.

"We'll see, won't we?" she replies. "Most guys either want to sleep with me because of where I work, or they want to leave because they are assholes who assume I'm a slut. For the record, I do it because I enjoy the way it makes me feel, and the cash is damn good."

"Don't worry, we're good," I say. "I mean …
I wanna sleep with you, but that's 'cause you are
super sexy, confident, and I like you. I don't think
there is anything wrong with working at a strip club.
In fact, I think it's kinda hot … but not in a slutty
way …"

"Or maybe it excites you," she says, leaning
forward, the curves of her breasts subtly emphasized.
"But I'm not the kind of girl you would take home to
meet your mommy."

How the hell should I respond? It feels like
she's baiting me, trying to seduce me while also
getting ready to throw a drink in my face. I turn to
look for the waitress to order another cocktail, but
she is looking in a different direction.

"Ummm, no," I pause. "Look, first of all, I
don't want to take any girl home to meet my mother.
Also, does that mean you want me to take you to
meet my parents? It's a little early for that, isn't it?" I
manage a smile.

She leans back in her chair with a self-
satisfied smirk. "Don't flatter yourself; you're not
exactly my type anyway."

"Oh, really, I seem to recall being just your
type the night we met," I reply, mirroring her smug
expression. "And you were quite flirty the other
night, as well."

"Perhaps my taste has evolved," she says, her eyes narrowing playfully. "Maybe pretty metro boys don't do it for me anymore."

"I'd say handsome and manly. Also, how am I metro? Is that even a thing anymore?"

"Well, look at you. Styled hair, fancy shirt, and those shoes, what did those cost?"

"I don't know. I don't remember how much they cost." Actually, I do. "But I don't think they were that much." Yes, they were.

"Where do you get your hair cut? A posh salon where they pamper your scalp and call you 'sir'?" she says with a bit of an aristocratic tone.

"That would be nice, but no, I usually get it cut at Rudy's. So, there." I give her a smile. "Rudy's isn't an expensive barbershop. In fact, they are a bit random in the quality of haircuts, depending on who I get."

"Mmm, yeah," she nods, her gaze lingering seductively as she kisses the rim of her martini glass, taking another sip from her drink.

The waitress returns to the table with our meals, interrupting our banter. We each order another cocktail as well.

I have a pork loin with potatoes and a couple of vegetables next to it. She has ordered an eggplant thing. Her food looks terrible to me. However, she says it's delicious and mine tastes good as well.

During our third round of drinks, as our meal slowly vanishes, I'm certainly feeling the calm that comes with a few cocktails and a satisfying meal.

"So, I have to ask. And this is in no way meant to be rude, but how did you get into stripping?"

She gives me a look that tells me she is tired of answering this question for people.

"I got bored sitting behind a desk staring at spreadsheets. And after seeing the money the girls were making at the club I auditioned. And then I started working a few nights a week for extra money. Now, I'm mostly there, dancing my nights away and making far more than I ever did behind a desk. And it's not just about the money; I actually enjoy it."

"Hey, I can relate to the whole *bored sitting behind a desk* thing. That pretty much sums up my job. And accountant to exotic dancer. That's an interesting transition."

"I usually just tell people I'm an accountant, depending on who I'm speaking with. People can be really judgmental sometimes."

"Hey," I hold my hands up. "No judgment here." I assure her. "Seems like your life's a hell of a lot more interesting than mine."

"Good, now that we've cleared the air about my job, let's get one thing straight. I'm not ashamed of what I do. If a guy's interested in me, he's got to be okay with it," she states.

I get the vibe that the people seated elbow-to-elbow next to us are listening to our conversation. The need for a smoke and another round of drinks is creeping up on me.

There is a bit of a pause before I ask, "So, why did you kiss me that night? When we met."

Her eyes narrow ever so slightly, a coy smile forming on her lips. "I kissed you because I wanted to. Simple as that. There was something about you, in that moment, that intrigued me."

"Oh?"

"I'd recently ended things with my girlfriend," she says, her eyes locking onto mine, a wry smile forming. "It was New Year's, and you looked hot and a little lonely. It made me want to kiss you."

"So, out of the three straight guys there, I was the best looking one?" I say with a bit of a frown.

"And, of course, you were the best-looking among the three," she adds, her smile growing wider. "Our little make-out session was quite nice. It's a shame you left so early."

"Best out of three, I'll take it." I smile, raising the remnants of my cocktail for a toast, and mentally kicking myself for leaving the party when I did. Our glasses clink as we both down the last drops and signal for another round.

As we sit facing each other, engaged in our flirtatious banter, I stare into her eyes, blinking to a slowing rhythm as the alcohol works its magic. Her movements glide through the scene in front of me with the grace of a ballerina. Her arms move with a fluidity as she raises her glass, puckers those lips, and sips ever so delicately, as if she's relishing every drop of the concoction. A mental checklist scrolls through my head.

Is super-hot = check.
Bisexual = check.
Stripper = check.
Drinks = check.
Is into me = crazy.
Crazy = great in bed.
Male fantasy = check.

"So, can I come watch you dance sometime?" I ask.

"If you're interested in seeing me, then show up at the club. Just know you're paying like everyone else. And if you act strange or cross a line, I'll have the bouncer show you the door. That'll also mean no second date."

"I take it that means there will be a second date?" I smile.

"Maybe." She teases. "We'll see how the rest of the night goes."

We're not ready to call it a night just yet, so we order another round, this time opting for one of the alternative concoctions from the drink menu. It's clear the bartender here takes pride in his cocktails, as the next drink surpasses the previous one in taste. Then again, it could be the alcohol has kicked in. Either way, I'm in no hurry to see this night come to an end.

"If you want to talk about something other than taking off your clothes in front of people, although, I'm perfectly happy to talk about that all night," I say with a wry smile. "I can talk about spreadsheets, algorithms, and data analytics with you?"

"As could I. I am also an accountant, remember?" She winks. "How about we skip the number-crunching and go straight to dessert?"

We split a cheesecake, followed up with one final round of drinks, before I pay the bill. She does the obligatory offer to split the check with me, and I do the typical, "No I got it" response, before looking at the huge number on the bill. I give the waitress my card and have trouble figuring out the tip, which makes me bluntly aware of how well-made the drinks are.

As we step outside, we are greeted with a gentle sprinkle of rain, adding an extra layer of atmosphere to the evening. Neither of us seems eager to call it a night.

"So, do you want to get another drink?" I ask.

"Sure," she replies. "How about we take it to my place?"

Sweet!

"Okay. Do you want me to follow you there?"

"I don't have a car," she says, "I live close enough to take the bus."

I want to ask her how she gets home from the strip club after the busses stop running, but that can be a conversation for another night – hopefully.

We walk to my car, and she gives me directions to her place. It is a quick drive through the city to Belltown, and then around the block a few times, before finding a parking spot. As we get out, I wonder if I will spend the night and at what time I will have to move or pay so as not to get a ticket.

She unlocks the front entrance of a large old brick building that I've probably driven past a hundred times and never really noticed before. The entrance has marble floors, or what looks like marble floors, and a large stairwell directly in front of us. To the left of that is an elevator. Getting in, she hits the button for the sixth floor. Stepping out of the elevator, I notice the smell of new carpet in the hallway that looks like it has been recently replaced, along with a fresh coat of white paint.

I follow her to a door where she unlocks a deadbolt. The door opens into a short hallway that leads into a decent-sized living room, which I can see has a large window facing the buildings across the street. She switches on a light in the hallway, kicks her shoes off, and hangs her coat on a rack attached to the wall. I do the same, following her into the living room, letting the door shut behind us.

The room has high ceilings with thick trim around the edges. It smells of flowers or some kind of other female fragrance. The furniture is nice, dark brown leather, and the floors are laminate wood. There is a large, off-white fuzzy rug under the coffee table. The room is dimly lit, with only the glow from the city lights filtering in through the window. Damn, it's furnished nicer than my place. I wonder if she owns or rents. In this neighborhood, this place can't be cheap. She wasn't kidding when she said strippers make decent money.

With the alcohol coursing through my veins, and drawn by her irresistible allure, I step closer, enveloping her slender waist with my arms, and give her a soft, lingering kiss.

Drawing back slightly, she smiles, an explicit invitation in her expression. Encouraged, I lean in for another kiss, this time with a bit more intensity, and she responds by pulling me close, her embrace pressing her curves against me. Our tongues mirroring that same magnetic dance they engaged in the very first night we met.

My hands hurry down her back, firmly holding her tight against me. She pulls my shirt up over my head before taking hers off. Then she takes my hand and leads me through a door to a bedroom. The bed is covered with a thick, purplish duvet, and a veritable mountain of pillows, which are quickly scattered onto the floor.

While on the bed, we continue to undress each other quickly, with her unbuckling my belt and I unclasp her bra. She has firm flat abs, and the most perfect tits I have ever seen. Not too large, not too small, just right. She reclines on her back, revealing her soft yet beautifully toned body in its entirety. I just want to kiss every inch of her. My right-hand cups one of her breasts, fitting perfectly as if they were designed just for me.

I climb on top of her, kissing her neck, and listening to her soft moans. I can't wait to feel the inside of her. "Where are the condoms?" I ask.

"I don't have any," she responds.

"Um—"

"It's okay. I'm on the pill."

It's not her getting pregnant that worries me. Although that would suck as well, it's more the fact that she practically humped me the night we met; she works at a strip club; she's fucking me on our first date; and she doesn't care if I use a condom or not.

Please don't have some disease, I think, just before sliding into her. She is boiling inside, her fiery juices inviting me further. Biting into my chest, she moans, and I can feel her nails digging into my back. The taste of her skin lingers on my lips as I passionately kiss her neck, her breath quickening with every touch. With my left hand I reach around and grab hold of the back of her hair, gripping it tightly, she moans louder, letting me know she approves, moving her hips in unison with mine, our rhythm increases and her legs move up and around so I can feel the heels of her feet bounce off my lower back with each thrust. The words "fuck me" escape her lips while I grind harder, as if trying to crawl as far as possible inside her. She rolls us over and starts riding me.

Her eyes flutter as if in a trance as she moves rhythmically up and down on top of me, increasing in speed. The thought of her bouncing so high she slides out and lands on my dick, snapping it, does a good job of giving me something to think about so I don't cum too soon.

Her nails dig into my chest as I grasp onto her nipples, squeezing them firmly, which she seems to enjoy, so I apply more pressure. She moans, which I interpret as her getting ready to climax, and I can feel the same building up in me as well. I'm ready to blow inside her like a fluid-filled jack-in-the-box.

Her head falls and her back arches as she climaxes, forcing her hips down and onto my cock.

As soon as she finishes and slows her pace a bit, I flip her onto her back, grab her legs and pull them over my shoulder. She continues to moan, building to another orgasm, as I cum inside her, blending our juices into a cocktail of spent sexual desire.

I pant as I collapse on top of her hot and damp body, struggling to catch my breath. The scent of alcohol and sex hangs in the air, mingling with our shared perspiration on her tender flesh. As we both lay there, basking in the afterglow, I slide out, and she releases a soft sad moan at no longer having me inside her. A satisfied smile spreads across her face, her hair a wild mess, as if a storm just passed through the room. We lay together, intertwined, silent – satisfied.

As the aftermath of our intimate encounter begins to wane, my dry mouth and vices inform me that I have an urge for some water and cigarette.

"I need a cigarette," I say.

"Sorry, no smoking inside."

Damn. I would have to go out to smoke, which means getting dressed and going downstairs.

"How about a glass of water, then?"

"That I can do," she replies.

I watch her naked ass get out of the bed, shaking as she walks into the other room, and I can feel the twitch of excitement building in my groin again. It won't be long before we have another round.

9

Ah, Monday, everyone's least favorite day of the week. In my case, even less so after a weekend, of bared skin and a passionate exploration between two new lovers. Saturday, we spent most of the day in bed, on the sofa, in the shower, and back in the bed, with some food delivery thrown in to keep us going. In the evening, she sent me home, having to work that night. I was stuck on the sofa watching TV with nothing to do besides think of her body sweating up on a stage, working her way around a pole while guys slipped her cash in exchange for a lap dance. I probably would have masturbated at the thought except my dick needed a break. On Sunday she was over at my place, where again we spent most of our time with our clothing off. The best thing about a new relationship is the stimulating cocktail of sexual excitement and desire, and the prayers that it will never end.

Monday rolls around and it's back to the cityscape; an unending panorama of monotonous paint-by-numbers office buildings that are sprouting up next to one another faster than it seems possible to fill them. The daily ritual of the drive, the coffee, and the onslaught of emails awaits my arrival. The vibrant weekend of passion is now a fading memory, replaced by a week awash in shades of grey.

Forcing myself to think about work, I wonder if the software release happened this weekend, or if it was pushed back again while I was busy burying my face between Sophie's thighs. With Outlook open, I see it finally happened. The notification of the completed software release, which is quickly followed by a deluge of congratulatory emails, each of my coworkers trying to outdo the other in a grand display of mutual admiration, all while reminding us just how supremely outstanding we are. So outstanding, and dedicated, that we have to send out congratulatory emails on a Sunday.

> *We are a go!*
> *Congrats!!*
> *Congratulations Everyone – We are live now to all users!!!!*
> *Great job everyone!*
> Etcetera, etcetera, and so on.

Fuck, people! Really! Do you really need to reply to the replies, congratulating everyone on a release and update to a product that didn't even include all that many new features and happened a month after it was originally scheduled? What I'd like to do is respond with a congratulatory email of my own:

Yeah, good job everyone. Way to go back and forth arguing over functionality so as to delay the launch. Especially considering that the PM's really had no say in usability and features and the developers more or less told us what we would get, making our job completely pointless. But on the plus side, we have plenty of job redundancy should someone leave.

Suck it up your asses!

Matt

I would then follow up the email with me standing on my desk, whipping out my dick and pissing all over my office before being escorted out of the building.

Okay. Deep breath. I begin deleting each email, waiting for the day to end just like every day.

"Bro." It's Jeff at my door. "Coffee?"

"Yes." I jump up, anxiously wanting to tell him about my weekend, and to get away from the desk and pointless barrage of emails.

At the coffee shop, our customary ritual unfolds as we engage in our usual bout of playful banter with Jessie while placing our drink orders and then, with our coffees in hand, we make our way outside for a cigarette.

Jeff starts. "You wouldn't believe my weekend. I was forced to dedicate nearly all of

Sunday to updating and publishing the how-to guides."

"Yeah, sucks to be you." I quickly interject. "I spent all weekend in bed with Sophie."

"The girl from the Garage?" he asks. His expression a mixture of shock and awe.

"Yep. We went out on Friday night. Fucked Friday night, fucked Saturday morning, fucked Sunday afternoon … well, you get the point." I smile with that smug smile that men do when bragging to each other.

"Good for you my brotha."

He offers a fist bump, which I tap.

"Yes. And it gets better. Check this out, she's a stripper."

"Like, at a strip club."

"Yep. Well, *exotic dancer* I think is the preferred term. I don't know, I didn't ask."

"No way!"

"Totally serious. She is a sexy, hot, stripper."

"I'm so jelly, bro. My weekend was spent juggling work and a visit to Bed Bath and Beyond with the wife."

"You know, I'm okay with that. While you were slaving away working and listening to your wife nag, I was busy having sex with a super-hot stripper chick."

I continue telling him about my weekend, relishing in that coveted envy from other men, the kind that every guy secretly craves – the look you get when you are strolling down the street with a beautiful woman on your arm. It's the reason that an octogenarian will marry a twenty-something. Not because he has anything in common with her or that they can even engage in stimulating conversation with each other. It is for the sheer "look what I have" joy of parading her around town like a shiny new Ferrari. Today, Jeff has that look in his eyes, and I have the Ferrari.

"Does she have any hot stripper friends?" he asks.

"Probably. Not that you get to touch any of them, married boy."

"Hey bro, nothing wrong with looking as long as you don't sample the goods."

"Whatever you say."

Back in the office, I try not think about Sophie by forcing myself to finish putting together a presentation for senior management outlining the feature set slated for inclusion in the upcoming spring release.

I want to know what Sophie is doing right now, to learn more about her by engaging in some online reconnaissance. However, she doesn't have Facebook, leaving the digital stalking avenue blocked.

That said, I can email her or text. The question is, should I? I don't want to appear too eager or clingy. After all, we spent all weekend together, and I don't want to come across as overbearing or needy. So, I hold off and exercise a bit of restraint. I check Gmail to see if she emailed me. Unfortunately, the inbox is disappointingly empty of messages from her. However, there is a subject line that catches my eye from Jennifer, titled "this weekend?" She was probably looking to hook up, which makes me feel a bit of relief that I didn't see it. Not that I would have replied anyway, thanks to the memorable weekend I experienced instead. Initially, I consider deleting it without looking at it, but my curiosity gets the better of me, and I decide to open it up after all.

Hey,

I got some "special vitamins" from a friend. If you aren't doing anything this weekend, you want to do some? For old times' sake ;)

Knowing what she is talking about, I feel a little excited reading her email. When we were together, we used to get ecstasy, some pot, then spending the entire night naked and having incredible sex. But, as with all great highs, there is the inevitable crash the next day. It was worth it at the time; now, I wonder how many brain cells I've destroyed in the process.

The email was sent on Friday, so I wonder if she meant this last weekend? But honestly, I couldn't care less at this point. My weekend with Sophie was nothing short of fantastic without the need for drugs. Yet for some reason, I don't delete the email as I should. I wonder if Sophie is into that. She probably is, she seems the type. The sex was amazing enough already, I wonder how good it would be if we were both rolling on E? I file away that tantalizing thought for a future conversation with Sophie and refocus on the task at hand: getting back to work.

Morning slowly drags on until I stroll over to Jeff's office to see if he is ready for lunch. His office is nicer than mine. He has a view that looks slightly past the building next to ours so he can see the Puget Sound in the background, just across the viaduct. His desk is facing towards the door, with the large window behind him. To the left is a bookshelf with a few books on it, none of them he has ever read. Most were given to him, in the same way I received the few in my office – at team events, trainings, or some other work function where they think that one of these books will inspire us to be better than we are. He also has a few pictures on the shelf – of him and his wife. One when they went on vacation to Hawaii and another from their wedding.

The door is open and Heather is sitting in the chair opposite his desk. So of course, I can't resist entering, interrupting whatever business they're conducting.

"Hey, guys," I say.

Heather is in an oversized button-up shirt that looks as if she swiped it from her husband. Her oversized glasses frame her face perfectly with chic precision, complementing her dark blond hair, which is pulled back into a ponytail. She has the look of someone who spent the night out, and hastily threw on some clothing in a rush before heading into the office. But maybe that's just me projecting.

"Hey, Matt," she responds, "You guys heading to lunch?"

"Yeah, you want to go with?" I don't expect her to accept.

"Maybe. Where to?"

"Probably just the sushi place."

"Sure. Okay. Let me go get my coat."

She leaves and I turn to Jeff with a smile and a raised eyebrow.

We walk together towards the usual sushi restaurant that we visit so often it's a wonder we haven't developed mercury poisoning. The familiar scent of fresh sushi and wasabi greets us as we enter the restaurant. Taking a table, we place our orders.

"Do anything interesting this weekend?" Jeff asks Heather after the waiter walks away.

"Worked mostly, getting everything out the door. You?"

"Ditto. How about you, Matt?"

"Nothing too exciting," I respond, not wanting to go into my weekend with Sophie in front of Heather.

Jeff doesn't let up. "What about that girl you went out with. Didn't you have a hot date or something?"

I know what he is doing. And of course, he knows it as well, probably thinking it is funny.

Heather jumps in. "Hot date? Oh, who with?"

"Nobody you know. She is a friend of a friend?"

"That's cool. Where does she work?"

I look at Jeff who is smiling in a way that shows he thinks he is being so funny.

What the hell. It's not like I have a chance with Heather anyway and she's always been pretty cool. "Actually, she's a stripper. She's a super sexy, hot stripper," I say with an acknowledging sigh.

I proceed to tell her the story of how we met, with a subtle insinuation about our exploits after the date by saying we had "a good time," allowing me to sound like a gentleman without delving into the details.

"We're planning to catch one of her performances one of these weekends," Jeff adds.

"No, *we* are not," I state.

"Come on bro, I've met her and she's cool. She's used to performing for audiences, so she won't mind if you bring along a friend or two to the show."

"I'd like to go, too," Heather adds.

"Really? Won't your husband have a problem with that?" I ask.

"No. I doubt it. He'll probably want to come with."

She has talked about her husband before. He works as a catalog photographer for some store, either Nordstrom's or Macy's. Yet I have never met him and I'm curious to see what kind of guy could rope her into marriage.

"Okay. First let me check with her and make sure it's okay. We don't know each other that well," I tell them.

"From the sounds of it, you know her *very* well," Heather taunts.

The conversation shifts back to work, as they pick up the discussion they were having when I walked into Jeff's office. I take my phone out of my pocket, since now I have an excuse to email her to find out if she wouldn't mind me bringing a few people to see her dance.

10

"Pretty sure it's this one," I say as we are driving through the cookie-cutter McMansions that line the streets of Jeff's neighborhood.

I'm not all that much into football, but when Jeff invited me to his place to watch the game, and I mentioned it to Sophie, she was surprisingly enthusiastic about the idea. When I picked her up she was wearing blue jeans with Nikes and a large Patriots jersey under a Levi's Sherpa jean jacket. Turns out, the girl loves herself some football. As she settled into the seat next to me the light fragrance of her clean jasmine perfume and bare neck delicately exposed beneath the pulled back bun of her hair, made me wish we had time to run inside for a quickie.

"Hey, come on in," Evelyn says, as she opens the door.

"Hello," I reply, while giving her a quick hug. "This is Sophie. And this is Evelyn."

"Nice to meet you," Sophie says, as the two of them do a quick nice to meet you hug as well.

"Nice to meet you too. I've heard so much about you," Evelyn says.

I'll bet you have. I smile to myself, wondering what that conversation was like between Jeff and Evelyn.

We obediently remove our shoes at the entrance. Evelyn takes our jackets, then leads us to the kitchen where Jeff is stationed next to the kitchen island, preparing what looks to be a feast for an army. Their kitchen features a contemporary layout, complete with a well-lit space and sleek stainless-steel appliances. A large island separates the kitchen from a spacious dining room with an oak dining table commanding attention with its central placement and six chairs neatly arranged around it. The table is polished, adorned with placemats at each seat, and a candle and flower display in the center.

"Hey buddy. Welcome," he says while slicing food. "Can I get you a drink?"

"Got it covered," I hold up the bag in response.

"I'll take that," Evelyn says.

I hand her the grocery bag and grab two bottles of Redhook. She goes to put the stuff in the fridge while I take out my key ring bottle opener to open the bottles, handing one to Sophie and keeping the other for myself.

Jeff sets down the knife and comes around the counter to shake my hand and then to Sophie he gives a big hug. "Good to see you again," he says.

"You too," she replies.

"Quite the food display you have going on here," I say when he finally releases his embrace of my date.

"True. I might've gone a little overboard on the food front. But hey, there's no such thing as too much grub, right?"

"Yes, there is," Evelyn adds with a mocking tone.

"Well, I think it's fine," Jeff shoots back. "Plus, a couple of our neighbors might swing by."

As if on cue, there is a knock at the door that Evelyn goes to open, returning with two people in tow. The guy's wearing a pair of well-worn, baggy jeans and a Seahawks jersey that doesn't do as good of a job covering his belly as he probably thinks it does. He has a short dark beard that matches the large curls of his graying hair which fall into his face. The girl is about the same height with dark skin and curly hair that hints of African heritage. She's dressed casually in jeans paired with a Seahawks hoodie.

"This is Patrick and Katie," Evelyn says. "And this is Matt and Sophie."

"Oh no! A Pats fan!" Patrick blurts out at seeing Sophie. He takes a couple more steps towards her. "I can't stand Tom Brady," he says it with a condescending smile.

I instantly take a disliking to him and imagine grabbing him by the back of the head and smashing his face into the counter a few times.

Sophie replies with a similarly mocking tone. "How did the Sea-chickens do last weekend? Oh, that's right, they lost. And the previous weekend? Oh, yes, a loss as well. The Patriots, if I recall correctly, have notched up wins in the past two games."

"That's because we don't cheat."

"Okay, everyone that's enough," Evelyn says. "We're all friends here."

"Oh, we're just talking smack," Patrick replies.

"Ummm, here, why don't you guys take this food into the TV room," Jeff says.

We each grab a tray of food and make our way to the other room. Besides the living room, there is a separate family room towards the back, with a large white leather L-shaped sofa against the wall on the right, a coffee table in front of it. To the left of the entrance are two matching leather chairs and a lamp between them. Against the far wall there is an entertainment center with a 52-inch flatscreen. The pre-game show is playing on low volume. The overhead lights are off with the light coming from the lamp and two large French doors that look out to the backyard bordered by a wooden fence.

The coffee table has a white cloth covering it, where we set the food down.

"You okay without me for a minute," I say to Sophie in a lowered voice. "I'm going to grab a quick smoke before the game starts."

"I'll be fine." She smiles.

I slip on my shoes and coat and head out to my car, glancing around as I walk to see if anyone is outside and looking in my direction. Opening the car door, I slide into the driver's seat, letting my feet dangle to the side as I retrieve my discreet one-hitter and a pack of American Spirits. I take another quick look around, double-checking for any onlookers, before carefully packing the little metal tube. Satisfied no one is watching, I ignite it, inhale deeply, briefly holding the smoke in my mouth before finally allowing it to fill my lungs, holding it in to get as much THC as possible before exhaling slowly, determined not to cough. After one more hit, I tap out the ash and put it away. Lighting a cigarette, I close the car door, lock it, and lean on the side, exhaling a plume of smoke into the chilly air as I finish my cigarette.

Mashing it out on the bottom of my shoes, I flick the butt into the street before heading back inside to find Sophie and Evelyn in the kitchen. I can hear the TV from the other room has been turned up.

Walking towards the girls, I can hear Evelyn saying, "I hear it is really good exercise."

"Feel my thighs," Sophie says while bending her knee, tensing her leg, and angling for Evelyn to feel.

Leaning down, she gives the leg a squeeze. "Oh, you *are* toned."

Deciding not to involve myself in that discussion, I turn towards the family room where I find Patrick and Katie sitting next to each other on the sofa. Patrick is leaning over the coffee table, a small plate in front of him with chicken wings and chips on it. Jeff is sitting in one of the chairs to the left.

"Hey bro, have a seat," he says to me.

I pick up the bottle of beer I had been drinking from the table and sit in the other chair.

"What are the girls doing?" he asks.

"Nothing, just talking in the kitchen."

"Evelyn isn't bothering Sophie, is she? I can tell her to leave her alone if you want," Jeff says.

"No, seems like they are getting along fine. Talking about exercising or something."

"That would be a nice change," Jeff says under his breath.

I pretend not to hear him, taking a long swig from the bottle.

The TV announces the opening kickoff.

"The game is starting," Jeff yells to the other room.

"Can you bring me another beer," I add.

The girls enter, Sophie has a bottle of Redhook in each hand, one of which she hands to me as she sits down on my lap. Evelyn sits on the opposite end of the sofa from the other two.

"We can slide down, if you and Jeff want to sit next to each other." Katie offers to Evelyn.

"I'm okay. Thanks," she replies.

"Let's see if Hasselcrack … I mean Hasselbeck will be able to make it a whole game without being injured today." Sophie says after the kickoff.

"Ohh, harsh," Patrick replies.

"Play nice, people," Evelyn interjects.

"She started it."

"Leave them alone," Jeff says to Evelyn.

She replies with a shake of the head and roll of the eyes.

It's not long after the kickoff that my beer is empty, so I give Sophie a little push, showing the empty bottle to her, letting her know to get off my lap.

"I'll get it," she says. "I need another as well."

She gives me a quick kiss, then grabs mine and her empty beers. "Does anyone else want anything?"

"Could you grab me another Bud Light," Patrick adds.

"Me too," says Katie.

"Here, I'll come with you." Evelyn gets up and the two of them go to the kitchen.

"Hey bro, sorry about Evie," Jeff says to me in a low voice.

"What do you mean?"

"Um, you know, bugging Sophie and all."

"I don't think she is bothering her. They seem to be getting along fine."

"Ok, well just saying."

Curios as to what he is talking about, I get up to check on the two girls in the kitchen.

"I love this counter," I hear Sophie saying when I enter the room.

They are standing on opposite sides of the kitchen island. On the countertop are two cans of Bud Light, a bottle of Redhook, and a white wine that Evelyn has been drinking with another empty glass next to it that she is filling.

"Hey," Sophie says at seeing me, "I decided to switch to wine."

"That's cool," I say while picking my bottle up and having a swig.

"How are things in there?" Evelyn asks.

"Oh, fine," I respond, "just wanted to stand up for a minute and stretch my legs. Plus, honestly, I

119

don't care that much about football. I know it's not manly of me and all, but I've never understood our obsession at rooting for the same guys that used to bully and pick on kids in high school."

"Speak for yourself," Sophie says. "I got along just fine with most people back in school."

"Well, of course not you. You were probably a cheerleader or something in school."

"No need for assumptions," she says, with a slightly amused smile. "I was a bit of a bookworm at school and mostly hung out with my close friends. I think we didn't really have the cliques that some schools are known for."

Evelyn says, "I'm going to run these into the other room."

She takes the drinks from the counter.

"Look at that, you scared her off," I mock.

"No, she's very nice." She lowers her voice, "She was asking me about pole dancing classes."

"Really?"

"Yes. It's great exercise. A lot of girls now are taking classes just for the fun of it."

"Hmm, okay." I move closer to her, place my arm around her waist and say, "Speaking of pole dancing, I don't think anyone will notice should you feel like taking a spin around my pole in the upstairs bathroom. If you know what I mean."

She grins. "A rock would know what you mean. And no. We're guests."

"Yeah, that's what it means when people say 'make yourself at home.' So, just like home let's do it on the counter," I joke.

"You're such a perve," she says, giving my chest a playful slap.

"Thank you."

"Mmm, what you guys doing?" Jeff asks, entering the kitchen.

"Mmm, nothing," I reply.

"Cigarette?" he asks me.

"Sure."

Sophie leaves us to go back to the game, while Jeff and I grab our coats and head into his garage to smoke.

Jeff pushes the button next to the door to open the garage door so as to let the air circulate.

After lighting his cigarette, he hands me the lighter, which I use to do the same, then pocket the cheap plastic lighter, without him noticing.

"So, how are things going with you and Sophie?" he asks.

"Fine, actually pretty good."

"I'm jealous bro." He lowers his voice. "All day Evie has been nagging me."

"Dude, she seems fine to me."

"You don't know what she was like before you guys got here. She was obsessing over making sure everything was clean and organized. Take a look at this garage. She had me organizing it just on the chance guests might wander in here."

The garage has two cars in it, the Volvo Jeff drives and a black Nissan Altima. On the right wall of the entryway, there are shelves filled with plastic storage containers along with a few cardboard boxes mixed in. On the far wall is a wooden workbench with a toolbox on it, and a few tools hung above it – a hammer and a couple types of screwdrivers. Everything looks as if it was placed by a real-estate agent prepping it as a show room for potential clients.

"Looks fine to me. How is this any different from how it normally looks?"

"That's my point bro, the place is always like this. I can't ever leave anything laying out. Everything has to be immaculately placed in its proper space."

"So?" I shrug my shoulders.

"You don't understand because you live alone. You have the freedom to do what you want, when you want. If you want to leave a coffee cup on the counter, you can. If I leave one on the counter, I get chewed out."

"I still don't see the problem. Clean up after your nasty self," I say.

"You just wait, you wait and see when you get married, nothing is yours anymore, and say goodbye to doing what you want. So, you better appreciate these good times with Sophie, because trust me, it won't last!"

"You know, I wonder that sometimes." I confess, taking a drag of my cigarette. "But, honestly dude, Evelyn seems fine. She's like a total sweetheart. She was even asking Sophie about taking pole dancing lessons. You've got to appreciate that?"

"Yeah, right. I'll believe that when I see it."

"You know what you need? You need to get stoned."

"Did you bring some?"

"Of course, I did. You really going to actually smoke with me?"

"Sure bro, lets' do it."

This is unexpected. In the past, whenever I've offered to get him baked, he says no. But today, it's a yes. He must be having a bad day.

I walk out to my car and get the little Altoids canaster I keep my stash in. Instead of smoking from the one hitter, I think it would be better to mix it with some tobacco. That way, he won't get as high, and it won't smell as much. Even though the garage door is wide open.

"I'm going to roll a couple spliffs to cover up the smell."

Walking over to his workbench I take out a couple of cigarettes from my pack and tear the filters off.

"Do you have any scissors or a sharp knife out here."

He opens the toolbox on the workbench, retrieving a pair of scissors that he hands over to me. I set them down and take the first cigarette, gently squeezing it to loosen the tobacco within. With the precision of a surgeon, I use the scissors to make an incision from one end to the other, opening it up to empty the tobacco. I repeat this process with the second one. Once the papers are prepared for repacking, I take the Altoids tin and extract some pot, carefully breaking it down with my fingers. Mixing the marijuana with the tobacco, I employ the papers to roll two spliffs.

Handing one to him and taking the other, we light up.

"This will make it easier for you to smoke," I say.

But that doesn't stop him from coughing after inhaling the first one. Which, of course, I laugh at.

While we are enjoying our upgraded cigarettes, I clean the mess from the workbench and put the tin back into my car for safe keeping.

I'm not feeling the effects quite yet when Sophie opens the door to the garage. "What are you guys doing out here. The Seahawks are winning"

"Nothing," I say, "just smoking cigarettes and BS'ing. You want one?"

Jeff chuckles.

"Oh really?" She raises her eyebrow.

"Yep. See." I take a drag, hold it for a second, and exhale.

"Yeah, just make sure you keep that garage door open," she teases. "Wouldn't want any of *that* sneaking into the house, would we?"

She closes the door, which causes Jeff to chuckle again.

"Take it you are feeling the effects?"

"No, I don't think so. I feel fine."

We finish our smokes, placing the final bits, along with the other butts, in the little soup can he has sitting on the shelf next to the door for that purpose, before heading back inside to join the others.

After standing in the cold, the heat in the room coupled with the inviting aroma of food, instantly ushers in a sense of relaxation. Or, maybe it's just the pot.

"Hello everyone!" Jeff announces.

They all turn and watch us enter, and I can feel my face get flushed at the sudden attention.

"What were you guys up to?" Evelyn asks.

"Nothing, just having a cigarette," Jeff replies, followed by another chuckle.

I go and sit at the same chair, squeezing myself next to Sophie who shakes her head at me with rolled eyes and a smile.

The Seahawks are playing pretty well this week, and the room erupts with every completed pass. Even I'm getting into the spirit of the game. The beers are swiftly replaced as they empty, and the mounds of food are being devoured and promptly replaced as well.

Halftime rolls around as we each take bathroom breaks or head to the kitchen to chow down some more.

Jeff and I head to the garage for another cigarette break.

"So, how you feeling?" I ask.

"Umm, pretty good bro. But I still don't think I'm high. I'm feeling pretty buzzed at the moment."

"Yeah, since it's your first time I didn't want to give you too much and get you in trouble with the wife."

Looking at his eyes, the telltale redness hints that he might be feeling the effects more than he realizes.

"It's not my first time. I smoked a few times in college."

"Oh, look at you princess. Experimenting in college. Is that also the time you made out with that dude during a game of spin the bottle?" I mock.

"Up yours."

"Want me to roll another one?"

"No, probably shouldn't."

"Okay man. Well, if you change your mind, let me know."

We stamp out or cigarettes, placing the butts with the others. Walking into the kitchen, we see Katie with a gun in her hand showing it to the others.

"What the heck!" Jeff says

"Oh hey," Katie says looking to us. "Sophie wanted to see my gun."

"What?" I ask.

"She said she had a gun in her purse and I wanted to see it," Sophie tells us.

Katie takes the clip out and doublechecks the chamber to make sure there is no bullet in it, then hands it over to Sophie who instantly strikes a pose with it. Her hand on the grip, finger on the trigger, holding it close to her face and pointing at the ceiling.

"How do I look?"

I don't get a chance to respond, as Jeff cuts me off. "I can't believe you brought a loaded gun into my house!"

"I always have it in my purse. You never know when you might need to protect yourself."

"Protect yourself? From what, exactly, around here do you need to protect yourself. A dirty look from someone for not parking close enough to the curb?"

"It's okay. I have my concealed weapons permit and I know how to handle it properly." She says with an offended tone.

"Yeah, that's what everyone says until they get shot in the face," Jeff says.

Sophie hands it back to her. "Sorry I asked to see it."

"Did you know she had that?" Jeff turns to Evelyn.

"Yes, but it's not that big of a deal. She keeps it in her purse."

"That's not the point!"

"Let's go have another cigarette," I say, while turning Jeff towards the garage again. He doesn't resist and as we walk away, I turn and motion the others to relax.

We quickly light up.

"Dude, you got really worked up about that? What's the deal?" I ask.

"I don't like guns, and I don't like it that people bring them into my house without telling me. Their dangerous and unnecessary."

"Yeah, I get it, but this is America, you know," I say as I head towards my car. He follows. "The country where people can recite the Second Amendment, but are clueless as to what the First or the Third are."

Opening the door, I take out the one-hitter.

"And Evelyn knew she was carrying it but didn't bother to tell me? That's so typical of her, always prioritizing what others think and completely overlooking my feelings."

We walk back into the garage as I pack the one hitter and hand it over to him along with the lighter.

"Is this my lighter?"

"Maybe?" I hold my hands up in mock ignorance. "Okay, but I think you might be overreacting just a little bit. Did you ever tell her that if someone has one not to bring it over?"

He lights it and takes a hit, which instantly results in a coughing fit.

"No," he says through coughs. "But still, she knows how I feel about guns. It's bull."

"Well, there you go. Maybe just be like, *hey next time don't bring that*. If they are decent people they won't and if not, well then fuck them and tell them to find another big screen to watch football on."

He hands the little cylindrical pipe back to me and I take a look at it to make sure it's finished. Seeing there is a little green left, I hand it back.

"Finish that off first."

This time he lights it up, taking a shallow drag, attempting to stifle the inevitable cough.

I tap the ashes into the small can filled with old cigarette butts, then proceed to reload it, enjoying a hit for myself. Much better this way than mixing it with tobacco.

We finish up our cigarettes as I return the one hitter to its hiding space.

"Good?" I ask.

A huge smile appears on his face. "Good," he says, while giving me a thumbs-up with his eyes so red it's as if they might crack any moment.

Back inside the game has restarted.

"Hey love," Evelyn says softly. "We had a chat while you were outside, and Katie's totally on board with leaving it at home next time they visit. Sound good?"

"Yeah," Katie adds. "Now that I know how you feel about it, I can respect your right not to want firearms in your home. As long as you can respect mine to have one."

We all look to Jeff for his response. However, it's evident from his bloodshot, glassy eyes that he's only loosely following the conversation and trying to decide how to respond.

"He's good with that," I respond on his behalf.

The game ends with a Seahawks victory, and as much as I couldn't care less about football, even I surprisingly found myself enjoying the game. The multiple beers certainly played a part in my newfound enthusiasm, along with the sensation of a full belly, a cozy warm room, and the presence of a hot new lover. Who for now, at least, is happy to hang out with my friends, drink, talk shit, and participate in some post-game nookie when we get back to her place.

11

Tonight is the night. I can't help but feel a bit anxious about bringing a group of people to see Sophie dance. Is it rude to bring your friends and coworkers to watch your new girlfriend take her clothes off on a stage in front of a crowd of strangers and give lap dances to sweaty old men? What is the etiquette in this particular situation?

We decide to meet at a bar in Bothell which is half full so we have no problem getting a table for the four of us. I order a double Makers and Ginger Ale from the waiter, hoping it will arrive sooner rather than later.

We are in a booth with Heather sitting across from me next to her husband. She is wearing a tight sweater, a skirt, and long boots with stockings. Her husband, Dean, is a tall guy with broad shoulders and short hair. Personally, I would have figured Heather for someone a little more alternative than the strait-laced former jock looking guy sitting across from me at the bar. I've never met a lacrosse player, yet this is probably what one looks like. He is wearing a black t-shirt that displays a portion of the half-sleeve tattoo down his left arm. The design ends just above the elbow. It looks to be some type of steam punk design, predominantly composed of deep blacks, with subtle touches of red and blue mixed in. If I had arms that solid, I'd probably have a few tattoos as well to show them off.

If they ever have children, they could probably enter them into some best-looking baby contest. What a tragedy that would be to happen to such a nice-looking body. Her tight waist would be stretched out and the pert breasts would get abused by the mouth of a baby instead of pleasured by the lips of a man. I bet she must have a few provocative tattoos concealed beneath that shirt somewhere. She comes off as too imaginative for something as cliché as a tramp stamp, but maybe something hidden below the back of her neck, tracing along her spine. Or perhaps on her upper arm or shoulder, some kind of punk-looking thing to go with Dean's. She must have an ankle tattoo. If I were to place a bet, that's where my money would go.

"Matt," Dean interrupts, snapping me out of my daydream about his wife. "How exactly did you and this girl meet?"

"We met a while back at a mutual friends party, and ran into each other again a few of weeks ago," I respond as the waiter returns with our drinks and I drain half my glass.

"So, did I tell you guys," Jeff interjects. "Since Tanya is leaving, they are going to bring in a contractor to take her place. And guess what? That contractor is going report directly to me."

"Tanya is leaving?" I ask.

"You didn't know," he responds. "I figured you would be the first to know since you have to work with her so often."

I turn towards Dean to explain. "Tanya works as a content writer on my team. I handle project releases and her job is to write stuff associated with the projects I manage. Her job is a bit redundant, honestly, which I've never complained about since she helps me out with some of my work. I'm not surprised she is leaving. She would often complain to me about not having anything to do."

"I heard she got a new job with some startup in Bellevue," Heather adds.

"She did—" Jeff starts.

"So, Dean," I interrupt. "Does it drive you nuts when you hang out with Heather's co-workers and all they do is talk about work?"

"I'm used to it," he responds.

"Really? I work there and have no interest in talking about the place."

"So, what would you prefer to discuss?" Jeff asks me.

"I don't care. I'm off the clock so if we can avoid the work talk, I'd be okay with that."

"Even if it's about me hiring some hottie," he says.

"Hey man, I've got a hottie. What do I care about who you hire?"

"You will when she realizes what a loser you are and dumps your ass."

"Story of my life, my friend, story of my life."

We toast to that.

The conversation turns towards other areas, as we continue to drink and eat our food with a nice alcohol influenced buzz happening around the table.

Following dinner, we pile into Dean's Expedition, leaving our cars parked at the bar. This turns out to be a good idea; I realize while the vehicle is in motion that I am experiencing the full effect of the multiple drinks. I crack the window open to let in a breath of fresh air. My lips feel dry, and I instinctively lick them. This is followed up with biting my lower lip, so that I slide my teeth across the stubble underneath, thinking about the night ahead.

It is one thing to introduce a girl you are seeing to friends at a normal having-a-drink engagement; it is a completely different thing to show up at her place of work after drinking, especially when that place of work is an adults-only dance club. A dance club that will have the woman I'm having sex with taking her clothes off and going into the corner with some nasty old dude to rub herself all over him for money, and the possibility of a tip or a second dance, assuming she does a good enough job of getting him erect. I'm not sure I want to go through with it anymore.

Of course, it's too late now as we pile out of the SUV in the club's parking lot. A group of voyeurs going to eyeball one of those voyeur's girlfriend.

"Sophie said she would leave my name. Matt Lewiston," I tell the bouncer at the door.

"Okay." He looks me over. "I can only let one in for free, but I'll let your friends get in for half-price tonight."

That's cool and unexpected, since she initially said that everyone else would have to pay regular price.

The bouncer goes through the rules. "No touching, no outside alcohol, must buy at least two drinks."

"Drinks," Jeff interrupts. "Drinks of what?"

"Soda or juice mostly."

"What are those, like ten bucks each?"

"If you don't want them, you can stay outside," he responds, letting Jeff know to shut up. "And no photography."

Entering the building, we are welcomed by the booming sounds of Bon Jovi blaring through the speakers. The large open space is dark, lit only by soft, ambient lighting. The only exception is the stage, which is well lit with an array of multicolored strobe lights that pulsate in rhythm with the music. Of course, my eyes are instantly drawn to the girl with her legs wrapped around a silver pole as she hangs upside down in the center of the stage. She is mostly naked, with nothing except for some lacy panties and white thigh-high boots. Intricate tattoos adorn her body, tracing down her back, arms, and calves. Around the stage are rows of chairs, and behind those are some tables. I can see one table of four, including two women. I guess Heather won't be the only female guest tonight. If smoking were allowed, I can easily imagine the place would be veiled in a haze of cigarette smoke.

To the left, raised above everything, is the DJ stand. There is a guy with long black hair pulled into a ponytail in the booth. He looks like the guy who was with Sophie and the other girl when we met at The Garage. Next to the DJ is a small bar with what I'm assuming is just soda, and a guy behind the counter who looks as if he spends way too much time admiring himself in the mirror at the gym.

"Ha," Jeff laughs, leaning in close, "if they're only serving non-alcoholic drinks, what is the point of the bar?"

"Looks, I guess."

Along the venue's right wall are small booths, with black leather or vinal seating, where the private dances seem to happen. Moving like a small group of in-sync animals towards a table near the stage, I'm trying to focus my eyes while scanning the room for Sophie. A girl is giving a dance in one of the booths that could be her. It's hard to tell with the light, clearly designed to give a sense of privacy to the guys with raging hard-ons and the girls shaking their asses for a decent tip.

We sit down and a waitress comes over to take our order. We all get a Coke, except for Heather, who gets a diet.

Jeff leans forward and remarks, "You know, there have been studies indicating that diet soda may be more detrimental to health than regular."

"I know," Heather responds. "But I like the taste."

Jeff is sitting opposite me at the table and turns around to watch the dancing. Dean pulls his chair around the side, moving closer to Heather, who is to my left.

We must be here early. Besides the group of four, there is the guy getting a lap dance in the back and a couple of guys near the stage on the opposite side from us. They look like two dudes who you would expect to see in a strip club, complete with neatly-folded bills on the stage in front of them waiting for the girls to crawl and collect.

Soft hands wrap around me from behind covering my eyes and a soft inviting voice whispers close to my ear.

"Hey sexy, in the mood for a little entertainment tonight?"

She slides around, before I have a chance to respond, wearing baby blue lace panties and a matching bra that makes her breasts look larger than I remember them. Over that she has matching thin lingerie.

Her scent is intoxicating, a new fragrance of perfume lingers in the air around her. Sparkles glisten across her chest and shoulders, adding a magical glow to her alluring presence. Fetishists must be emptying their wallets at her impeccably manicured feet.

"You smell nice," I say.

"Thanks. Who are your friends?" she asks as she moves to sit in the chair next to me.

We do introductions and I sense a little jealousy in Dean, or perhaps that could be me projecting again. Fuck, I need another drink and I'm kicking myself for not slipping a flask into my jacket pocket when leaving home earlier. But I was worried the bouncer would search us before letting us in. I'm surprised women can make a living doing this in a state that doesn't allow alcohol in strip clubs. When I was 19 and could drink legally in Canada, we used to go up and get drunk there, back in the day when it didn't take hours to get through the border. The best of both worlds: booze, and scantily clad women, compared to the prudes here in Washington.

After chatting with us for a bit, Sophie says, "I have to go get ready. Maybe a dance on the house later." She winks at me before sauntering away.

"Nice pull, Matt. Even I'd hit that," Heather says, elbowing me, with a deepened voice.

I've never seen this side of Heather. I like it. But, would she actually be up for 'hitting that?' Maybe she also goes both ways. She looks like the type of girl who does. Or, perhaps she was being sarcastic and making fun of me for going out with a girl who spends her evenings rubbing her cooch in the face of lonely perves.

"Thanks," I smile in response.

There is a new dancer on the stage. This one is doing the naughty school girl, with a short plaid skirt, glasses, and her blond hair pulled back into a ponytail. She loses a few points for authenticity with the caked-on makeup in an attempt to mask the bags and wrinkles around her eyes. And the faded tribal tattoo coiling around her left ankle and calf that matches a similar design on her left shoulder, doesn't help her look any younger.

It isn't long before one of the girls roaming the place sits in the chair at the table next to us. She is speaking softly to Jeff, who seems to enjoy the conversation. She is a bit pudgy, with great tits in red and black lingerie.

After the girl on the stage finishes her two songs, we hear, "Coming to the stage next, brace yourselves for the captivating allure of the Persian princess – Zora!"

"Pony" by Ginuwine begins to play. Shitty song, yet my heart jumps a beat as Sophie works her way out on the stage. She's added a matching lace scarf that complements her outfit, and she has switched into high heels – or were the heels always there? Either way, she struts across the stage, picks up a rag and spray bottle to clean down the stripper pole (because good hygiene is important amongst strippers, apparently). Somehow, she makes even that look sexy. She moves gracefully across the stage, swaying in rhythm to the beat of the music, slowly peeling off the scarf, which she floats across the faces of those next to the stage. Watching the guys breathe in, I'm reminded of her scent, that has now faded. The guys on the other side of the stage have already placed a couple of bills for her, and I feel like I should do the same.

"Is it rude of me not to put some cash up there, or would she find that offensive," I ask the table.

"I don't mind," Heather responds and moves from our table to a chair near the edge of the stage.

"And that's why I married her," Dean says with a smug grin on his face.

"Well, now I definitely have to go up there," I say.

I take a seat in a chair beside Heather, at the edge of the stage. However, when I reach for my wallet, realize I have no singles and need to go to the bar to make change. Watching from the corner of my eye, Sophie continues her routine. She slowly peels off the layer of lingerie, revealing glimpses of her smooth, toned skin. Back at the stage, I extend two ten-dollar bills, folded together, and wait for her to move towards us. It is money well spent, as I'm sure she will show her appreciation later in the night. Or should I have put twenties out? It's too late to reconsider now. I'll save the twenties for the private dance later.

She moves towards Heather first, each sway of her hips and twirl of her body a tantalizing display of femininity, up until she buries her tits in Heather's face. Maybe a foursome isn't so out of the question, assuming I could stand the idea of Dean fucking Sophie. She's had sex with guys before me; I would assume some of them might look like him. Looking at the two girls together, a three-way would be like stepping into some kind of heaven.

Sophie gracefully shimmies towards me, takes the bills, then slides close and pulls my face between her breasts as well. Mixed in with her perfume, there's a subtle hint of sweat that's exhilarating. She pulls back and turns around, stands straight with her legs spread, positioning her flawless ass directly above my head. She bends over, looking between her legs at me. The money has disappeared, and her hair is hanging over her head. I can see the two guys on the other side watching and I know they want to be me, as she squats, bouncing her ass on my forehead. My heart races, giving me the urge to just bury my face between her cheeks; unfortunately, or fortunately, she moves on before I can act on the impulse.

Next, "Closer", by the Nine Inch Nails, begins to play. This is a much better stripper song, in my humble opinion. She is spending more time at the pole for this one, doing the upside-down thing like the girl was doing when we arrived, and more bills have been flung on the stage. Looking to my right, there are more people in the bar now, another girl with a guy over at one table, and another group of three guys at the table near them. A third guy has joined the two at the opposite side of the stage, possibly the one who was getting the lap dance earlier.

Sitting so close to Heather, the body heat coming off her is arousing. She has taken off the sweater she was wearing earlier to reveal a tank-top shirt and a vine tattoo wrapped around her upper right arm. *Called it.*

After Sophie finishes her show and collects the bills strewn over the stage, Heather and I move back to the table with the others. Jeff is nowhere to be seen and Dean seems to be having a good enough time on his own, drinking his overpriced soda while chatting up the occasional stripper that stops by the table offering private dances. Now that Heather is back, it isn't long before he buys her a lap dance and she not-so-reluctantly goes off with the bitchy blond stripper from the other night to enjoy a dance. Talk about great ideas for foreplay. Buying your wife a lap dance at a strip club is the way to do it.

The air in the room must be draining the alcohol from my system, as if they've installed ventilation specifically to filter booze from men's bodies while managing to retain the faintly intoxicating aroma of perfume.

When Sophie returns, she takes my hand to lead me to a back space for the private dance offered. We pass by the first booth, which has a large black leathered chair or love seat. To each side are walls painted in a dark burgundy. Past that is another booth with the same design. This one, however, has a girl straddling some guy. I turn my head, not looking to give them a bit of privacy and avoid feeling like a pervy voyeur.

Sophie leads me in the next booth.

"So, how does this work?" I ask as she guides me to the seat.

"Like you don't know."

"I don't actually. Don't get me wrong, I've been to strip clubs before, I've just never had a private dance before."

"You just sit back, relax, and enjoy," she purrs seductively

"That is something I can definitely do."

"And no touching." She shakes her finger at me.

She begins by taking a step back, her hips swaying in time with the music as her hands glide up her body, stopping at each breast, gently squeezing and caressing them.

"So, this is the VIP area, eh?"

"Oh no honey, even you have to pay for the VIP room, and you don't want to do that."

At this point she gyrates toward me, leaning forward, moving close enough to touch, which I instinctively reach out to do. She pushes my hands back to my sides, while staring me in the eyes, a seductive yet domineering smile, and shakes her head no. Then she steps away, straddling me in the same way as the girl and guy we passed.

"Why not?" I ask. "You don't think I can afford it?"

"It's your money, you can spend it however you like. You pay extra to see me in a different outfit or naked, which you can do anytime you want for free. But if you really want, I can take you there for a private dance."

With the heat radiating off her body, and the pressure of her weight on my lap, I can feel myself beginning to get an erection. Thankfully, the angle in my jeans is causing a bit of pain, preventing me from getting a full hard-on. She runs her breasts up my chest – the sensation sending shivers down my spine. I can taste her sweet breath as she leans in close, her lips dangerously close to mine. Just as I lean forward to kiss her, she moves away, a knowing grin on her face.

"Guys pay by the hour in VIP rooms. Girls have different costumes for those occasions," she explains. She grinds against me and I squirm uncomfortably. "But you'd be amazed at how often they just want someone to talk with in there," she adds with a sly smile.

She turns around in a reverse cowgirl move that is impressive – both in her ability to do it on the little sofa, and ability to do it to the music, which is now "Cherry Pie". She must notice my boner by now. I mean, isn't that the point of a lap dance? To get the customer aroused and send him home wanting.

At the moment, I am more preoccupied with the sensation of her grinding against me than what happens in the VIP room. It is almost like she is a different person tonight, exuding confidence, more dominating than usual. Dress her in a leather outfit with a whip in her hand, and I would probably be on my knees, more than happy to lick her boots.

"Do guys ever come in their jeans when you do this?"

"Do you really want to know?"

Since that pretty much answered my questions, I respond with, "No."

I take a deep breath, filling my lungs with the scents of sweat, perfume, and arousal that surround us, and willingly let my dick work to proper erection in appreciation at what she is doing.

12

Holy fuck! The air is stifling, making it a challenge to breathe, and I'm fighting the urge to vomit – a result of the multiple beers and stench of weed and cigarette smoke that fills the room. We are in the house of who I assume to be the bouncer or perhaps the DJ from the club. Sophie is sitting on the lap of another woman, in a large armchair to my left. The house is brightly lit and there is loud bass-filled dance music pounding against my eardrums, adding to the feeling of suffocation. My butt doesn't want to move from the tattered brown sofa I'm sitting on. The cloth is worn down and the cushions are all caved to the center, forcing the four guys, including myself, sitting on it to fall inward. Through the haze of smoke, I can see the girl who Sophie is sitting on running her fingers over Sophie's thigh. I don't recognize the other girl. I'm assuming, from the look of her, she must be one of the strippers from the club. They seem to be enjoying themselves, laughing and talking. The large brown chair seems to have aged better than this thing that I'm currently trying to escape from. My heavy arms, along with the rotating room, are making it a challenge to dislodge myself from the sofa, which appears to have molded around me. *Please*, I silently beg, *don't let me get sick*. My stomach is churning at the thought.

Focus, you douche-bag. Here I am, in a room with two totally hot chicks feeling each other up, and one of them just happens to be the girl that I am sleeping with. *These are the kinds of nights you fantasize about, and if you puke, I will literally have to punch you in the nuts.*

The guy jammed into the sofa to the right of me holds a joint in my direction, which I wave off. He reeks of cologne. Remembering there is a can of beer on the floor near where I am sitting, I reach down and pick it up off the wooden floor to take a drink. Blah, cheap, shitty and now warm, but at least it's liquid. Fresh air! I need to get up; I need to go outside; I need to join those two girls in the chair.

With my left hand on the armrest, right hand on cologne man's shoulder, I push, and my ass rises from the sofa thanks to an additional nudge from cologne man. *Thank God.* The door is around behind the couch, which continues to provide support while I flounder my way outside onto the front porch. A rush of cool, refreshing air greets me as I step outside. Instantly, I begin to feel better. My legs wobble as I move over to lean against the side of the house, and my hand instinctively reaches for the pack of cigarettes that are not in my pocket. Fuck. At least the beer is still in my hand. Finishing off the warm remnants left in the bottom of the can, I then stumble to the other side of the porch to release my guts into the bushes over the railing. That feels better.

As I lean over the edge, trying to wipe away the long lines of bitter drool sticking to my lips, the base from inside vibrates along the railing. I can't believe the neighbors haven't complained or called the police. I'd be super pissed if these people lived next door to me.

I think I've managed to spit out the remains of the beer and acidic flavored food chucks hiding in the crevices of my mouth. Standing straight, another big breath of fresh air helps me fight the swirlies that hit me. One more deep breath and I'm feeling much better. All I needed was to get the cheap alcohol out of my gut.

The empty can is discarded into the bushes to join the vomit that someone other than me is going to have to deal with. The thought of checking my car for a cigarette briefly passes through my mind; however, the more intriguing thought involves the two girls inside and the possibilities they present.

Back inside, the music seems louder, the air thicker, and my mouth tastes like someone just took a dump in it. Sophie sees me, giving me a smile as the two of them get out of the chair, moving in my direction. She takes my hand and guides me down a hallway behind the other girl. Like a child who was just offered candy from a stranger, I obediently follow.

"Wait. I have to piss," I say.

Letting go of her hand, I turn to what looks to be a bathroom.

"Better hurry," she says teasingly. "Wouldn't want to miss out on all the fun?"

Nope, we definitely do not want that to happen.

Into the dingy run-down bathroom, I flick the switch to turn on the light, to be blinded by the super-high voltage bulb hanging in the center of the room without a cover to dim it. I relieve myself in the toilet, feeling impressed with my ability to successfully hit the target. From the looks of the floor, it seems I'm one of the few guys to piss in here tonight that has managed to aim correctly. Now to the sink to wash my hands, splash some water on my face, and drink the cold refreshing liquid straight out of the faucet. The medicine cabinet has a rolled-up tube of toothpaste in it. I grab it, squeeze a bit onto my finger, and hastily scrub it across my teeth and tongue. After a quick rinse, I feel somewhat rejuvenated, as the lingering taste of decay on my tongue is replaced by a fresh minty flavor.

"Okay, you fucker. Cowboy the fuck up," I say to the not so good-looking reflection in the mirror.

Using some of the water, my hand works through my hair to straighten it out before turning the light off and heading back into the hallway.

Three doors to choose from. Two closed and one cracked open. Makes sense to check out the open door first. The light is on overhead, revealing a bed with a worn brown blanket covering it and a bunch of coats piled on. No women in here. The second door, however, turns out to be the right one. This must be the girl's room. It has just enough space for a full-sized bed, a small table with a computer monitor on it, and an old wooden dresser with a bunch of girly items covering the top. A dim lamp on a nightstand next to the bed casts a soft golden glow of shadows around the room.

Sophie and her very attractive friend are on the bed, each in nothing but a bra and panties. The girl is laying on her back with Sophie on her side next to her, posed as if ready for a Playboy photoshoot. The female playmate has tattoos down both legs in intricate designs, along with a massive one around her upper arm that connects to a design down her side. Sophie has one arm draped over her, displaying her luxuriously smooth, dark skin. They both look at me and smile. I'm instantly erect.

Unbuttoning my pants, I stumble towards the bed, trying to take them off before realizing my shoes are on. As my body falls to the floor, I attempt to move in the bed's direction to pad the fall, and fail. With my hands still tugging on my pants, there is nothing to lessen the impact of the wooden floor, except for a thin rug, which I only become aware of when my face suddenly meets it. It smells of dirt and mildew – not the most pleasant welcome.

"Are you okay?" one – or maybe both – of them asks.

"I'm fine," I mumble, rolling onto my back and kicking my shoes off before sliding my pants the rest of the way down.

It takes both of them to assist me in getting onto the bed and out of my shirt. *Best night ever*, I think as my head sinks into the soft, fragrant pillow.

13

My eyes open reluctantly. I know without looking where my sore, rotten body is lying. The memory of last night passes through my throbbing skull, along with a vague recollection of being pulled to the bed. A body, presumably Sophie, lies next to me. As the lingering fog in my vision clears, her face is next to mine, her mouth hangs wide, exhaling stale morning breath. Not that mine is any better from the taste of it. The remnants of her dark makeup are smeared under her eyes. My head feels like a ton of bricks, and each vein is throbbing as if someone plugged an air compressor into the back of my skull and is now filling my cranium like a thick balloon waiting to blow.

Raising my head slightly, I see the girl on the other side of Sophie. They are both under the covers, preventing me from discovering if they are naked. Thoughts of the two of them having sex enter my mind while my organs reject any notion of being sexually aroused. Instead, my body is telling me it would prefer to piss, shit, and vomit all at the same time.

With a surprising amount of difficulty, I succeed in crawling out from the bed without waking the two sleeping girls. Wearing nothing but my underwear, I quietly find my way to the bathroom. The light in the hallway accentuates each flaw of the dilapidated house. The walls wear a pale cigarette-stained tint of off-white, and the wooden floors throughout are covered with the scars of countless feet and dirt and garbage having been drawn across their surface. They seem better suited for a bonfire than a floor. When I open the door to the toilet, the smell of piss and lingering shit bitch-slaps me in the face. There is no turning back now; the imminent explosion waiting inside me is happening. Locking the door, I rapidly take some toilet paper to wipe the seat of the toilet before lowering myself to cleanse the various bits of nastiness that are anxiously waiting to exit my bowels. While adding my own wretched scent to the room, there is an odor of mildew that lingers in the air, likely from the old worn shower curtain draped over the bathtub. Looking around, there is mold growth along the bathtub's edges, partially obscuring the caulk, which makes me wonder when last it was cleaned.

Feeling nauseous from the combination of odors attacking my nostrils, I flush, not wanting to clog the toilet and knowing there is more to come before my burning ass will let me stand up. My stomach curls at the blend of stink in the room, forcing me to grapple with the urge to swap my ass with my face and vomit into the shit-soaked, piss and pubic hair-covered toilet I am currently seated on. Thankfully I manage to avoid throwing up, as the remaining solids and liquids burn their way through my digestive system and exit my body. Eventually, I muster up the courage to wipe my ass, stand up, and flush the toilet.

The idea of smoking a cigarette makes my lungs hurt, as I'm hit with a coughing fit, and something that looks like a yellow blob of ooze works its way up my throat to be spit into the sink. On another level, a cigarette sounds fantastic; however, it would also involve finding one. *I really need to quit smoking.* Having no idea where my coat is, or if there is a pack lying around somewhere, I decide to give up on that idea, and open the bathroom window. Something I should have done sooner. I start digging through the cabinet in search of aspirin or any other type of headache medicine, anything that will make the pain go away. Fuck yes, a bottle of ibuprofen. Amazed that anyone in this crap-hole of a house would buy some, I drop four of the little pills into my hand and my mouth guzzles down water from the tap to wash them down. Splashing some water on my face, I avoid looking at myself in the mirror, ashamed of what I will see in return.

Entering the bedroom, I am greeted by the warm retched air, thick with stale sweat and alcohol that hangs after a night's restless sleep of three drunken bodies. This time she wakes up as I crawl back into bed. She doesn't say anything other than rolling over and sliding towards me so that I can wrap my arms around her, warm and still wearing the panties and bra she had on last night.

You would think after the night we had, it would be easy to drift back asleep. It's not. My head throbs steadily; my aching stomach informs me with each turn how miserable it is; and the cottonmouth only adds to the overall misery. All I really want is to go home and crawl into my bed where I could shut my eyes and wallow in hours of uninterrupted sleep. How these two women can soundly sleep is beyond me. Eventually I give up, find my pants and other articles of clothing before deciding to wake Sophie, to see if she wants to come with me or stay here.

She blinks, rubs her eyes with the palm of her hand. "Sure, I'll go with you. If you'd like?" she says.

"That's why I asked."

She rises from the bed, and the other girl rolls over, briefly opening her eyes just long enough for Sophie to say goodbye. In the living room, some guy is sleeping on the dilapidated brown sofa. I don't recognize him, or care. The room is littered with empty beer bottles, cans, and plastic cups. The bottom of my shoes sticks as I walk through. I remember there being a decent number of people, but the place seems more trashed than possible for that number of guests. In the kitchen is a table painted black with four matching wooden chairs. My jacket is draped over the back of one of them. Retrieving it, I can feel wetness and smell the beer that someone must have spilled on it at some point during the night. Fortunately, my car keys are tucked in the pocket where I left them.

The freezing air provides a welcome relief as we walk outside to my car parked on the street near the house. Tossing the jacket in the back and looking around, I have no idea what part of town we are in. It's only when we begin driving with the heater cranked on high that I realize we're in Ballard.

"You want me to take you home, or you coming back to my place?" I ask Sophie.

"Do you want me to come back to your place?"

Why the hell does she keep answering questions with a question?

"I wouldn't have offered if I didn't mind you coming with me. But just so you know my plan is to shower and go back to sleep."

"Are you mad about something?"

"No."

The reality is that I am in a pissy mood, and I'm not sure why. Is it because of her and that girl from last night? Is it because I want to know if they had sex or not? Or is it simply because I feel like crap and just want to go home and take a sleeping pill?

"You seem mad?" she says with a hint of frustration.

"Maybe it's you asking me if I am mad or not that is making me mad."

"Fine, just take me home."

"Fine."

We drive silently to her place, and I can feel the anger and tension building up in me. I want to yell, but I'm holding back. I'm waiting for her to say something, anything, that would give me a reason to shout and curse. However, she remains silent, staring out the window, not saying anything, ruining my desire for an angry outburst, which only fuels the tension.

Pulling up in front of her apartment, she gets out, then says, "Just so you know I didn't fuck Tracy last night because you passed out. And I wouldn't do that without you. Asshole! So, if one of us crossed a line it was you!"

"How the hell should I know. After all, you lie to people for a living, making guys think you are whoever they want you to be!"

She slams the door and walks away.

"Thanks for slamming my door!" I yell. Of course, she probably can't hear me.

"Cunt," I mutter under my breath while slapping the car into first gear and hitting the gas, causing the tires to spin on the damp street as I speed off.

Back home, one of the Lunesta I picked up off a friend and saved for situations just like this enter my mouth, along with another long drink of water. After a quick shower, it does not take long for the sleeping pill to kick in and the memories of the night and ache in my body fade away.

14

I spend the rest of the weekend lazing around the house, replaying the events of the previous night in my head, flipping through TV channels, and attempting to force down a couple of leftover slices of pepperoni and mushroom pizza.

If anyone crossed a line, it was her. Fuck her for telling me, *I crossed a line*. Crossed what line, the line of someone who passed out, or the 'didn't have sex with two girls' line? It wasn't even my idea! They were the ones all over each other; plus, they were the ones who went into the room. More like *she crossed a line*. She didn't bother saying anything to me about having a three-way in advance. If she had said something, I'm sure I wouldn't have drunk so much and been more aware. What makes her think I would want to do that in some random house with some random girl, anyway? Who knows where that skank has been? She takes her clothes off for a living and is willing to fuck a couple of people at a party. If one of us crossed a line, it was her, not me. If she wants to call me and apologize, then fine, I will accept it. However, I'm not going to call her first. Despite that, the rational voice in my head (which I rarely listen to) is telling me to swallow my pride and pick up the phone.

Nothing changes by Monday, leaving me caught in this waiting game. A game where each player waits to see who will be the first to crack and contact the other. Except it's a poor game to play, really, because I know how women are. Once they commit to ending a relationship, they move on quickly. How do I know she's not in the process of mentally checking out of this relationship already, or at least going through the mental checklist of why she should end it? We have only been seeing each other for a few weeks, so it is not like things are that serious. Sure, it's fucking hot to date a stripper now, but what if I take her to a work function and it turns out she gave a hand-job to Chris in the back room of her club for a few extra bucks? That is a vomit-inducing thought. It probably would be for the best to end things now. Enjoy the ride while it lasted and get off at the first stop.

"Hey player, how was your weekend?" Jeff says, stepping into my office and snapping me out of my trance.

I look up and sigh. "My weekend sucked big harry balls. How about you and your lap dance from the fat chick?"

He shuts the door behind himself and takes a seat across from me.

"She wasn't fat."

"Dude, she was definitely pleasantly plumper than the other girls there."

"No, she wasn't, and I think she really liked me."

"Ha," I laugh. "So, when did you leave then? I don't remember you leaving."

"I'm amazed you recall anything. Those drinks barely had any mixer in them," he remarks. "You were pretty hammered when I left."

After leaving the strip club, we headed back to the bar to retrieve our cars. And, since it was still open, it only seemed logical at the time to have a few drinks. Drinks that the bartender made with a hefty amount of liquor into each glass. From that point my memory of the evening is a bit of blur.

"Yes, yes I was," I respond with a sigh.

"So, what happened?" he asks.

"Well, when the bar closed, some of Sophie's co-workers invited us to some ghetto-ass house party. Which seemed like a good idea at the time. That was until I ended up getting so drunk that I passed out instead of having a three-way with Sophie and some other hot chick."

He bursts into a fit of laughter. Eventually, he regains his composure. "Bro, that's rough. You manage to snag a winning lottery ticket and then lose it. Only you could be so lucky and unlucky at the same time," he says, still struggling to catch his breath.

"Yep," I nod in agreement.

"I just headed home when the bar closed. Seeing you with Sophie and Heather with Dean, I felt like the odd one out."

"Really? Because I recall you spending a lot of time asking Sophie about the fat chick. You didn't try heading back to the club for a few more dances, did you?"

He rolls his eyes but refrains from responding, leading me to wonder if that is in fact what he did.

After a bit of a pause, I say, "So, yeah, Saturday morning Sophie and I got into a bit of a fight about it, and I haven't talked to her since."

"I don't understand," he says. "What was it you fight about? It sounds like nothing happened."

"I was just tired and cranky and then she snapped at me. Which pissed me off. And … yeah … I guess that's it. There really isn't much else to say." I let out a resigned sigh. "I suppose I'll have to give in and call her."

"No, you can't do that," he says sharply.

"Why not?" I ask, surprised at his change in tone.

He leans forward, saying, "Relationships are all about power struggles. If you give in and admit fault now, you'll be doing that for the rest of your life together. Look at *me*. I can't eat or drink what I want, and the only time I get to watch what I want on TV is when she's not home."

"That's not true."

"It's mostly true."

"Whatever," I roll my eyes.

"I'm telling you, bro, I speak from experience. You need to wait for her to make the first move. Believe me, you'll appreciate it in the long run."

"And what if she doesn't?"

"She will. I've seen that way she looks at you. She'll be the first one to give in."

"Yeah, we'll see," I say. "If she doesn't, you will be receiving a swift kick to the balls."

"Don't fret my broheem. Relationships are like a game of chess. Surrendering too many pieces now will bite you in the ass later on." He remarks, rising from his seat and making his way back to his office.

After he leaves, I genuinely begin to do some work, which continues for about an hour until I see an email from Sophie. I guess he was right.

Matt,

You were the one talking about a three way because you've never had one. I tried to give you that and you get pissed about it. I figured I would let you cool off this weekend, however since you didn't call or message me, I don't think it's the right time for us. Plus, you seem like you've got a lot on your plate and I don't want to stress you out any more than you already are. There are things I need that you just can't give me right now and I think this is the best option for us.

It's a shame. At least it is still early in the relationship, so better to end it now instead of later.

> *I wish you the best,*
> *XXX Sophie*

I feel like I just got punched in the gut, each letter a sharp jab to the chest, and my heart aches reading her email. *Damn it, Jeff. I knew I shouldn't have listened to you.*

I turn around and look out the window towards the building on the opposite side of the street. Directly across from me is a matching office space, with a man sitting behind a desk, his back to the window, fixated on a computer screen in front of him. Every day, he follows the same monotonous routine as soon as he enters: he removes his suit jacket; takes a hanger off a coat hook on the wall; places the jacket on the hanger; then hangs it up. At the end of each day, he reverses the process, removing the hanger and putting his jacket back on as he leaves. Mr. Suite, as I call him, follows the same repetitive cycle, day in and day out, with the same three suits: one gray with stripes, one solid gray, and one dark blue. I imagine he lives in some bland white house somewhere – Bellevue most likely, or Queen Ann or Green Lake. He is married to a woman who was reasonably attractive in high school or college when they met. Over the years, she has gained a few extra pounds, which she attributes to the two kids they have together, and not to the overindulgence of food and wine. She's fully aware of her weight gain and often comments on it, expressing her desire to start going to the gym if she could only find the time. Time that she never seems to find.

"Hey Matt, got a sec?" The message from Chris pops up on my computer.

"Sure." I respond.

"Can you come to my office?"

Great. I'm totally in the mood to listen his nonsense today. Or hear about the latest thing I did wrong.

I walk over to Chris's office.

Trying to maintain a friendly demeanor, I casually ask, "What's up?" Taking a seat in the opposite chair.

"So, I got an email from Nick Westford about an email you sent him."

Oh, now I know why I've been called into the principal's office. One of the things that you should never do with a severe hangover first thing in the morning: get into an email argument with someone at work.

He goes on, "He forwarded me what you sent him, mentioning that your reply to his request for more details was unprofessional."

"Did he forward you the whole conversation?"

"Yes, he attached the email thread."

"So, you can see that he was being an annoying douche."

The wrinkles on his forehead crease in frustration. "That might be the case, except for he deals directly with our clients, so if he is asking you for help with how to respond to them, you can't respond with 'isn't that your job'".

My hands tighten into fists and my voices rises. "Well, it is. As you can see in the email, he was basically asking me how to do his job. My job isn't dealing with clients. I'm a project manager, not a client manager or customer service representative. I gave him the answer to the question of what is going to be included in the next release. And he didn't like the answer that a feature the customer wanted would not be included. It's not my job to tell him how to explain that to the client. It's his job. Simple as that. He basically wanted me to type up the response so that he could copy and paste it to the client."

"Understood, but part of your role here involves collaborating with colleagues who assist our customers. The manner in which you responded was both discourteous and unprofessional."

I have to take a deep breath to calm myself before responding, "Okay, sorry, your right. Do you want me to email him or something?"

"Yes, I would. And I would like you to reflect on how your actions are perceived by others. Lately, you seem like you don't want to be here. Which is fine, but if you don't, I would recommend seeking opportunities where you might find more fulfillment. However, if you want to stay, it would behoove you to show that commitment," he states, his voice oozing with condescension. "You know, it is important to me that everyone be fulfilled with their role here. You're a smart guy, Matt, and I respect you. However, I also have a responsibility to consider the wellbeing of your peers, and the company, and your recent conduct has been disappointing."

He leans back in the chair, visibly pleased with the gravatas of his lecture, while letting me know it is over for now.

"Got it," I state, knowing that if I continue to speak, it will result in an outburst that would most likely get me fired. The anxiety of wondering what I would do for money quells that notion.

I swing by my office to grab my jacket and decide to take a walk to clear my head.

The Starbucks is empty, with Jessie behind the counter as usual. While waiting for her to complete my drink, I ask, "How was your weekend?"

"Nothing exciting," she responds. "I worked Saturday, then hung out at home on Sunday doing laundry."

"Oh, laundry day. Fun stuff." I smile. "So how come you never mention your boyfriend?"

"Because I don't have one."

"That surprises me," I respond.

"Why?" she asks over the sound of steaming milk.

"I don't know, because you seem pretty smart, and fun to talk to. And, not too bad to look at." I think I made her blush a little. "Well, if you are interested in maybe grabbing a drink or something sometime, I would be down for that."

Without missing a beat, she responds, "You know, Matt, you're a really nice guy and all, but I don't think it would work. I mean, you're quite a bit older than me."

"I don't know if I'm that much older, and what's that matter anyway?"

"Well, how old are you then?" She asks.

I hesitate to respond, trying to decide if I should say I'm younger than I actually am. My guess is she's in her early twenties, so if I say I'm in my late twenties, she couldn't complain about my age. Most people seem surprised when they find out that I am thirty-one, often assuming I'm younger.

"I'm thirty-one."

"Oh my god! You are soooooo old," she teases with a playful smile.

If a person's heart could literally drop to their gut mine just did.

"Ouch," I say, while trying to sound like I'm still in a lively mood.

"I'm just kidding," she says. "You're not that old, but I'm only twenty-two, that's almost ten years difference."

"When will you be turning twenty-three?"

"In July."

"Hmm, well that doesn't work. I'll actually be thirty-two in April."

Thankfully, I'm saved from this humiliating conversation as another customer enters the shop, giving me a reason to leave and return to the office. Although, it's a toss-up which is worse, doing my job, or a conversation that's making me feel old for the first time in my life.

Sophie,

I know I should just give it some time to let you calm down but the more time I give it the more likely it will be that we don't talk again. I know we have only known each other for a couple of weeks, but I want to let you know that—

"Matt, can you get with Lance about that?" Chris states, taking my thoughts out of the email I am typing and back to the person sitting across the table from me.

We are in a small conference room with a round wooden table between us. One other chair at the table has Kerry sitting in it. We are reviewing the feature list. A spreadsheet is projected on the overhead that has a ranked list of changes.

"Sure, no problem."

I have only an inkling of an idea of what he wants. Something about consolidating one of the items in with another. It doesn't really matter; he'll probably forget what he just asked me to do, anyway.

"If we can find a way to combine the two that would be ideal," Kerry says.

"Yep, making a note of it right now," I lie.

"It's not like if you call into the cable company for an issue with your cable, they are going to send someone to fix your TV," she continues.

"What?" I ask.

"You know, if you have an issue with one thing you don't fix something else."

"I know. However, I think you are using that phrase wrong, is what I'm saying. 'You don't call the cable company because your TV isn't working,' is how it goes. So, like in our case, just because they have our software installed, they shouldn't call us because their computer isn't working. And honestly, I don't see what that has to do with this anyway."

"We know the saying, Matt," Chris states. "We're simply trying to drive home a point."

"Um, okay. Sorry," I mutter, considering that I was only half paying attention to their conversation in the first place. Maybe the misuse of that expression was correct to whatever they were talking about. I can already sense the ass-reaming that will be delivered to me later.

As expected, around an hour after that meeting Chris calls me to his office.

"So why are you the only one I seem to have problems with, Matt? This is the second time today!"

It is a valid question. Why am I the only one he has problems with? What makes me different from everyone else in this company? But then again, why is it so wrong to stand up for yourself and express an opinion? Why is it we have to kiss ass to move ahead in this world and everyone just accepts that because that's the way it is? If the meeting were with Jeff or Heather, they wouldn't be offended at me pointing out the misuse of a phrase. They wouldn't be outraged, accusing me of having behavioral issues. Yet, whenever I do it to someone with authority over me, I'm the asshole.

"I don't know," I hunch my shoulders in response. "She was using the phrase wrong and out of context. It's not like I was wrong in what I said."

"It's not just the content of your words, it's the tone. You say everything with a negative attitude."

"So, you have a problem with the sound of my voice? There really isn't much I can do about that."

He pauses for a moment. In what appears to be an attempt to hold back what he wants to say.

Inhaling and exhaling deeply, he says, "I don't want to have to do this, but at this point, I have no other options. I've already cleared it with Kerry and she concurs. Please read through and sign at the bottom." He slides a piece of paper across the table towards me. "This is a formal write-up addressing your ongoing attitude issues. It states that we've discussed the matter, and any further behavioral problems could lead to termination."

My hands are clenched on my lap as I go through it. The document points out my behavior, citing it as dismissive and rude, specifically highlighting my negative attitude and argumentativeness. Attached are dates and summaries of past lectures he has given me. Apparently, he has been planning this write-up for a while. I think about saying something, but decide it's not worth it, knowing that if I were to open my mouth now, I wouldn't be able to hold back. So instead, I sign at the bottom and hand it back over.

"Do you have anything you would like to add?" He asks.

"Nope," I say through clinched teeth.

"Okay, well, I want you to go home for the rest of the day. When you return tomorrow, I expect to see an improved attitude. Hopefully, this will be the last discussion like this that we need to have."

"Okay."

I get up and leave the room, go back to my office and grab my jacket before heading out the door.

15

Lying on the floor, embracing the soothing effects of the Vicodin I've swallowed, I wonder what makes artists, musicians, and creative people different from the rest of the world. What separates Vincent van Gogh from John D. Rockefeller? Why is it Beethoven can create beautiful music, while some random guy in an elevator struggles to hum the Jeopardy theme in tune? And thanks to the nausea that often accompanies Vicodin, why is it that creative people are more prone to alcohol and drug abuse? Jimi Hendrix, a self-taught guitarist, would drop acid before going on stage, and he's considered one of the greatest rock musicians of all time.

They say "left-brain" people are more logical and analytical, while "right-brain" people have a more subjective view of the world. I've always thought of myself as a left-brained person. It was that rational thought process that led me to a business degree. Yet it turns out that I despise my office job, which one would assume is the type of work for a logical thinker. My office job involves sitting at a desk all day, and doing what I'm told, along with my co-workers, who, logic would dictate, are also predominantly left-brained thinkers. Most of the people I work with seem relatively content with what they do. Yes, they might bitch and complain occasionally, but at the end of the day, the paycheck, the job security, and a stable life take priority over individuality. I've always faulted these people, wanting to stand up and scream, "What's wrong with you! Don't you see how fucked up this is!" To them, this isn't fucked up; this is the way life is supposed to be. This is the way the world works. And they're right. Without the corporate office monkeys, where would we be? Wandering around San Francisco, advocating free love? We've seen how well that played out in the '60s. An office job pays for my car, my rent, my clothes, my food, and all the trappings of a comfortable, yet unfulfilling, existence.

  I haven't decided what to do about work yet. I should probably start showing up with a positive attitude and pretend to care. Instead, I'm thinking I should post my resume on Monster and apply for a few jobs. It can't hurt to look and see what else is out there. Plus, I can't hum the Jeopardy theme in tune, so picking up the guitar and busking on Pike Street is probably a bad idea. I rushed through business school to get where I am now. However, now that I am doing what I thought I was supposed to do at this point in my life, I'd rather be sitting at home laying on the soft carpet of my living room floor with a Vicodin and a bottle of Sam Adams.

As a child, I used to watch the TV show *Family Ties*, thinking I wanted to be like Michael J. Fox's character, Alex P. Keaton. He wore suits and was going to make a lot of money someday. Back then, I had it in my head that people who wore suits and were entrepreneurs had a corner office, drove a nice car, and lived in a fancy house. Even though I had no idea what an entrepreneur actually was. There was also *The Secret of My Success*, where Fox's character started in the mailroom and pretended to be some guy in a suit so that he could move up within the company. Teaching us that to be successful in life, you need to con your way to the top. Being a con man could work as well, as it did for Dana Carvey in *Opportunity Knocks*. So, in a nutshell, my entire path in life can be attributed to watching too much TV and too many movies. And I don't even own a suit.

In high school, I wanted to go into science or chemistry. The idea of delving into scientific mysteries and conducting experiments interested me. Mixing things together, pulling things apart, and making discoveries that would change the world. That's what fascinated me. So, I did none of that, going for a business degree at CWU as quickly as possible, leading to where I am now: laying on my floor, staring at the ceiling, wondering how I ended up here.

The laptop resting on the coffee table, with my Gmail account open, is casting a soft blue light in the dimly-lit room. I glance up to do a brief scan and notice an unread email from Sophie in my inbox. It appears to be a response to the message I sent earlier. I sit up fully, inhale deeply, holding the breath for a moment before releasing. Staying on the floor, I lean against the sofa, and double-click to read her message. Even though I should feel relaxed with the meds in my system, my heart is racing.

Why do I feel a need to make you understand me? It's like a constant struggle between who I am and who you think I am because of what I do. It's just a job, it's not who I am. I knew this would happen. I knew that if I tried to be what you want, then you would think less of me. That you would be mad, and you were. I wish I could understand why you are so angry all the time. I just hope that someday you will find what you are looking for and can be happy.

Wishing you the best,
Sophie

I start typing my response:

I don't want things to end between us. I guess I don't know where this relationship was heading, I know where I wanted it to go. Honestly, I was super hungover and yes, you're right, I was being jealous. But not even that, I was angry at myself. I've never had a three-way and finally have a chance and I get drunk and pass out.

I wonder if a VPN would allow me to sign up to a poker site in another country. Then I could make money from my winnings.

I just want you to know that I'm not mad anymore. I mean I wasn't really mad actually, it just seemed like I was, but then …

Searching now, I can probably do that, except what about the payment, would it be linked to my US PayPal account or checking account? And if so, could I get hacked or something?

… it seemed like you were mad then that made me mad, and I was tired, and yes I totally want to have a 3 way with you.

Here is one called Paddy Power. Hmm, I wonder how secure it is. Christ, I'd have to get up and get my credit card. But, if I use my card, it can be reversed if it gets hacked, so there is that.

We haven't really ben seeing each other that long so I guess we just need to … I don't know. Its not like it is that

serious, is it. Like um, I don't know what I'm trying to say
here.

God, I sound like a moron. And why am I having this conversation in email. I'm so tired.

Can we meet sometime this we ek and just get a coffee or something?

After hitting send, I shut the laptop and climb onto the sofa before drifting off to sleep.

16

After passing out on the sofa hopped up on painkillers and alcohol last night, I forgot to set my alarm, waking up later than usual. Add to that the rain and commuters driving at a snail's pace because they couldn't see, or for whatever other reason it is that causes people who live in a city that rains more often than not to drive super slowly, as if they had never seen water fall from the sky before. Heading down I-5 this morning was like race cars jockeying for position, except that the racers were barely inching along at about five miles per hour with their windshield wipers on high. The day is off to a perfect start.

"Good morning, Matt," Heather says from behind me, as I'm waiting on the coffee machine to grind the beans. I turn around to see her standing on the opposite side of the island that separates the kitchen from the seating area.

"Hey. Haven't seen you around lately," I respond.

"Yeah, I've been tied up with offsite meetings all week. How are things going with Sophie?" She asks.

"Good."

I could tell her that things are not going that well at the moment, and she would probably offer to sit down and talk about it. But the last thing I want to discuss with a co-worker is my relationship. Even if that co-worker looks inviting, wearing a tight-fitting tan sweater, with long sleeves with a rolled turtleneck at the top. The slight hint of her perfume mingling with the freshly brewed coffee, makes me want to wrap my arms around her, bury my face into her neck and breathe in the intoxicating fragrance of her morning skin.

Plus, when a girl has slipped a few dollars into your girlfriend's G-string and had an intimate view of her breasts, there is a special connection that allows for deep relationship conversations.

Instead, I say, "You know, as good as can be, I guess."

"I like her. We had a lot of fun the other night," she says with a grin.

"Yeah, it seemed like it," I say, smiling at the memory of Heather at the club.

"I'm assuming we can keep all of that between us."

I know what she means. In the business world, one learns who they can share personal experiences with and who they can't. Most people fall in the second category.

"Oh, of course. Don't worry."

I press my right hand against my closed lips and twist, as if locking a key into place, and then fling the imaginary key over my shoulder.

My coffee is done, so I top it off with some milk and sugar while she moves to place a cup and hit the buttons that will grind her a fresh cup.

"See ya later," I say, heading to my office.

"Bye."

Back at my desk to do a quick email check, which involves deleting most and moving others into folders for possible future reference. Only a handful remain that require a response at some point throughout the day. With the majority of today's work complete, it seems like a good time for a cigarette break. I head over to Jeff's office.

"Smoke break?" I say, sticking my head around the door.

He looks up from his monitor. "Sure."

He grabs his overcoat from the wooden coat rack he has in the corner and we head downstairs. The rain has stopped. The two of us walk around to the usual spot between the two buildings.

"Did you leave early yesterday?" he asks as we light our cigarettes.

"Yep. Chris sent me home."

"He did? Why, what happened?"

"I was being a smartass to Kelly during a meeting."

From there, I tell him about the events from the previous day.

"Geez. What are you going to do now?" he asks.

"Nothin' much I can do," I say, exhaling smoke through my nostrils. "Just take it up the ass and smile, I guess. When I get back upstairs, I'll probably start looking for another job, but honestly, I don't see the point. The fucking job market sucks right now. Plus, honestly, would any other place be any better than here?"

"I don't know, bro. Before working here, I worked in customer service. If you want to know about a dreadful place to work, try doing that all day. People never call to tell you how happy they are. They only call because of a problem, and the management there is really strict about what you can communicate to customers. They monitor your calls and all you can do is tell the customers what you are told to say, reading from these scripts written by monkeys with typewriters."

"Welcome to corporate America," I mutter.

We continue smoking in silence for a while. It's nice to have someone who doesn't spout off useless advice about "staying positive" or some bullshit like that.

Deciding that I will not be applying for any customer service jobs, we stomp our cigarette butts into the cement, then head back inside. At my desk, I set up an account on Monster to submit my resume for a couple of open positions.

Let's see, I have rent on the townhouse, a car payment, utilities, credit card interest, and a few other things. If I quit now, I'm fucked. So, that's out as an option. I wonder how long it would take them to fire me. Do they have to go through any more steps – maybe a second writeup before they can? Businesses nowadays are always worried about being sued, which might benefit me. Of course, I could always just begin doing some work and shut my mouth. After all, that is what I'm getting paid for.

"Come on dude," I say to myself. "Just stop being a jackass and keep your mouth shut."

I check my Gmail to see if Sophie has responded. Unfortunately, the only new item showing is an email from a Nigerian prince in need of financial assistance. Jennifer hasn't replied either, to see if her offer about last weekend still applies.

Now, how about getting some work done for a change! First things first, that requirement's document. This shouldn't take all that long, since it mostly involves copying the template I have and swapping old text for new, as the features don't change that much in AdMatics. Honestly, it's not that bad of a product for web ad creation. The script loads faster than what other companies offer.

After working for about an hour my head begins to throb. Needing a break, I decide to head to the break room for some aspirin and fresh cup of coffee. Just as I'm about to stand up, a notification pops up on my computer screen, accompanied by a ping. It is from Joline. Despite my initial instinct to ignore it, I read it.

"Matt, can you come to my office?"

Her office is just around the corner, on the same floor as mine. She could easily get up and walk her podgy ass to my office in the time it took her to type that message.

"Why? What do you want?" I type back.

"I want to talk to you about the testing schedule. Can you come here, please?"

"Why can't you come to my office?"

"Because I want to show you something," she replies.

Oh, well, of course then. I wouldn't want you to strain yourself by walking to my office. Nope, instead, I'll just drop everything I'm doing, and go to your office.

I walk over to her cramped nest. "What?"

"I want to see if you can change the testing schedule?"

"And you couldn't come to my office to ask that, or just say that in your message?"

"Look, I have to show you," she waves for me to walk around behind her desk.

I don't want to breath in the pungent air that hangs around her, like the sour odor of mildew clinging to clothing that wasn't dried properly. But the sooner I do, the sooner I can leave. Her desk has little bobblehead dolls of various Mariners' players, along with pictures of her and her husband. Seriously, who would marry this woman? And, of course, a picture of her dogs. She also has stacks of notepads, printouts, and a couple empty diet Coke cans.

"I'm looking at the calendar and it looks like we have plenty of time between the bug bash and release. So, could you push the testing dates back two days?" she asks, her stumpy sausage finger pointing at the screen.

I take a deep breath.

"You do realize," I respond, "that the schedule was set months in advance so that everyone could get it on their calendar. Which means, if I change the dates, I'm changing it for everyone. So, *everyone* else has to rearrange their schedules."

"Yes, I know," she says. "But I have a conflict on the day."

I take another deep breath before replying, "No. I can't change the schedule. We need that time between the bug bash to get the results over to engineering so they can put any fixes in place before the release. Any time reduced between the two reduces the amount of time they have to get their work done."

"I don't see why two days would make that much of a difference?"

That's because you're a moron.

"Well, first of all, it would be a pain in the ass trying to find time on multiple people's calendars where they are all available for a half-day to sit in a conference room and run test scripts. Then the engineering team would complain about not having enough time to implement fixes. So, I'm sorry if you can't make the bug bash." I take another large deep breath. "How about you just send me your test scripts in advance, and I'll see if someone can run them for you?"

In truth, the engineering team spends little, if any, time fixing things before the release. That's the joys of Scrum Project Management. Release now and fix it later. Mostly, it is her pretentiousness that irritates me. Just because she is large enough to have her own planetary gravitational field doesn't mean everybody else's schedules actually revolve around her.

I excuse myself with a fake smile to get that aspirin.

The workday has ended, and we are sitting at Ozzie's tavern, having just finished a couple cheeseburgers and fries.

"What's the latest on the job situation?" Jeff asks. "Sacked yet?"

I take a sip of my third Jim and Ginger, impressed that he made it this long before bringing up the subject of work.

"No, obviously, not yet."

So far, we have discussed the hot bartender who made us our drinks and played a bit of name that song with the music playing in the background of this dimly-lit run-down dive bar.

"I don't want to talk about work. Let's talk about something interesting."

"Yeah, okay. What would you like to discuss?"

Not really having anything in mind other than work, I say, "If you could have sex with Heather, would you? The catch is afterward her husband would kick you in the balls as hard as he could."

He chuckles. "It would hurt for a while, but I've been kicked in the balls before. The pain eventually goes away."

I shake my head with a mock disapproving smile.

"Actually," he leans over, lowering his voice, "I think they have an open marriage?"

"Oh, really?" I say, imitating his lowered voice. "Did they invite you and Evelyn over for a key party?"

"No." His volume back to normal, "I was looking at hookup ads on The Stranger last night, and I'm pretty sure she has a profile on there."

"Okay. First of all, what are you doing on The Stranger's personals?"

"I wasn't on the personals. I was on the Lustlab. The people looking for hookups."

"And even more shocking. What were you doing looking at Lustlab hookups? I've met your wife and I don't get the impression she would be okay with that."

"I was merely browsing, bro. I would never actually do something."

As he continues, I roll my eyes.

"I came across one in the casual encounters section and I think it was her. The girl in the picture was wearing glasses with pointed corners and the color was identical to the ones she wears. Her head was turned, but by what you could see of her face, it looked like her. And remember how they were at the strip club – he bought her a lap dance, bro."

Now he has me interested in jumping online later. Talk about the ultimate threesome with her and Sophie.

"Ummm, hmmm. Well, go for it," I reply, knowing he never would.

"No, I can't. I'm married."

"Aren't you supposed to say, 'I can't because I love my wife'?"

"Of course, I love my wife," he says, unconvincingly. "I just sometimes wonder if we should be married. The most we ever do is an occasional dinner. Even then, she only wants to go to one of the local places. She says Seattle has gotten too unsafe. Her ideal evening involves staying at home. When we first met, she wasn't like that. She was fun. For our wedding in Hawaii, we rented a scooter and toured the island. Now, I mention getting a motorcycle and she says I can't."

"How does that work?" I laugh. "If you showed up at home on a motorcycle, would she leave you? She'd be like, 'That's it! Divorce!'? But hey, if she does, that solves your problem with hooking up with some chick you met on Lustlab."

I wonder if Sophie would be like that if I got a motorcycle? She seems super cool, like she would have no problem with motorcycles – not that I want one, but if I did, she would probably be up for it. And talk about someone that would look great in tight leather pants. If we got married, would she change or do what most women do and try to change me? I'm sure Jennifer would hate the idea of a motorcycle. She would probably be happy to buy a new outfit for it, but to ride on one – I doubt it.

He continues, "I just thought about it. I don't think I would actually want a motorcycle. But, it's just like things have changed, gotten boring."

On the stage in the back of the bar, a few guys had been setting up band equipment. The music playing through the speakers cuts off, letting the bar know they are about to start.

"Darn, it got late quick." Jeff points out after looking at his watch.

"Do you need to be home?"

"I took the bus today, so I just need to make sure to leave in time to catch the last one."

I'm not quite ready to head out just yet. The amount of alcohol in my system is at that perfect point to where I'm feeling good and want to hold on to it a while longer. At home is nothing but emptiness – a reminder of the fact that I am over thirty and working at a shitty job that I am probably going to get fired from, have no stable relationship, and the nagging suspicion that I might have a slight drinking problem. Not wanting to acknowledge any of those things, the best solution at the moment is to opt for another drink.

"You are more than welcome to crash at my place." I offer. "Assuming your wife will let you."

"I don't *actually* need her approval to stay out, you know."

"Sure you don't. It's okay buddy, you can go home and lock yourself in the bathroom with your laptop and rub one out to the girl on Lustlab. Or, even better, you can stay out with me, have another drink, listen to some music and crash at my place. It's not like anyone would notice if you show up to work in the same clothes tomorrow. Most people try to avoid eye contact with your wardrobe as much as possible, anyway."

"What's wrong with this?"

"The shirt is fine," I say. "But those purple pants are horrible."

He is wearing purple jeans with a black t-shirt that has an old Atari logo on it.

"They aren't purple, they're plum."

"Plum! That's even worse," I laugh.

"Let me see."

He heads outside to call his wife. While he is gone, a waitress comes by the table, and I order us each another round. The band on the stage starts playing. There are five of them. Lead singer, guitarist, bass, keyboard, and drums. They start up with a cover of "One Way or Another" by Blondie. It isn't that bad of a version they are doing. They've rearranged it enough to work with the lead singer's voice.

Jeff returns about halfway through my drink. I've been watching a pair of blondes on the dance floor slightly past their prime. Based on their dated hairstyles, bad dye jobs, and outfits, they seem to think it is still 1985. Which must be why they are here, as 80s music is the only thing the band is playing. *Stuck in the 80s with these guys, for those who were alive then and are alone now.*

"Yeah, I can stay out," he tells me.

"Cool. Drink up." I nod to the glass in front of him. Leaning in and lowering my voice a bit, "Hey check these two at the table next to us. I looked over there earlier and the girl gave me a smile. Do you think they are swingers? They have that look to them."

There is an older couple at the table. The man is balding, with long gray hair pulled into a ponytail in the back. Next to him is a woman with faded tattoos down her arms, baggy eyes, and a mouth that looks like she has sucked so many dicks she lost count.

He turns and looks while I continue, "I mean, you are looking for some strange on the side, right? Maybe you could go home with them tonight. Get down and dirty with her while he wanks-off on the bed next to you. And don't worry, I'll cover for you with Evelyn."

He smiles. "Nasty bro. I'm not that desperate."

"You guys want to dance?"

The two girls who had been out on the floor have walked over to our table. Closer, the shorter one is not as bad looking as initially suspected. The lines and bags around her eyes suggest she's had her fair share of partying adventures. As long as I properly bag my meat, she might be a fun hookup for the night.

"Oh, I don't know," I say. "I'm not really much of a dancer. Plus, my friend here is married and if his wife found out he was dancing with another girl, he'd probably get spanked."

"I would not," Jeff retorts.

"It's just a dance, guys. Come on. No spanking unless you ask for it. I promise," she smirks in my direction.

She is grabbing my arm, pulling me away from the table. I could easily stop her, but what the hell. The band is playing a decent sounding cover of "The Power of Love." Jeff has willingly let himself be dragged out by the other girl. Even the creepy swinging couple has moved to the dance floor.

"Not a bad cover of this song!" I yell, leaning in.

"Yeah, they're great. The keyboardist is a friend of mine."

"Oh, cool."

I don't really care enough to ask if by 'friend' she means boyfriend or fuck buddy, or just friend. What would really be nice at the moment is getting my hands on some coke. I wonder if her friend the keyboardist can hook us up? Or if she can?

The song ends, transitioning into a cover of "Major Tom." The catchy melody and beat fill the bar, drowning out conversations and drawing more people to the dance floor. Then the chorus hits as everyone begins to yell out, "Four, three, two one …"

This girl is nice and close, swaying and gyrating with the beat, her warm body against mine. As the chorus hits again, she jumps back, raising her hands into the air, singing along. I can't help but get swept up on the excitement of the room, bouncing with my hands in the air as well, singing along.

After a few songs, I realize I need to rehydrate and make my way back to the table with the girl following close behind.

"What's your name?" I ask.

"Angela," she says, leaning in for a half hug.

"Matt," I respond.

I take a long swig from my glass just in time to catch the waitress. Being the gentleman that I am,

I offer her something. She orders a vodka and cranberry juice.

"So do they do original music or is it just covers?"

"They do original stuff, too, but places like this book them to do covers because that's what people want. They have a show coming up in a couple weeks at the Tractor doing original music, if you are interested."

"Yeah, maybe. What type of music is it?"

"It's kind of like an alt-country or indie type stuff."

"Cool? Do you smoke?" I ask, with two fingers to my lips.

"No."

"Okay. I'm going to go have a quick one. I'll be back in a minute."

She moves back to the dance floor with the others while I head to the door.

Outside, past the bouncer, there are a handful of other smokers like myself. Knowing some mooch will ask for a cigarette as soon as I pull my pack out, I move a few feet down the sidewalk, turning my back to the group to light it. I slip my phone from my pocket, shooting a text to Kai and my dealer, Renton, to see if they have any coke. Renton is not his real name. It's a nickname someone gave him at some point that has stuck.

Back inside, the drinks are flowing strong, and it's clear that Angela is good-to-go for the night. On the dance floor, she's pressed up against me, and my hands are all over her. She turns her back and grinds her ass into my groin while my arms are around her. I cup her breasts. They're being held up nicely; however, I expect if I let them out, they would hit the floor like a ton of bricks. But they say with age comes experience. Plus, as an 80s cover band groupie, she might have connections to hook us up with some blow, since Kai or Renton haven't messaged me back. The band works through the top of the classic rock playlists, from CCR to the Pretenders. The four of us create a partial circle, jumping up and down to David Bowie's "Let's Dance."

"I love this song," Angela yells into my ears. "I saw him in concert once. It was the best!"

I give her a double thumbs up rather than yell over the music back to her.

The blue, red, and green lights pulse through the room; the dance floor is jammed with people bouncing to the music. In contrast is Jeff, who moves awkwardly. His feet shift left and right in some type of two-step, with his arms defensively crossed over his chest, albeit with a big smile on his face. Angela's friend appears more interested in dancing with her than anyone else. Angela is spinning and twirling with a huge smile on her face, clearly enjoying being the center of attention. No one seems to mind the heat from the bodies pressed together, bumping into one another, all caught in the carnivalesque atmosphere.

I look around with that whisky fueled buzz that I love so much. It's that sweet spot in the night where everything is vibrant, the people around me are a bit hazy, and the frustrations of everyday life has faded away.

The band is clearly having a good time with the crowd. They undoubtedly think they are the shit at imitating the look of 80s glam rockers. The lead singer struts around the stage in tight leather pants with a thinly-knit sleeveless t-shirt that highlights his dangerously thin frame, almost as if he's on the verge of an overdose. He occasionally turns his back to the crowd, singing to the drummer, a move copied from some rocker in the 70s, and passed down ever since, a symbol of indifference towards the audience. The lead guitar and bass player are sporting the long 80s butt-rocker hair, whipping their sweat-soaked locks along to the music. The crowd on the dancefloor is enjoying a moment in a memory of themselves back when they were young, or in my case, drunkenly moving to the beat of the drum with a girl who knows all the lyrics.

"I'm going to the ladies," she pants with beads of perspiration streaking her makeup.

It is getting warm in here, so I use that as an opportunity to head out for some fresh air. Outside, after I've lit a cigarette and given one to some jackass in a tattered green army jean jacket asking to bum a smoke, a cop car rolls up with two officers inside and the windows rolled down. They park and get out of the car while the guy with the army jacket takes a couple of steps towards them.

"How's everything with you, officers?" he asks, taking a drag from the cigarette.

The one who stepped out of the passenger side of the car responds. "Fine. And you?"

"All good. You lookin' for anyone specific, or just patrolling the area?" The man flashes a wide smile.

The officer shifts his weight slightly, his hand resting near his belt as he scans the area.

The man continues with a snarky tone, "Some shady characters hanging around here tonight." He shakes his head. "Always wise keeping an eye out. That's what I say."

I decide to walk a few steps further away, not really having any interest in engaging the police in conversation. Looking at my phone, there is still no response from either of the guys. It's fine if neither of them has anything, but a text back wouldn't hurt.

I'll have to see if Angela can hook us up for the night. There is no doubt that the lead singer partakes.

There is a sudden commotion from where the cops are standing and I look to see one of them tackling the smoker, flipping him over and jamming his knee into the guy's neck.

"I said don't move!" he hells.

"I'm not moving," the guy says, struggling.

He is moving, but more in an involuntary struggle because some cop is throwing all his weight on him. The other officer is standing with one hand on his pistol ready to draw, the other arm up, making sure that the crowd gathering around stands back.

"Please … I can't breathe," the guy continues to sputter out as he struggles under the weight of the cop.

The officer pays no attention to the man's breathless pleading, instead seizing the guy's hands and forcefully twisting them behind his back. The guy cries out in pain. With his handcuffs ready, the cop releases his knee from the man's neck, clasping them around the wrists. He moves quickly, not giving the guy an opportunity to resist. Not that he could put up much of a fight, judging by the look of him. As he regains the ability to breathe, he gasps for air. The still-lit cigarette he was smoking now rests just inches from his mouth on the ground.

There is a woman in the crowd yelling, "He didn't do anything! Let him go!"

The other cop, preoccupied with controlling the onlookers, doesn't see his partner forcefully drive his knee into the man's back, knocking the wind out of him.

Some stocky guy moves forward, yelling, "Did you see that? He just kneed him for no reason! Did you see that!"

The other cop pushes him back. "Sir, you need to stay back!"

"Your partner just assaulted that man for no reason," the guy continues.

I stamp out my cigarette and head back inside instead of getting caught up in the riot that looks about to break out with more people gathering around.

Inside the band has stopped playing, with the music now blaring from the speaker system. I spot Angela at the table with the other girl.

"Hey, what happened to Jeff?"

"Don't know," the one he was dancing with says.

It's decision time. Do I ditch the girls, close out my tab, and track down Jeff? Or do I stick with the girls, and the possibility of a night with Angela, and forget about Jeff altogether? Angela is swaying to the rhythm of the music, her inviting raised eyebrow and a playful smile in response to my internal dilemma.

Decision made.

I lean it close to Angela. "So, what's your plan for the rest of the night? Want to take off?" I nod towards the door.

She turns and slings an arm around my shoulder. "Jamie and I are going to finish our drinks and then I'm going to head home," she says with a smile. "Thanks for the dance, it was fun." She gives me a quick kiss on the cheek then turns back to her friend.

I have to pause for a second to process that. "Ok," I respond, not interested in calling her out for the nappy tease she is. "Have a good night."

I give them both a friendly wave and head to the men's room for a piss before leaving.

Outside, the scene has expanded to include an additional police car parked alongside the first. Its rooftop lights are flashing, giving the impression that the party has spilled out into the street. One of the new officers has his notepad in his hand and is speaking to the bouncer that was at the door, idly standing and doing nothing, the whole time. The guy that the cop arrested is sitting in the back of the first police car while the one who arrested him is speaking with the newly arrived cop. The crowd has grown, though the mob seems to have died down, now that more officers are on the scene. Except for the woman who was yelling earlier in the man's defense. She is gesturing loudly to an officer who doesn't seem to have any interest in what she has to say.

Good thing the guy isn't black, I think, turning to have another cigarette and text Jeff to see where he went.

The next day I swing by Jeff's office. He's sitting behind the desk.

"What the hell happened to you last night?"

He looks up. "Oh, I called Evie and she came and picked me up."

"Dude, I was looking all over for you. I thought you passed out in an alley somewhere."

"Oh, I'm sorry. I had a bit too much to drink and headed home."

"Well, you could have said something before you left."

I expect his wife was not pleased about having to drive all that way to pick his drunk ass up in the middle of the night, so that makes me feel a bit better about him ditching me.

"Sorry bro, once I called Evie, I just zoned out. What about you, did you hook up with that chick?"

"No, once you bailed, I decided to take off."

"Seriously? She seemed like she was ready to jump your bones."

"Yeah, but it turns out she wasn't," I say, then change the subject. "Did you see the commotion out front?"

"I saw the police there. I wasn't able to catch what occurred. Did you?"

"Yeah, a bit," I say. "Lunch?"

"Sure."

"Cool. I'll fill you in then," I reply, then head to my office to see what fun the day has in store for me.

17

"You want some shrooms?" Renton asks.

"No, man. Just the weed thanks," I reply.

"Are you sure, I'll give you a killer deal."

He pulls a plastic grocery bag with a QFC logo on it full of mushrooms from his kitchen cabinet.

"Holy shit, dude," I laugh. "That's a lot of fucking shrooms."

"A guy I know up in Granite Falls grows them. He turned a shed into a mushroom farm. How about some candy, then?"

"Candy?" I ask.

"You heard of candy flipping?"

"No, I guess I'm just not that cool."

"It's MDMA with a just a dash of LSD."

"Really?"

"Dude, you need to try it. You get the upbeat feeling from the X mixed with a super positive acid trip. It's like being in a magical fairyland. Trust me." He says, with a smile that reminds me of the Joker in a Batman comic.

From a drawer he takes out a zip-lock bag half full of purple pills.

"You buy ten or more and I'll let you have them for ten each."

"Dude, where the fuck do you get all this shit?" I ask, amazed at his ability to get such large quantities of narcotics.

"I have my sources," he says with an evil grin.

At ten for ten, I could probably sell them for twenty or twenty-five and make a few bucks. Maybe that's what I should start doing when I lose my job. I should become a dealer. The guy has a pretty decent house in Rainer Valley. It's not super huge or anything and a faint musty smell lingers in the air. Nothing a good remodel wouldn't solve, especially in the kitchen with its outdated dark brown cabinets and yellow countertops. He could probably turn a decent profit if he were to sell it. I wonder how hard it is to become a real estate agent.

His biggest problem is that like most dealers, he does too much of his own product. His gaunt face and thin blond hair only add to the look of someone who spends his nights cracked out and malnourished. But he has always been reliable and never fucked me over with any product.

"Yeah, okay," I say. "I'll take twenty."

After failing to talk Kai into meeting me at a bar in Columbia City, and driving around forever to find parking on the hill, I'm back in Percy's shitty little apartment waiting for the drugs to kick in, selling each a pill for twenty bucks.

"I'm not feeling anything yet," Percy says.

"Dude, you just took it like ten minutes ago," I respond, annoyed. "Let's smoke a joint. That'll relax you into it."

I take a joint I rolled at Renton's out of my cigarette pack. The distinct smell of marijuana smoke fills the air as the joint is lit. I take a long drag, relishing the first hit before handing it over to Percy.

"Do you call it flipping, or candy flipping, or candying," Kai says after taking a hit then passing the joint back to me. "If you are on E, you are rolling, so I guess flipping kind of makes sense. You roll, then you flip." He laughs.

I might have to ditch these two at some point.

I think it would be nice to flip with Sophie. *Great, now he has me saying it.* I look at my phone to see if there are any messages from her. She's probably working tonight. Or out with someone else. My heartbeat picks up at the thought of her out with some other guy. Fuck! Why did I have to be such a dick?

We've migrated to The Chapel and the drugs have kicked in. I'm standing at what used to be the gallery overlooking the dance floor below. The lights of red, white, and green create a pulsating kaleidoscope of color. Below the people merge and morph into a mesh of vibrant 3D animated cartoons. It's amazingly beautiful, like something out of a psychedelic dream. The bass thumps through the floor, vibrating up through my body into my chest. Even if I wanted, I don't think I could convince my body to stop moving to the beat.

My parched mouth forces me to turn and return to the table where Kai and Percy are sitting. Sliding into the seat next to Kai, I can see he is feeling the effects of the drugs as well, with a massive smile on his face and hands sliding over the cool surface of the table.

"Mike … Matt … Matt, hey," Percy says, correcting himself while leaning over Kai to talk to me. "These are my friends … ummm, and they want to buy some …" He trails off with a lisp.

Sitting to his right are a guy and a girl. I think. Yes, I blink a few times in order to bring them into focus. He's got dark, curly hair, and a youthful face that looks like he shouldn't have been allowed in. She also looks young, with long blond hair that runs down her shoulders. Her fair skin reflects the pulsating light, like an angel.

"Hey, hey." Percy forces my attention back to him. His face is distorted into a lumpy form of shadows. His cheeks are bulged into nasty boils, his eyes sunken into nothingness.

I feel a hand touch my leg and look down to see his hand stretched over Kai with some cash in it. I take the cash and slip it into my pocket, then take out my little bag of pills and hand him two in return.

He turns towards the little angels and I see the boy turn towards the girl, sliding it to her under the table. They both look around to see if anyone is watching, then lift a hand to their mouths. The guy takes a quick drink from a beer bottle while the girl does the same from a glass of something. They make scrunchy faces, reacting to the taste of the pill that begins to dissolve in their mouths before swallowing.

Jack Johnson is playing while we wait for the second pill we have all taken to kick in. The church was turning into an obnoxious sensory overload, so now we are in a small apartment that smells of scented candles, two of which are sitting on the coffee table in front of me, sending light and shadows dancing across the tables surface. I've settled into what must be the softest sofa in existence, with cushions that feel like sinking into fresh warm dough. It would be absolutely perfect if it weren't for Percy seated uncomfortably close to me.

He is speaking in some form of language or gobbledygook. I'm not sure if it's his speech or my hearing distorting the words as they pass through the gaping black hole in his face. The young couple are resting comfortably together in a large armchair. Actually, the girl is sitting in the chair, the boy is on the floor in front of her. He is leaning back while she runs her hands through the large curls of his dark hair.

Somehow, she still shines magically. I wish I could shrink her down, hold her in the palm of my hand, and suck on her like a popsicle.

Trying not to stare creepily as I watch her body snakelike move to the music, I take out my phone to message Sophie. Damn! The screen is bright, almost blinding. After a bit of messing with the settings to turn it into dark mode, I manage to open a text message. It's funny in typing this how the screen brightness has changed my mood. Feeling up, feeling good, letting my imagination run wild at thoughts of the young girl to serious thoughts at the dark screen with letters that have turned into bubbles.

What is this music playing? Some girl singing. It's relaxing but emotional, it's like she is speaking to me directly. However, it is a challenge to listen over the sound of Percy, who is still talking!

"Quiet," I say, holding my hand up to his face. "Who is this?" I ask the couple.

"Star Anna," the boy says. "You like her. I just got it."

"Yeah."

I lean back to stare at the dimly lit lamp standing next to the chair they are sitting in. Looking around the room, I realize it must be their place, or her place. The cleanliness of the apartment is enhanced by the white walls and the feminine touch of flowers on an end table. The only thing that implies a guy lives here is the entertainment stand. A TV sits in the middle with a stereo receiver that has an iPod dock with someone's iPod rotating through the music we have been listening to. Not the music I usually play when rolling, but it certainly works great for flipping.

Kai is sitting on the floor, leaning against the wall with his phone to his ear. With the music slowing down, I can hear him describing his circumcised dick to someone, or to a voice mail. I have a feeling he will be off to the bathhouse soon, hopefully taking Percy with him. But then I'll be left with the couple who might want me to leave. Then where would I go?

Sophie, right? Message Sophie. She's probably home by now. What time is it anyway? My phone is a blur. *Focus eyes.* Wow, it's after two already. Sophie would be home by now. Or would she? What time does she work till? Maybe I should go to her work. I'm okay to drive, probably. If I can remember where my car is.

The voice of Kermit the Frog starts singing "Rainbow Connection." I look at the couple who slide in and out of focus like a camera lens that is adjusting the image into sharpness.

"Someday we'll find it, the rainbow connection, the lovers, the dreamers and meeeeee" We all sing in unison.

I love these two. I want them to be my new best friends. I need to get their names and phone numbers. Phone. Right. Message Sophie. Back to my phone. Message Sophie.

"Dude," I state, "You need to stop talking and slide to your side of the sofa. Seriously, back the fuck off."

Percy looks shocked, not knowing how to react. The mood in the room has turned again.

"I'm sorry," I add, "I'm trying to send a message and I can't focus while you are talking so much. Okay. Thank you."

"Sorry," he says, offended, while sliding to the other side of the sofa.

Fuck, I am so thirsty.

"Um, could I get some ice water?" I ask the couple.

"Yes," the girl says, getting up. "Does anyone else want anything?"

Everyone responds with a yes.

"I'll help you," I say, following her to the kitchen that is set to the side of the living room. Watching her fill the glass with water, the light reflects a vibrant rainbow over her face. It's so fucking adorable I want to squeeze her until her head explodes.

"Are you okay in there?"

How long have I been standing here staring at the water in the bowl of the toilet trying to force my useless dick to let go of the piss annoyingly stuck inside? It's like, right there ready, but just doesn't want to happen.

"I'm fine," I say. Then silently whispering, "Okay, fuck you dick, if that's the way you want to be about it, you don't get to go."

Flushing with embarrassment, I make my way back into the living room. Kai and Percy seem to have left. The young guy is sitting in the chair, as the girl sits on the armrest next to him.

"Where'd those two go?" I ask.

"They left," she says.

"Oh, I guess I should get going, too," I say.

"You're welcome to stay if you want," she says.

What do they mean by that? Do they want to have a three-way? I'd totally be down for that, although I don't think my dick would work. I'd be perfectly happy to taste what's between her legs.

215

"I put a pillow on the sofa and a blanket for you," she says.

I look, and there is a pillow and a folded red blanket.

"Oh, that's okay, thanks. I don't want to be a bother."

"You really shouldn't be driving," the guy says.

I could probably take a taxi to Sophie's or Jennifer's. If I could think clearly enough to tell the driver where they are. Kai doesn't live far, I don't think. But he's probably not at home. And the idea of spending any more time around Percy is revolting.

Somehow, this sofa has become even more comfortable than before. The fresh scent of the pillow and the softness of the blanket wraps me in a warm soothing cocoon. The curtains are moving like slow ripples in a lake. Turning, the girl is now sitting on the lap of the guy, whispering something in his ear. He shakes his head. She probably wants him to go to bed with her. I try to speak to let them know they can leave me, but I can't speak. Normally, that would probably be an issue, but not tonight. Tonight, it's not worth the effort. Although, if I could speak, I would request something other than Fish to listen to, the Grateful Dead of my generation.

Would I be happier if I finally accept that what I dreamed will never happen? Maybe that's my problem. Maybe I should stop looking at these jobs as something I don't want but as something I want. As something that would contribute to happiness in my life. I wonder if there is actually wind or maybe the heater causing the curtains to move, or if it is just my drug-addled brain creating the impression of movement.

The morning light is beginning to peek through the curtains. The couple left at some point, turning out the lights, blowing out the candles, and shutting the music down. And the coming down phase begins. The worst phase of any trip, when you begin to see things as they are, dull and dreary. Occasionally a wave returns, reminding you that you are still a bit high, but it's just a wave, and the dips last longer and are more noticeable. The colors fade, the movement of the shadows recedes, until all you really want is to sleep. But your mind won't let you. It's time to leave.

Breathing in the chill of the morning air feels nice, so I take out a cigarette, light it, take a nice long drag, then bend over into a fit of hacking as the phlegm in my lungs is expelled into spit on the ground. After the coughing fit, I smash the rest of the cigarette out, and try to orient myself to where I am and where my car is located.

The worst part is where all you want is sleep, but sleep never happens. When the height of the experience is over but not so far gone you can go to sleep. You give up on sleeping and lay on the sofa as the morning turns to day, and the day to evening, while flipping through the channels, not paying attention to anything on television, just wishing that you could fall asleep.

18

"You know what the problem is with your apartment?" I say, looking toward the window.

The thick curtains are open while the thin white sheers underneath have been closed, allowing the light from the city to filter through, casting a gentle glow that hangs in the air like a thin mist. Adding to the soft glow are the fairy lights draped around the headboard above us.

We are lying naked under a lone white sheet that remained on the bed after the evening's passion. Her head is on my chest, my right arm wrapped around her.

"I like my apartment," she replies.

"I do, too. Except that you don't have a balcony. So, I can't go outside to smoke a cigarette."

Without turning her head, she says, "Hmm, well, you could always consider quitting."

"Yes, but you getting a balcony is probably more likely to happen."

My gaze drops to the contour of her nose and the curves of her cheeks. Most of her face is concealed by her dark hair, now tousled with strands sticking out in all directions instead of its usual silky smoothness. Looking further down to the outline of her body under the sheet as one long sensuous curve from head to toe, I slide my hand up from her waist and over her breasts to feel the warm softness of her flesh.

"Oh, again?" she says in response to my action.

"Give me a minute," I say. "If you don't mind me smoking and blowing it out the window, maybe even less."

"No smoking in my house. You know the rule."

I grunt and get up out of the bed, looking for my clothes.

"If you want," she says, "You can go up on the roof to smoke."

"You have roof access?"

"Yes, it's nice. You can see over the building next door to the Sound."

She rises from the bed, and each of us reaches for our scattered clothing, the items tossed to various locations on the floor. Once we are suitably dressed, we move to the door where my thick navy-style peacoat and her yellow North Face jacket are waiting for us. It was plenty cold earlier when she agreed to meet at the Cuban restaurant for dinner, mojitos, and a talk. The food was excellent; the talk was friendly, and the waitstaff quickly replaced the drinks, which led us back here.

Exiting the elevator on the top floor, I follow her down the corridor and around a corner to a small flight of stairs that leads us to a thick metal door. With a bit of resistance, the door creaks open to a rooftop terrace. There are a few wooden outdoor chairs around a matching table. Opposite to that is a good-sized built-in barbecue. More chairs are scattered about. The roof offers a decent view of the buildings across the street, one of which is the same building visible from her bedroom window. The late night cold has most people at home, leaving little noise rising from the streets below.

"Nice view," I say as I take out a cigarette, offering her one, knowing that she will decline it with a turned-up nose.

"Over this way."

She leads me to the other corner of the roof where we can see the Puget Sound. The view is crystal clear in the brisk night air. There is a ferry crossing from one of the islands, leaving a small wake as it flows along the smooth black surface of the water. West Seattle on the other side is unmistakable, with flickering lights from homes and a few cars moving along the shoreline, like a scene staged for some cheesy chick flick. If we are still together by the summer, I will have to talk her into having a barbecue up here. If this even counts as back together and not just a drinks-and-fuck night.

She has the hood from her jacket up over her head. It frames her face perfectly, like a snow bunny on her way to the slopes. I wrap one arm around her to pull her close. Even with the thick jacket between us, I can feel the warmth working through the dense material. I tilt my head down and lay it on hers with the hood making for a nice pillow. These are those little moments in life that are often ignored and rarely remembered. I don't have to think about work problems, financial problems, relationship problems, or other people's problems. I can simply breathe in the clean cold air coming off the Puget Sound and enjoy the view and the warmth from someone who cares. No longer interested in finishing my cigarette, I flick what remains of it off the building to the street below.

"Don't do that," she says, breaking the silence.

"Do what?"

"That might hit someone."

"I doubt it, and even it does, it's not like it's going to start their hair on fire. It will just bounce off."

"It's rude. And you're littering. Look there is an ashtray right there." She points.

I roll my eyes and nod. "Well, I think paving the streets hurt the environment a bit worse than a cigarette butt … but, okay, I promise to start using the ashtray." I give her a quick kiss on the lips.

She scrunches her face at me. An exaggerated reaction to the cigarette smoke on my breath.

"Do you want to sit down, or go back inside?" she asks.

"I'm okay to sit for a bit if you are."

We move over to one of the large lounge chairs. I sit first and she nestles between my legs, leaning back into me so that I can wrap my arms around her and slip my hands in the large warm pockets of her jacket. She does the same, interlacing her fingers with mine.

After a few moments sitting I can tell it won't be long before my ass starts to hurt on the wood.

"A cushion would be nice," I say.

"They have cushions on them in the summer but during the winter they store them."

"Makes sense."

We sit in silence for a bit.

"Tell me something about yourself?" she asks, breaking the silence.

"What do you want to know?"

"Are you from Seattle? Do you have brothers or sisters? Stuff like that."

"More or less. I have one brother. My parents are divorced and my mother lives in Snohomish, that's where I grew up."

"That's north of here, right?"

"Yeah, a bit northeast. I take it you are not from here then?"

"No, the UK originally. My dad is Iranian and my mother is English."

"There is a picture of them in my living room."

"You mean that place we pass on our way to your bedroom."

She lightly smacks my leg in response. I know the picture she is referring to. It's a framed family portrait. Her father is wearing a suit, while Sophie and her mother are both wearing dresses. Sophie was probably ten or eleven when the photo was taken.

"How come you don't have an accent?"

"My parents met in London, then they moved to New York when I was six. I can do a New Yowk accent." she says, going into the typical idea of what a New Yorker sounds like. "My fatha worked in text-uhls before retieng."

"Textiles?" I reply, not acknowledging her accent.

She drops the accent. "Yes, cloth and stuff, imports from the middle east. He owned a jewelry store in Iran but then had to leave after the uprising. That's when he went to London."

I laugh. "Wow, that sounds much cooler than my parents' story. The most international travel they have ever done, I think, is a visit to Canada. So, what brought you to Seattle?"

I assume it is because of a boy, as that is usually what causes a girl to move across the country on her own, but don't want to say that.

"Work."

"Really. You moved to Seattle to be a stripper?"

"Nooo." She smacks my leg softly. "I got a job in the Contracts department at Boeing and moved here. Except, I hated it. Then I went to work as an accountant for the company that owns Dolls. Then I started dancing."

"And you get along with your parents and stuff?"

"Yes, no daddy issues if that is what you were thinking."

"I wasn't thinking that."

I was

"Funny story. At the club the other night a couple girls were complaining about that. They were like, 'I hate it when guys assume I have daddy issues or was abused as a child. One said, I never even met my dad.' And the other was like, 'I haven't spoken to mine since it was ten.' It was so funny we all broke out laughing."

"That is pretty funny."

225

The chill in the air is becoming more noticeable, and even though my arms are wrapped around her, and my hands are keeping warm in her pockets, it is probably time to head back inside.

"This jacket isn't really as warm as it looks," I say. "Do you want to go back inside?"

We get up and I feel warmer already after removing my ass from the stone-cold chair.

"Actually, I probably should get going," I say once we are in the building. "Unlike you, I have to work in the morning."

"You can stay here if you want."

"I would, but I don't have a change of clothes, and my car is parked on the street. I don't want to get towed in the morning if I'm not up in time. So, Sophia," I say intentionally mispronouncing her name, "Was this like a one-time thing, orrr …"

Her lips curl in a wicked smile. "It can be more than a one-time thing. Plus, if you ever piss me off again, I always have the voice message you left as blackmail."

"What message?" I ask.

"The one you left the other night when you were all tripsadick."

"Tripsadick. That's a new one. But honestly, I thought I only texted," I say, referring the simi-incoherent text that she replied to when agreeing to meet me.

She laughs. "You don't remember."

"No, I'm sorry," I say embarrassed. "I remember thinking about calling."

She takes out her phone and plays it for me:

I'm always thinking about the past worried that I will forget. But does doing that make me less present? Yes, it does. Especially with me because when I think about the past it makes me sad. But thinking about the present and future does as well. I keep thinking about the past as if they were better times, but I was just as sorrowful then as I am now. My mind is a carousel, spinning around the axis of time. But the future looks better than the past because the past is back then, and the futured is now. The past is in stone while our futures retain their fluidity right here, in this moment—

"Ok, that's enough." I say, grabbing the phone from her hand to end the replay.

"But your mind is a carousel, spinning the axis of time," she laughs historically.

"Okay, okay. I vaguely remember leaving that message now, although at the time I really feel I was on the cusp of some major philosophical breakthrough." I have to laugh a bit as well.

"You were, honey," she says, her tone dripping with humorous condescension. "Just wait until it gets to the part about the fluidity of water in the future. Or something about water flowing and the future." She bursts into a fit of laughter again.

"In my defense, I was in the bathroom at the time, so water was on my mind. And I think I read that carousel thing in a book."

She laughs even harder, "And I thought you came up with that yourself."

I give her a kiss, her lips, warm and soft, cause me to briefly rethink my decision to leave and go back home.

Driving north, I think that maybe I should start keeping a change of clothes in the car for situations like this. Or even better, maybe she should come to my place more often. It is closer to where she works. *No, don't be thinking that shit. Next, you will give her a spare key, asking her to move in, and then what?* If we keep seeing each other, she will eventually meet my parents. My mother is about as conservative as a person can get. When we were kids, she would take us to church. Not that my brother or I became better people for it. She only goes now for Christmas mass and Easter. But if asked, she would say she is a good Christian. Whatever that means.

Hey mom. This is Sophie. She gets naked and gives men lap dances for money. We met when she came up to me at a party, stuck her tongue down my throat and told me she also loves cock.

Yep, that should go over well.

19

I should not be here right now. But if I weren't, where would I be? At home alone? Out with Jeff or Kai? In my defense, I made these plans after Sophie broke things off with me. So, technically, it's her own fault if she calls and gets my voicemail. She had all week to ask me if I wanted to do something this weekend and she chose not to.

"What are you thinking about?" Jennifer asks me.

"Nothing. Just waiting for the effects to start kicking in. You know, what we need is some music." To get Sophie off my mind.

I rise from my spot on the sofa and plug my iPod into her stereo. A song by Soul Asylum picks up where it left off, providing a bit of distraction from my racing thoughts, and relaxing my restless fingers with melodic guitar chords. I settle back onto the plush warmth of the sofa. The warm color tones of the apartment, and the familiar scents lingering in the air with the light fragrance of those dried rose petal potpourri things she has in a bowl, provide a comfort in this little apartment that I have visited hundreds of times, helped her move into, and experienced several nights of passion in. It is also the sense of ease that comes with being here. When I step through the door and remove my shoes, setting them to the side, the soft light brown carpet under my feet lets me know I can relax. However, I'm not as relaxed as usual – in fact, a bit of anxiety is crawling on me like a growing rash.

"You want to get stoned while we wait for it to kick in?" I ask.

Without waiting for a response, I get up and take the little glass pipe out of my jacket pocket, along with the black plastic film container I often use to store my travel weed.

"Sure," she replies, as she gets herself some water from the kitchen while I pack the pipe.

The layout of her apartment is small with an open floor plan, so there isn't a separation between the kitchen and living room, only a small dining table dividing the two sides of the space.

"Do you have a Coke or Pepsi or something?" I ask.

"Sure. Do you want it in a glass with ice?"

"Yes. Thanks."

I just have to remind myself not to slip up and say the wrong person's name at some point tonight. At the moment, it won't be a problem, however I know once the drugs take effect, I might get chatty. Speaking of the person I don't want to accidently mention, I power my phone off and stick it in my jacket pocket. This way, if Sophie calls, I won't answer it, or if I develop a desire to call her, powering the phone on might slow me down. If she calls and asks later, I can claim the battery died and I was home but didn't notice it. That's a better excuse than saying I was out and having to come up with a story about where I went. If she asks, I stayed home tonight and vegged in front of the TV and maybe got a bit too stoned or something. She will believe that. Unless, of course, she decides to show up unannounced, and I'm not home. But I doubt that will happen. She's never done it before.

Jennifer has done the surprise visit many times in the past. She did it when I was home by myself, so no complaints about her booty calls. And she never seemed to question it if I wasn't there. Assuming she stopped by at a time when I was out.

Jennifer returns, placing the glasses on the coffee table. I hand her the pipe and she takes a baby hit, coughs, and hands it back to me. This is when, instead of my phone ringing, hers does. She glances at the caller ID and answers it.

"Hello," I overhear her say. "No, probably not … At home … Ummm … Well, I'm hanging out with Matt actually … Yes, I know …"

I take a long hit off the pipe while she continues to have her conversation. Evanescence is now playing. I haven't listened to them in a while.

"Leah wants us to go have a drink with them at the Bottle Neck." She has her hand over the phone and whispers, "I don't think it is a good idea to tell her about us … you know. What should I say?"

I didn't think my brain would be forced to make decisions tonight. On one hand, going out would get me out of the moral conundrum of sleeping with my ex-girlfriend. Yet the idea of drug-fueled sex is tempting. And there is something exciting about it being with an ex, the whole it-might-be-the-last-time aspect of it. Plus, staying in means there's less risk of running into anyone I know.

"Matt," she says.

"Um, I don't know. Where is the Bottle Neck?"

"It's just down the street. Like a 5-minute walk."

That's not bad. Sophie lives in Belltown and works up north in Lake City, so even if for some reason she does go out tonight, the odds on her coming to The Hill, and to the same bar a few minutes away, are very unlikely. And we will probably be back here shortly after the E kicks in anyway, long before she gets off work.

Jennifer looks at me with a 'say something' expression.

"Okay, sure, yeah whatever."

"Really. What about … you know."

"How about this? We go and hang out for an hour, just long enough for the E to kick in. And then say I'm not feeling well and want to head home. And I didn't drive, so you need to give me a ride home."

She tilts her head. "They aren't going to believe that."

I raise my shoulders in response.

She gets back on the phone while I take another hit from the pipe. After hanging up, we both put our shoes and coats on.

As we are leaving, Jennifer says, "I don't want to drink anything. I don't want to mix alcohol with the E."

"No problem. Just go to the bar to order drinks and get a 7-up and say it's a vodka and 7."

I've never had a problem mixing my narcotics and alcohol. That is the fun part sometimes, to see how the reactions differ in different situations – a bit of an adventure. I'm already feeling good from the weed, plus adding a drink to the mix might be an interesting combination. Not too much though, I don't want the depressants in the alcohol to overpower the stimulants of ecstasy.

Stepping into the bar, it is instantly apparent why they named this place "The Bottle Neck." The place is already packed full of people – most of whom are standing – despite the fact that it is only a quarter past nine. Along the back wall is a well-stacked bar with an array of bottles, and two bartenders hustling back and forth, mixing cocktails for the crowd. The crimson walls and red-tinted lighting create a casual atmosphere. Disco music pulsates through the speakers. Leah is sitting at a small table to the left, waving us over.

"Hi Matt, how have you been?" she gets up and gives me a hug.

"Good."

We sit down in the other two chairs.

"Thank God you guys are here. Everyone keeps trying to steal the chairs."

"It's why I hate being the first person at a place sometimes," I respond. "Where's Steve?"

"He's on his way."

"Do you want a drink?" I ask Jennifer.

"Sure. I'll have a vodka and 7-Up," she replies.

"How about you?" I ask Leah as I'm getting up.

"No, thanks," she says, gesturing to her drink – looks like some type of martini – on the table.

Moving to the bar counter, I line up, jockeying for placement to get the bartenders' attention. Eventually, one of the bartenders looks in my direction. I order a couple of Sprites as they don't have 7-Up. The ice inside the glass chills my hands as I pick them up.

Sitting back down, I hand Jennifer hers and take a long refreshing drink from the soda. The cold liquid is a welcome relief to the heat in the cramped space.

The girls are talking, so I use that as an excuse to get up and go outside for a cigarette and some fresh air.

Standing outside, I turn my phone on to see if I have any missed messages. I don't. I consider messaging Kai to see if he wants to join us, but decide against it, still waiting to see how the night ends up. So, I switch the phone off and slip it back into my pocket.

Just as I'm getting ready to head back inside, Steve walks past. He doesn't notice me at first.

"Hey," I say.

He turns, and it takes a second to recognize me. "Matt. Hey, buddy. How are you?" He holds his hand out.

"Not bad," I say as we shake hands.

"Fancy seeing you here," he says.

His eyes move back and forth, wondering if I am here with someone and just happened to run into him. He is most likely debating whether he should mention that he is there to meet Leah and Jennifer. The wheels in his head are undoubtedly turning, wondering what the odds are that we would all be at the same place tonight, just randomly meeting each other.

A decision, made he hesitantly says, "You here with Jennifer?"

"Yeah. They're inside." I drop my cigarette butt on the sidewalk, smashing it with the front of my shoe, gesturing for him to follow me.

It isn't long before all four of us are crammed next to each other. I can feel my mouth drying up as I yell to be heard over the noise. The sweat is beginning to roll down my back as the ecstasy takes effect. I look over to Jennifer and can see from her drowsy eyes that it is hitting her as well. She has a slight grin forming on the corner of her mouth. I can't believe she isn't as annoyed at being here as I am. The place is cramped, stifling, the music is loud, and people keep bumping into me. You know what I need? I need to smoke some weed.

Knowing that Steve is a pot smoker, I lean over and give him a bump on the arm and gesture. He gets the hint and nods.

"We'll be back in a minute," Steve yells to the girls.

We put on our coats and head outside to look for an out-of-the-way area. I left my pipe at Jennifer's, so I take out one of my cigarettes, break the butt off it, and start peeling it apart to turn into a joint.

"What's with you and Jennifer?" he asks as we walk.

"Nothing. Why?"

"Last I heard from Leah, you guys weren't talking."

"Yeah. Now we are trying this let's be friend's thing."

He nods his head, expressing his lack of belief that the just friend's thing will work, or that he believes it at all. Either way, he doesn't follow up the line of questioning as I light the joint.

As the night rolls on and our initial attempt at escaping seems to have failed, we have migrated to Neighbors. There is some old troll standing next to me speaking so closely I can practically taste the lingering stench of his beer-scented breath which hangs in the air like a virus. I turn my shoulder to him, hoping he will get the hint.

He doesn't, so I turn and say, "No, really, I'm not interested."

"Is it because I'm old?" He tries to look sad. "That just means I know what I'm doing."

He's slightly shorter than me, dressed in a tight dark green t-shirt and jeans. His face has the look of a guy who grew up in an era where he couldn't be himself. Now that he can, he seems to have taken it too far in the other direction.

"You see that girl there?" I say, pointing to Jennifer, who is dancing with Leah and Steve. "I'm with her."

I'm taking a break where there is a slightly raised floor, separated from the dancers with a metal railing. It's a spot for those who want to stand and observe, or attempt shouting in each other's ears to have a conversation, or to have a quick drink. By this time of night, the club is full of people who have consumed their fill of booze or whatever drugs they were planning to swallow, or are possibly in the search for more. I'm not sure when I lost interest in going back to Jennifer's place, maybe around the third drink. Or perhaps when I switched to double Jack and Cokes instead of singles. Regardless, here I am, in a packed dance club, with booming music and flashing strobe lights, being approached by the club's senior citizens, or 'trolls' as Kai calls them.

"Then why aren't you out there," he says, gesturing to the dance floor. "How about you let me buy you a drink, lovely?"

A free drink would be nice; however, I'd like to avoid the roofie he probably plans to slip in it.

"No, I'm good, thanks."

I turn my back to him and he eventually gets the hint and squirrels off, searching for his next potential victim. There is a touch of sympathy in me for the guy as he skulks away. Maybe it is the image of me as him in the future that does it. A sad, lonely old man with nowhere else to go, who still remembers the days when he could hit the disco and blend in perfectly.

They announce last call over the speakers. I also realize the need to take a piss, so before the bar, I work my way towards the men's room. There's already a line of guys waiting ahead of me. Some talking to each other, while most are probably just trying not to think of water in any form as the late-night drank-too-much pisses kick in. I can't help but watch the man in front of me, fidgeting as he rocks back and forth, a behavior that I find myself mirroring, struggling to suppress my own desperate need to relieve myself. Passing through the door, the heightened senses brought on by the ecstasy are still present, amplifying the powerful smell of urine and body odor that permeates the crowded space. I try not to breathe through my nose, but then I wonder if it is better to inhale through the nose and hope the nose hairs catch the shit and urine particles floating in the air, or to breathe through the mouth.

Thankfully, one of the urinals opens up and I can think about something else. But this isn't any better, I seriously have to pee, and these guys standing right around me are making me nervous.

Have I been standing here for a really long time? It feels like I have been standing here forever. Time seems to have come to a stop, or perhaps speed up. *Come on, dick, do it, go! Relax, just relax. Breath in and out, in and out. Wait, no, don't breathe in.* Breathing means inhaling the air in the room, the air humidity and scent of human excrement. I think the guy in the urinal next to me is looking at me. *Is he trying to look at my dick or just wondering what is taking me so long? Come on, dude, you can do this. Close your eyes, don't think about anything else happening around you, just go to the bathroom. Breath in, now out, and go. Almost there. One more time, in and out and go …*

Having completed what felt like the most intense and lengthy piss of my life, I swing by the bar, to discover that time did not speed up, or slow down, while I was in there and they are still serving. I order one last double Jack and Coke, close out my tab for the night, and then head out to the dance floor in search of the others.

I'm feeling pretty good. The lingering effect of the ecstasy is still working its magic on my system. The music is pumping, my body feels light and fluid, and I'm eager to hit the dance floor once more.

I weave through the dense crowd to where I'm pretty sure the three of them were, only to find the space filled with other dancers. Taking a sip of my drink and almost having it spilled on me by some blonde with dreads, I move towards the edge of the dance floor and do a lap, looking for the group.

Maybe they went for a drink? From the floor, I squeeze through the mass for the bar, looking for a final drink for the night. The bartender is cleaning up and I can see him turning people away now.

"Come on man, just pour one more beer and you can pocket the cash." Some pretty boy is saying to the bartender.

"Piss off, the bar is closed," the bartender responds without even looking at the guy.

"Fuck you!" the man yells as he turns around and storms off.

From there, I make my way around towards the outside of the dance floor with the watchers.

"What the fuck?" I mutter to myself.

The trolling old man from earlier spies me heading in his direction. I look towards my left as if I don't see him and walk past. Downing the last of my drink, I swap my empty cup for my jacket, then make my way towards the door.

Outside there is a slight haze of rain in the air.

There are a few people huddled against one wall under an awning, having a cigarette. Reaching into my jacket for the pack of American Spirits, I open them to find only one left. I tap the last one out, mashing the empty pack into a ball, before putting it back into my pocket. Feeling for my lighter, I can't find it.

"Can I get a light?" I ask the extremely tall, goth-looking guy next to me.

He takes out a lighter and passes it to me. I light the cigarette, inhaling the harsh smoke that fills my lungs. As I exhale through my nose, a plume of gray smoke floats off into the night. Handing back the lighter, I lean back against the frigid cement wall behind me.

Checking my phone, there is a text from Jennifer.

Where are you?

Outside. Where are you?

The rain isn't too bad at the moment, so I start walking towards the gas station a couple of blocks away to get a pack of cigarettes and a new lighter. I don't remember if they close at some point, but I'm pretty sure they are open all night.

I slowly stroll towards the station – a refreshing relief from the overcrowded dance club. The pavement glistens with a wet shimmer reflecting the lights from the surrounding buildings, providing a nice distraction as I walk.

Sophie should be home by now, and her place isn't that far. The best thing to do right now would probably be to grab a cab to her place and pick up my car in the morning. However, I could just quickly drive down the hill.

With my phone in my hand, I text her.

U home? Up?

Some guy mumbles something to my right. I Look up from my phone, placing it into my pocket, to see some black dude in a large blue ski jacket and dark red hat.

Judging by his location next to the building, right on the edge of an alley, I know exactly what he said, without knowing the exact words. I stop and take a step in his direction.

"Maybe, what you selling?"

"Whatcha want? blow?"

As a general rule of thumb, I try to avoid buying narcotics from some random dude on the street. But, what the fuck. Let's see where this goes?

"Can I get a sample first?"

"Sure." He tilts his head, motioning for me to follow him down the alley.

Looking around with plenty of people passing by, I feel somewhat reassured that he won't try to mug me. Besides, I've probably only got less than ten bucks in my wallet. So, if he is planning to mug me, he won't get much.

He leads me between two brick buildings, covered in graffiti, lined with overflowing garbage bins and reeking of rotting food and piss. A small bag of white powder is now in his hand. Opening it, he takes out a small pocket knife, dips that into the bag to draw out a sample. I wonder if using the knife is trying to send me a message. He holds it towards me.

Taking the knife from him, I place it under my nostril, keeping an eye on him to make sure he doesn't suddenly get the urge to shove it into my face. A quick inhale through the nose and I feel the burn and tingles that go along with it.

Handing him back the knife, I say "Okay. How much?"

"Hundred a gram."

"Hundred a gram, fuck that," I start to walk away.

"Okay." He stops me. "For you, eighty."

Yeah, for me, or for everyone else who isn't interested in spending a hundred bucks buying some mediocre coke from some street dealer.

"I don't have any cash on me. I'll need to hit the cash machine."

He shrugs his shoulder and follows me as far as the corner of the building where we met. I finish my walk to the station, hit the cash machine, and withdraw a hundred dollars, all in twenties. I step inside the station to buy a pack of American Spirits and a lighter while I'm at it.

Leaving the station, I consider forgetting about the coke. Really, it's not like I need it, but you never know, I can always hold on to it for another night. Or, just sample a little tonight. It is still early after all.

Walking back to the street where the guy is still standing, he nods at me to follow him back down the same garbage-strewn alley as before. I follow.

"Good?" he asks.

"Yep."

The eighty is placed in my right pocket with my wallet in my left, and phone in my jacket pocket. We watch each other as I pull out the cash and he does the same with the bag of coke. With one hand, we exchange the drugs, with the other we exchange the cash. He starts to walk away, counting it as he walks.

Looking around and seeing that I am alone, I figure I might as well sample a bit before heading back to the club to meet the others. I open the bag, taking my car key out of my pocket; dipping it into the bag, I inhale to experience the burn of something that is clearly not cocaine.

"Mother fucker!"

I throw the bag against the wet brick wall, then sprint to the street, looking left and right to see where that bastard ran off. A couple of guys look at me apprehensively as they walk past.

Making a choice, I turn to the left and do a slow run down the street, looking for him. He clearly has done this a few times before. He probably ran into one of the open bars or some slit between two buildings, like the cockroach he is. I turn the other way and jog down the street, looking, but he is nowhere to be seen. He made a few bucks, now he's on his way home or to another one of his spots to scam some other half-drunk sucker like me.

No longer in the mood to socialize, I start walking to my car. My high and drink seems to have worn off, thanks to that jackass.

At least there is a new pack of cigarettes in my pocket, which I immediately open.

In my anger and frustration, it doesn't take long to get to the car. The heater is turned on and I notice how wet my shoes are. My toes, slightly numb from the cold, tingle as the warmth from the heater dries them. "Our Endless Numbered Days" by Iron and Wine plays, so I lean the seat back to relax while my body dries out.

Looking at my phone, there is no response from Sophie, so I text her again. She had better be at home, because if not, that would mean she hooked up with someone from her work. Where else would she be this late? That's what she's doing right now.

She is probably riding some dude in the back of a car in the parking lot for some cash and a ride home. *Don't think like that. You are just going to piss yourself off some more.* A couple of quick tokes off the one-hitter and then home if she doesn't reply. She might have simply gone home and to sleep, or she might be out with her coworkers. Coworkers who also work at a strip club and probably fuck people for money in the back room. *Shut up, brain!*

I wake up to light filtering through densely fogged windows dripping wet with condensation, a sore back, and a brutal case of cottonmouth. I lean the seat forward, every muscle protesting as I sit up in the cramped car. Thankfully, I must have had the presence of mind to turn the engine off before falling asleep. Turning the ignition, the little car purrs to life, and I step out to stretch my legs while the engine warms up and the windows defrost.

Looking at my phone, there is a voicemail notification and a text from Sophie. I read the text first.

"Hey on my way home now. Tired, but feel free to stop by if U R still out."

I decide not to respond right away, and listen to the voice message.

Jennifer's voice comes through with distant music in the background. "Hey, not sure where you went. When we were leaving, we noticed your coat was missing, and I don't see you outside. I'm heading home now. If you're still out, please don't drive. Come over to my place instead. If I'm asleep, just wake me up."

Not in the mood to respond to her either, I ignore the messages to head home for a hot shower and a nap.

20

The curved walls stretch endlessly upward, disappearing into the bright white light that fills the space. My body drifts counterclockwise, my gaze inward, down towards the ground below. In the center is a pillar leading up. It seems as if I'm gaining speed, although there is no sensation of wind. Maybe I've always been moving at this pace. Looking down is Humbug, his shaggy fur hangs wet, ears perked up, tail happily wagging, his nose near the ground as he explores. Continuing to swim against the current of the empty air, moving my arms and kicking my legs as if fighting the buoyancy of water, I struggle to reach him. Closer and closer as the scent of freshly-washed dog fills my nostrils, the familiar smell of shampoo and clean fur. I can feel him now, the soft wet hair on my hands scratching his lower back. He is much larger than I remember, more like a medium-sized bear. His long fur a mix of brown and black with a patch of white on his chest, just like I remember. My fluffy bear. He wags his tail happily as I pet and scratch his back. But I'm still hanging in the air, attempting a breaststroke to swim closer, so that I can wrap my arms around him. He continues circling the room, nose focused, engrossed by the unfamiliar scents. Finally, I am able to get a proper hold. His bulk dwarfs me as I wrap my arms and legs around him, embracing his massive frame. Burying my face into his soft fur, I inhale the familiar warm scent that reminds me of my childhood. I squeeze his massive frame, my legs unable to fully encircle him – he carries me along.

Knowing I'm in a dream, I don't want it to end. A tall escalator is now attached to the pillar. He follows his nose to the steep incline. When he reaches it, I lose my grip and I'm floating back out to the circular walls of the silo. Fighting, knowing that if I hold on, he won't leave. Struggling to swim back to him, the invisible current pulls me further away, watching as he steps onto the ascending escalator. Not wanting him to go, I am awoken by the sound of a doorbell.

Rubbing the sleep from my eyes, my thoughts on Humbug, and wondering what happened to him, I slip on some sweatpants and a t-shirt to open the door and find Jennifer standing there.

"What are you doing here?" I ask, as my eyes struggle to adjust to the hazy light filtering through the clouds outside.

"You didn't respond to my message. I was worried. Can I come in?"

I step aside to let her through the door. She walks to the living room, removing her heavy blue

251

coat, tossing it on a chair. She is wearing jeans with a thick wool red sweater, her hair pulled back into a ponytail.

She turns to me and asks, "What happened to you last night?" Her voice with a hint of worry.

"Nothing," I mutter, sitting down on the sofa. "I lost track of you guys. I thought you left, so I came home and crashed. I was going to message you later today. But as you can see, I'm sleeping off a bit of a hangover."

She sits next to me. "I'm sorry. We looked for you but couldn't find you. I left you a message to come back to my place. I was really worried about you."

"Yeah, I know. I got your message."

"You could have at least texted me," she says, clearly irritated.

I stand up to get a glass of water from the kitchen.

"Yeah, sorry. But I would like to remind you that we are not in a relationship. So, there is no requirement to reply to you, you know."

"That's rude. We may not be in a relationship, but that doesn't mean you can't be considerate and let me know you are okay and not sleeping in a gutter."

Returning with my water, I sit on the opposite end of the sofa, taking a long drink from the glass, the water rinsing away some of the lingering taste of last night's hangover.

"Yeah, I said I was sorry. Anything else," I say with an exasperated shake of my head.

There is a long pause as her eyes flitter back and forth, thinking of what to say next.

"Well, since I'm here, do you want to do something today? Maybe see a movie?"

"Seriously? No. I feel like shit. I don't want to see a movie, and again, we are not in a relationship anymore. In fact, I find it a bit irritating how you keep showing up unannounced, as if we are."

"I know we're not together anymore!"

She gets up to collect her coat.

"Take a breath, okay." I exhale deeply, following my own advice. "I don't think this is working. This back-and-forth thing we keep doing. It's not working. We need to just acknowledge it isn't going to work between us and just end it. Maybe someday we can be friends, but I think we need some time apart for a while."

She sits in the chair, clutching her coat to her chest. "But what about last night? We had fun last night. Hanging out with all four of us like we used to do."

"Last night wasn't real. Last night was chemicals and holding on to the past," I say in the kindest tone possible. "Look, can we talk about this some other time, please? I'm hungover and cranky and I don't want to get into an argument." As I say this, I stand up and walk over to her. "Let's just take a day to relax. I'll call you later."

I won't call.

Guiding her up, I can see that look in her eyes – the fighting back of tears, mixed with a bit of hope at my offer to call.

"Yeah, that's probably a good idea," she says, her voice wavering slightly. "Let's get some rest and talk more later."

She kisses me before leaving, a soft, hopeful kiss on the lips that I return.

I relax into the sofa's cushions as I lean my head back, the memory of why we broke up the first time returns to me – a reminder of why letting her go now was the right thing to do.

We went to breakfast at a nearby café, barely speaking, before heading back to her apartment, where we sat mindlessly watching TV. We could have been out at a coffee shop, park, movie, anywhere really, yet we weren't. The relationship had settled into a stagnant routine, devoid of excitement or genuine interest, and I didn't know why she wanted to be with me, nor I with her.

"The thing is, I've run it through my head a hundred different ways and I don't see how it will work. It's just not there anymore, you know," I told her.

I knew it was the right thing to do, although at that moment it didn't feel like it. I could think back to when we were happy together, back when we first started seeing one another. But, as relationships often do, it went downhill. The exact moment it happened? I don't know.

"And we argue all the time about the stupidest stuff," I continued. "This morning you got mad at me because I put a coffee cup where the glasses are supposed to go—"

"Well, you should know by now," she interrupted.

I threw my hands up in frustration.

"Can I finish?"

She paused, letting me know to continue.

"Or that time you got mad at me because I threw away some hair scrunchie that was on the floor of my bathroom. Seriously, those things aren't expensive. I could have bought you a dozen of them for a couple of dollars."

Technically, I threw it away because I wasn't sure who it belonged to, but I didn't want to tell her that part.

"How about you?" she said. "You are constantly complaining if I leave something at your place. Like I'm some needy girl trying to take over your life."

> Yes, I know it takes two to fight, yet it only takes one to start it, and she was that one.
> "Where is this coming from? I thought things were going really well between us."

They had been that day. However, between the arguments over me still having an ex's phone number in my phone, or the random lies she would tell for no reason other than a desire for sympathy, the thought of wasting the rest of my life with her was depressing. I could imagine the two of us in a house, two or three kids running around, cats and dogs, and me going into that gray cement building every day to pay for all of it. Jumping off a bridge sounded more appealing. She would let herself go, because that's what happens when people get married. She would have stretch marks, saggy tits, and would blame me for it, because I was the one who put the babies in her.

And, the lies! The lies, the lies, the lies. They made no sense. She would lie about the most insignificant things. Did she think saying what she thought I wanted to hear would make me happy, or keep me around because of some insecurity of hers? Honestly, the reason for the lies never made sense to me. Like the time she told me about some stalker she had. She showed me a Facebook page of this person and a note he left at her door. Of course, I then spent more time at her place to *protect her*. Oddly, the guy disappeared after that. Never to be heard from again. And she would always be vague about her answers when I would ask questions about him. According to her, they went on one date and that was it. That must have been some amazing date! The only thing I could find about him was that Facebook profile. The profile that only showed the one picture because it was set to private. He didn't have a LinkedIn profile or any other social media account with that name and picture.

Or the time she asked me to help her look for a new car? She was driving a VW Jetta. It was in good condition and had no issues. We went around to four different dealers so she could test drive cars, not a single one she was interested in getting. And she never replaced the car, in the end leaving me to assume she just wanted to spend the day together as she never brought it up again. Because we couldn't just spend the day together like normal people, she had to make up reasons to spend time with one another. This is the girl that told me she had a cat as a child, then when we were with her parents and I asked about it, they said she never had one. Then she was like, "I never said that." What kind of person makes up stories about childhood pets?

I continued, "Things are going well between us *today*. But that's today."

"Not just today. We haven't gotten into an argument in weeks," she protested.

"Exactly. Two weeks. And the fact that you know that says something. We argue all the time, and it's just not there anymore. I spend most of my time when we are together just dreading the next argument. Wondering what I will say that will piss you off."

I thought about bringing up the lying; however, I felt that would just turn this into a full-on argument. And I didn't want to fight with her. I just wanted to be alone. What I really wanted at that moment was to go home and relax and not have to think for the rest of the weekend. I wanted to roll a joint, get super baked, and play video games. Whenever I tried doing that, she wanted to come with me, then she would complain that I was sitting around playing video games and smoking pot instead of talking to her. Being in a relationship with her was suffocating. When we weren't together, she would want to know what I was doing. And when we were together, we never did anything interesting, anyway. Occasionally we would meet up with friends, but those times seemed to grow further and further apart. Sure, the sex was nice but even that seemed to be drying up. It had probably been a week or two at that point since we last had sex.

"Okay. If that is what you want," she whimpered.

I could see she wanted me to say something else, but I didn't know what to say. I had nothing to say. She wanted me to say that I loved her, that I wanted to be with her, that I didn't want to end it. That I changed my mind after a temporary moment of indecision. Except for I didn't love her, and I didn't want to be with her. When I wasn't with her, it's not like I thought about how much I missed her. I enjoyed my time away.

"So, I guess I'll be going now."

"Can I have one last hug?" she asked, with slight tears bubbling in her eyes.

"Yes, of course."

I felt bad at that moment, bad about hurting her, bad about leading her on in a way that implied the relationship could have been more than it was. Maybe it would have been easier if I texted her or sent her an email? That is probably what I should have done. However, the words just kind of slipped out of my mouth. The thoughts had been there for days and finally the words jumped from my lips at a quiet moment when it was just the two of us and I wanted to leave.

Relationships, in my experience, follow a limited timeline. In the beginning, you are getting to know each other and it's exciting – it's new. This is usually around three to six months. Then, from six to nine months, people get comfortable with each other, the gloves come off. There is no longer a need to be overly considerate to one another. That is the point that women often try to mold men into who they want them to be. From nine to twelve months is the downside of the relationship. Both, or at least one, begins to realize that the relationship will no longer work, yet they keep it going anyway in some attempt to make it work out, because they have invested so much time into it. Jennifer and I were in the eleventh month.

She moved slowly, looking for answers, for something to say that would change the moment, a lie she could tell. But I didn't have any answers to give her. I didn't know what to say or do. Usually, when it comes to ending relationships, the girl breaks up with me. Which is much easier. So, all I could do was hug her in return and to let her tears soak into my shirt.

After what was a long and uncomfortable moment, I eventually let go of her, feeling like a total jackass, like that guy that leads women on, gets what he wants, before eventually ditching them.

At the door, just as I was getting ready to go, she gave me one more long hug. An embrace that when we let it end, I expected, would be the end. I let go, looked to the floor and said, "Goodbye," turned and walked away, not feeling as good about my decision as I thought I would.

A few days later, she called me up and told me she was sick and asked if I could swing by the store for her. I didn't ask why she didn't call her parents or one of her friends. At the time, I was still feeling guilty for breaking up with her. Maybe the stress of it made her feel ill. I asked her what she wanted. She replied that she wanted some soup and cold and flu medicine.

"Okay, I'll swing by the store and get some for you. And some juice."

Before going to her place, I picked up some NyQuil, orange juice, chicken noodle soup, and a few other things. I knocked on the door and she let me in wearing pajamas and looking miserable. I made the soup and sat with her on the sofa, under a blanket, in front of the TV watching Friends reruns. As it often goes when sitting next to a cute girl in her white and pink flowered pjs, one thing led to another and we were both naked, doing the thing that two naked people do together.

She might have actually been unwell. However, she didn't have a runny nose or cough, and her mood certainly picked up after the orgasm. So, it is possible my jizz has miraculous healing powers. Or, more likely, she was lying about being ill just to get me over to her house.

"Well, I've got to get going," I said, putting my clothes back on.

"You're welcome to stay longer if you'd like," she offered with pleading eyes.

There are pros and cons to being a man. One downside is that our dicks often have more control over our actions than our brains. On the flip side, once the dick is done doing what it wants to do, rational thought returns to the male. After the hormones have been cleansed from our system, a guy can go back to making decisions without the influence of the opposite sex.

I made up an excuse about having to go visit my mother and scuttled out the door like a man with commitment issues.

It was remarkably freeing for her to do that to me, pretending to be sick. The final straw, the last lie, it was the perfect justification to truly end things between us. Prior to that, I had been wrestling with guilt, drinking more than I should have, and wondering if I had made a mistake by breaking up with her. I was feeling the loss in my life and had been missing her those past few days. Her laugh, her soft touch, the times we would spend snuggled up on the sofa. But that was gone, thanks to that one last lie. That last time of her manipulating my sympathy, as if fucking me would be all that it would take to make me forget and forgive. So, I left her again, this time, not feeling all that bad about it.

21

I arrive at work with a newfound motivation to not be such a terrible employee. Maybe it's the feeling of relief that comes from breaking things off with Jennifer, and a renewed commitment to Sophie. Maybe it was the sun shining on my drive while listening to a new CD I picked up by Ray LaMontagne, reminding me that Sophie is "the best thing" to happen to me.

As usual, I swing by the breakroom for my morning coffee. There is no one around and sitting on the counter is a coffee cup I recognize. A cup that belongs to a person I despise! A white coffee mug with text on the side. There it sits, perched alone on the breakroom counter with no one to keep it safe. Now the question is, what to do about this opportunity before me? While it would be easy to trash it, he might come around the corner and find me here. It's likely he just left it to take a quick piss break, given that I typically only see the cup either in his hand or on his desk. A gift from his wife, he told me once.

Unfortunately, I don't have enough time to whip my dick out and run it around the inside of the mug, plus it's not like we are the only two people in the office at the moment. Someone else could catch me, and indecent exposure is probably not the best way to lose a job. So, I lean over and spit in it, a nice glob of my saliva for him to enjoy. Casually, I swipe my finger around the inside to spread the sticky liquid evenly so that it is less noticeable and dries quicker. After that, I proceed with the original reason I came here. Placing my cup under the machine, I press the button to select caffeinated and the quantity. The machine grinds the beans, while I step back, waiting for it to finish as the air fills with the aroma of fresh coffee.

Chris walks around the corner, clearly coming from the men's room.

"Good morning, Matt," he says flatly.

"Morning," I reply, intentionally dropping the word 'good'.

"You are here early?"

No, I'm here at the same time I usually arrive, which I should point out is earlier than most of my coworkers. However, still standing on shaky ground with the jackass, I decide not to say anything and simply nod in agreement with a grunt.

I grab my cup and step to the side to add some sugar and cream. Mentally crossing my fingers that he doesn't notice the glisten of my saliva on the stained white ceramic, and that he doesn't rinse it first.

"Do you want the creamer?" I ask.

265

"No, thanks."

He doesn't look into the cup while I hold the creamer in his direction. He places the cup in the machine, pressing the same buttons I did a few minutes ago. Watching from the corner of my eye, I put the creamer back into the fridge while fighting a smile on my face.

"Have a good day," I say while walking away.

"You too."

22

The kids dress up in costumes and get candy, while the adults dress in costumes and get alcohol. Sophie and I are hanging out in Lower Queen Ann for our first Halloween together. I'm dressed as a priest, willing to give confessions to any bad girl in need, while Sophie is wearing a sexy cop costume. She has a tight button-up top accentuating her cleavage, short shorts, knit stockings and, of course, thigh-high black boots. She also has the cheesy police officer hat on with her hair tied in a ponytail. And of course, what police woman outfit would not be complete without a pair of handcuffs hanging from the belt? She emits an air of authority that, judging by the looks as we walk, many people would be more than willing to submit to.

We are starting the night at Chopsticks. Rachel the bitchy blond, and Henry the DJ from the club, are here as well. The guys haven't started the piano show yet. And we are waiting for Kai to arrive, who should have something in a pill form for the party. Until he gets here, I hold myself over with a rum and coke.

Rachel is dressed appropriately in a hot bumblebee outfit, wearing black high heels with knit stockings, a short black ballerina skirt, and yellow and black striped top, sleeveless to show off her arms. Her blond hair is parted on the side and pulled back into a ponytail on the other side. And no bee outfit would be complete without silly little wings on the back and antenna on the top. If a three-way with her is a possibility tonight, I will not fuck it up this time. I'm taking it slow on the drink, and when Kai gets here with the E. I will switch to water and be ready to go should it happen, which hopefully it will. When Sophie mentioned Rachel was going to be here, I brought the subject up of possibly trying the three-way again. She stated she wasn't interested in doing that anymore. Then she added it was a moment that has passed and since we got into an argument last time, she doesn't want that to come between us. I tried to explain that wouldn't happen this time, but dropped the subject. So, we will see how the night plays out. I'm hoping once we get the drugs into the girls, it will get them in the mood and they will be ready to go. I just hope that Henry doesn't try to participate.

"How do you get a job as a DJ anyway?" I ask to break the silence.

"I've always been into music. When I was in high school, I picked up an old turntable and records. From there getting a mixer and speakers. I used to DJ parties and shit. And worked my way from there."

"That's cool."

He is a tall, lanky guy with a funny narrow nose that has a large lump on it. My guess is, it was broken at some point in time and not fixed correctly, as it is also angled to his left just a bit. He has his curly black hair hanging down tonight in a floppy mess. He's dressed as a pirate. I'm assuming he has the costume at home for D&D nights with his friends.

Halfway through my second drink, Kai texts me he is outside. I head out to meet him.

"Heeeyeye," he says in a high-pitched voice.

"Hey."

He is dressed as a cowboy. Well, mostly as a cowboy. He has jeans, boots, a gun and belt, a cowboy hat, and a vest. The only thing missing is the shirt.

"So, were you able to get any E?" I ask.

"No, he didn't have any. But he did have some coke so I got that instead."

I am a bit disappointed, but coke can be fun as well. And on my list of things to do before I die is snort coke off a girl's ass. And as asses go, Sophie has one I would love to snort lines from.

"How much were you able to get?" I ask.

"I bought a gram. Happy with that," he smiles.

Beggars can't be choosers, so yes, I am happy. Kicking myself for not bringing the rest of those pills I got from Renton.

We walk across the street where there is an entrance to the door of a used record store that is closed for the night. Kai keeps a lookout while I open the baggie, and dip a key from my key chain in, hold one nostril with my thumb and take a snort. The burn in the nostril hits me right away, followed up with tingles and the sniffles. I dip the key one more time for the other side. The nice thing about coke is how quickly it hits you. Sniffing, my eyes blink a few times and my heart jumps a beat, letting me know it is ready to go for the night. I swap places with Kai while he takes a dip, and we head back to the bar.

The dueling piano guys started playing while we were outside. Up on the stage are two full-sized pianos sitting across from each other. Each one has a guy at it singing "My Humps" by Black Eyed Peas.

With one of them singing, "What you gonna do with all that junk. All that junk inside your trunk?"

Followed up by the other guy singing the next lines, "Imma get, get, get, get you drunk. Get you love drunk off my hump."

Everyone in the bar is singing along, including the people at our table. The table we have is crammed to the left of the stage, with people standing around the bar packing it to the limit.

"Hey girl!" Kai chants as we head up to Sophie. "Don't you look good."

"I love your outfit," she replies, while opening the vest to check him out.

He moves over to Rachel and gives her a hug.

Everyone sits as a waiter comes around and takes drink orders. Henry turns back to watch the guys on the stage, while Kai and Rachel grope each other's costumes. Rachel is opening Kai's vest to check out his chest and Kai looking down Rachel's shirt, because he is gay and can get away with it.

"Hey, I've got some coke if you are interested?" I quietly tell Sophie.

"What!"

"I've got some coke. You interested?"

"Oh, no thanks, I'm good for now."

Good for now? What the hell. This is some pretty decent shit. I'm feeling jazzed. My fingers are dancing on the table to the music, my toes are bouncing to the beat, and I'm ready for a bump. The two of us could hit the bathroom for a couple of lines. Do people still do that, or was that just an 80s thing? It would probably be pretty damn hard nowadays to snort a line of coke off the back of a toilet. Honestly, who would want to? Talk about a nasty place to stick your nose.

"Hey all!" One of the piano players interrupts my train of thought. "You know how this works – scribble your song on paper, slip a tip, and we'll orchestrate your tune. The heftier the tip the sooner the song will get played."

"And, of course," the other one interjects, "If you want us to stop playing a song toss a 20 up here and we will stop immediately and start playing yours!"

"You know what I think?" the other says.

"What's that?"

"I think it is time to bring Sexy Back!"

A bunch of people cheer as they go into a rendition of "Sexy Back". I don't get the impression they know the whole song but it sure is impressive how they can jump right into it.

"Are you sure?" I lean back over.

"I might do some later, just not right now."

I could see if Henry or Rachel want some, except it's not like I have all that much to share for the night. So, fuck them! If my plans for a three-way work out, I'll share a bit with her, but that long schnoz of his is not going anyway near my bag.

"Okay," I say with a possible tone of annoyance.

I make my way to the men's room, weaving through the sea of nurses and doctors, fairies, cats and dogs, all dancing and singing along with the dueling pianos.

In the john I have to stand to wait for the stall, feeling like a jackass when a urinal opens up and I let the next guy take it. He probably thinks I need to take a shit. But once I'm in the stall, I take out the little baggy. Instead of using my key, I take the cross from my neck, employing it instead for a quick bump, and one more time for the other side. Thank you, Jesus, for your sacrifice. I'm feeling fine. I can hear in the bar the guys have moved to "Have you Ever Seen the Rain." A classic – and I sing along with the chorus. After all, who hasn't sung CCR while snorting coke in a public toilet?

Man, I live in the Pacific Northwest, of course I've seen the rain. I've seen more rain than an Indian Rain Dance. I've seen those cats and dogs falling from the sky many, many time. I've driven in the rain, walked in the rain, fallen asleep at night to the sounds of the rain. I've seen rain that I thought would never end to rain that was gone in the blink of an eye. When it comes to moisture in the sky, I've seen it all. However, my friend, I have not seen the rain tonight. Hallelujah!

Back at the table, the others are singing along, except for Henry. He doesn't seem much like a singer. He is nodding along to the music, seemingly enjoying himself. I wonder if he ever gets with any of the girls at the club.

"Hey, Henry. It must be awesome working at the club with all those girls. You ever hook up with any of them?" I ask, leaning in.

"No, once you have seen the women's bathroom there you lose all interest."

"Oh, come on."

"Really. They are some of the messiest people. There is shit everywhere in the changing room."

I have a feeling it doesn't have as much to do with his opinion of the girls as it has to do with him. Maybe they aren't into a former AV club kid who wears all black and probably has Star Wars action figures on display his house. In the original boxes of course. He probably tries regularly and gets turned down.

"Plus," he continues, "the time most of the women are there tends to be rather short. These two have probably been there the longest, which is why I'm friends with them."

"So, you are saying that if tonight Rachel was like, 'you and me, my place.' You wouldn't do it?"

He pauses, a grin appearing on his lips, telling me everything I need to know. I smile back.

Hell, I would snort a line off Rachel's ass if I could. Then lick it clean.

"Cheers," I say, grabbing my drink and toasting it to his.

This tastes like shit. The ice has melted in it, and it is all watered down, warm, and flat.

"Sweet Caroline everyone!" The piano players announce. "And remember, a twenty on the table will get us to stop playing it."

Ugh. The song on its own is fine. It's when they reach the chorus my eyes roll into the back of my head. Every face hole in the bar begins belting out the lyrics at the absolute top of their lungs.

"Sweet Caroline, Good times never seem so good … bum, bum, bum." The crowd chats in unison.

"Do you want another drink?" I yell to Sophie as she sings along with the rest of them.

She nods here head in response.

Fortunately, it seems I'm not alone in my contempt for the song, as someone tosses a twenty onto the piano, bringing the music to an abrupt halt. Half the crowd erupts in cheers while the other half groans in disappointment. The guys quickly transition into a rendition of "(I Can't Get No) Satisfaction."

Returning to the table, Sophie is glowing. Her smile envelops her face, her flawless teeth, gleaming like a beacon, drawing me in. And, of course, those bewitching dark eyes – eyes in which a man could easily find himself lost. Leaning in, I kiss her on the lips, as I place the drink in front of her. The warm wet lips that soften to my touch. Followed up by one on the cheek, savoring the feel of her velvety-smooth skin against my lips.

A few blinks later, we find ourselves at a bar in Belltown. It is a large space in an old brick building.

Not long after Henry left, we met up with one of Kai's friends, Nicholas, at Chopsticks. Nicholas is a short, immaculately dressed, Asian, who is the MC for a fashion show going on tonight, in whatever bar it is we are in.

Cutting to the head of the line, we followed Nicholas past the bouncer as if we were celebrities.

"You okay?" the bouncer asked, stopping me.

"Yeah. Why, do I not look okay?"

"Just checking."

It is not like I'm stumbling all over the place, not to mention I'm with one of the people in the show tonight. And Kai, who walked in ahead of me, has been drinking heavily since we met. Yet he lets *him* go inside. Well screw you too bouncer douchebag.

Inside, they have cordoned off a section of the floor to create a space for the models to parade about. Three guys with fancy looking cameras, flashes firing intermittently, strut around as if they are the shit, jockeying for position to get the best shots as the show kicks off.

Nicholas is in the middle of the floor with a microphone in his hand. His voice has changed to a slighter higher pitch than the one he had when we met.

"Welcome, and thanks for coming out tonight! We've got a fabulous lineup of lovely ladies for you tonight. And judging by this amazing crowd, there's no shortage of style here either." He strolls over to a guy dressed in military attire. "Hey there, soldier! What's your name?"

The guy in the military costume replies, "Emery"

"Emery, I'll be sure to show my appreciation for your service later tonight," he says with a sly smile.

The crowd laughs, and the soldier guy holds up a plastic rifle he has to accompany the costume. From there Nicholas goes back out to the floor and looks at a piece of paper in his hands.

"First up we have Emma! She is rocking the runway in a sizzling ensemble by VME Designs."

Emerging from a side door, saunters forth a slender girl, wearing a dark green fairy costume with a short skirt attached to a matching corset. Her hair is fashioned into an elaborate updo. She strides confidently in a massive pair of matching heels that makes me wonder how she manages to stay upright while gracefully making her rounds. The audience cheers and the camera guys are snapping pictures while bouncing around to capture her from various perspectives.

Nicholas introduces the next model. "Here we have Bella, sporting a creation by Reputation, representing the home team in this dazzling Seahawks-inspired ensemble!"

She is wearing a short jersey that bares her toned midriff, oversized shoulder pads, blue short shorts, matching thigh-high stockings, and heels. She is holding a blue football with the Seahawks logo on the side.

"Who's up for a quick game?" Nicolas queries the crowd, instigating a round of applause.

We stand to observe the show as a few more models take their turn. My high is wearing off and it is time for another taste. "You interested in joining me for a little—" I tap my nose to Sophie.

She tilts her head as she gives it a little thought. I think she might say no again, instead she responds with a positive nod. We work our way towards the restrooms. Moving towards the girl's room first, we see two women in line waiting. Holding her hand, I pull her into the men's room. There is a guy in a faded jean jacket looking down at the percaline urinal. Swiftly, we make a beeline for the stalls. There are only two, so we head for the one farther away from the entrance.

Scrawls and markings cover the stall in a mix of markers, pens, and scratched-in messages. Pictures of dicks seem popular, along with text next to the dick. One says, 'fuck me like you hate me.' Another saying, 'Big fat orange dick' with a picture of a big fat hairy dick drawn underneath it. Of course, there is a phone number written to the right, while another person drew some sperm coming out of the big fat orange dick.

There is no lid to cover the toilet with; however, it is not as nasty as expected. Yes, there's pee splattered around, but, thankfully, it doesn't reek, and so far no one has left a floater or smeared surprise in the toilet bowl.

I pull out the bag and use the system that has been working so well tonight, spooning some up with my cross. I hold it out for her and she leans over, holds one nostril with her finger, and quickly inhales with the other. Doing the sniff, sniff, that cokeheads know so well to make sure it is all in, she leans back. Damn, she looks good. I dip in a bit for myself before giving her another go at it. Then back to me. I add some to the other nostril, stick the cross into my mouth to make sure none is wasted, before retying the almost empty bag and putting it in my pocket. Kai and I took a dab on our way over. I run my tongue over my gums, staring at her as she glows radiantly. Her wide, sparkling brown eyes meet mine. Our faces draw close, lips brushing against each other, and I catch a hint of her sweet, alcohol-tinged breath.

Softly pushing me away, she says, "You taste like an ashtray."

"I don't mind," I smile.

I feel my heart beating fast as her hands grab my hips and pull me closer. Her hands are running up and down my sides, feeling every inch of my skin. I can hear her moaning softly as she takes my hand and guides it underneath her shirt.

I turn her around, pressing my body against hers, my hands tracing the contours of her figure, stopping at her breasts. Instantly I have an erection. She grinds her tight ass against me, releasing a pleasurable moan. Moving my right hand down, I undo the top button of her shorts, slipping my fingers to the warmth between her legs. Leaning forward, she positions her legs apart. Steadying herself against the side of the stall with one hand, her other deftly slips between us, massaging my crotch.

I'm firmly teasing her nipples, enjoying the softness of her cleavage, while my other hand slides her shorts down, exposing her bare skin. Undoing my slacks, I let them drop as well. While trying to maintain balance, our pants down to our ankles, she leans forward, allowing for better access, as I step back and slide between her legs. She reaches down, skillfully guiding my cock into its rightful place. With each moan, she pushes herself more firmly into the wall, grinding her backside into me. Grabbing her by the waist, I thrust into her while also trying not to fall over.

"What's taking so long in there?"

There's someone trying to open the stall door.

"I'm in here," I yell back.

"Hurry up."

Trying to ignore him, I hear, "There's someone in there. Look there are two people in there."

A head pops up over the door to the stall. "What you doing?"

"Goddamn it!" I shout.

Sophie moves so that I exit her. "This isn't going to work," she says.

I sigh.

We pull our pants up and open the door to leave the stall. There are a bunch of guys standing there looking annoyed at us. This men's room managed to get extremely busy in a short time.

"Assholes," I mutter as we leave the room.

They don't seem to care. The guy that looked over the side of the stall at us quickly goes in. I guess he really had to pee.

Avoiding eye contact with anyone in the restroom, I take Sophie's hand and pull her through a sea of men with anxious and annoyed expressions. Back in the main area of the bar, we make our way toward Kai and Rachel. The venue is wall-to-wall people now. My eyes dart around, searching for the two of them among the masses. Nicholas's voice announces another model. The people watching applaud, while all around are the sounds of conversations, one voice talking over another. Dance music plays as the models parade from back to front, flaunting each outfit. Two guys are standing shoulder-to-shoulder, neither of them dressed for the night. We squeeze past them plus another dressed as the hulk, some girl in a slutty nun costume, and more in various costumed states. I navigate through the crowd, holding onto Sophie with my hand, unwilling to lose her in the horde of partyers. The room is hot with the breath and body heat from the surrounding mob. Sweat beads on my forehead, itching, so I wipe it away, a useless endeavor as more sweat instantly replaces it.

Finally, we make it to where the others are supposed to be. They're not here. I look across the partitioned area and the surrounding crowd. The flashes from the cameras are going off constantly, and it is impossible to see anything with the flash, leaving tracers as the photographers move around in front of the people. Flash, flash, move, flash, flash, move, flash. Like hyperactive wasps, they are up, flash, then down, flash, sideways flash, turn the camera and flash. The model, as she walks, looks to one, flash, flash. And into another flash again. I have to turn away. I feel like I am at an amusement park, but I am not in any way amused.

"Where'd they go?" I holler towards Sophie.

She shakes her head in response, so we work our way towards the other side. I'm trying not to look at the lights that are now preventing me from seeing clearly. Where people should be, I see white spots.

"Let's go," she shouts.

There is no need to respond to her. I swiftly head for the exit, turning sideways to slip past the people as we make a quick exit. The entrance has people jammed all around it, some waiting to get in as those of us who have had enough make our escape. Stepping outside, I see, not far down the road, Kai is engaged in conversation with some guy. I'm blinking to get the white spots out of my eyes as we walk up to him.

"Where'd you two go?" the words ooze out of his mouth with an undertone.

"To the bathroom," I tell him in a way that I hope he takes it to mean to the actual bathroom.

I'm almost out of coke and don't want to share any more with him.

"What happened to Rachel?" Sophie asks.

"She left. She said to tell you she will see you later. I think she went to meet some people. What are you guys up to now?"

"I think we are just going to head back to—" I pause as the smell of the hotdog stand hits me, "Oh, hotdogs. I'm starving." I hadn't realized how hungry I was until now, so without hesitation I let my nose carry me, like a cartoon character, to the delicious aroma of barbequed meat product in a bun.

Kai and Sophie follow. The dodgy guy Kai was chatting with stays behind, leaning against the lamppost. At the end of the street, on the corner, is one of the greatest inventions known to mankind: the late-night hotdog stand – a haven for those drunken souls in need of some food to end the night. The scent of sizzling hotdogs and onions wafts through the air, drawing a small crowd of a dozen or so people who are milling around, as some wait for a relish and mustard covered dog while others are scarfing theirs down, and a few just loitering around, soaking up the scene.

We get in line. "You want something?" I ask Sophie.

"No, I'm good."

Kai orders before me, while I get a bratwurst with cream cheese. We pay and move to the side, waiting for our food. People are coming and going, and eventually, he hands me mine. With the first bite, a medley of meat, cream cheese, mustard, and ketchup, snuggled within a warm bun, explodes in my mouth. I'm on my second bite when I hear some girl next to me say to the guy working, "Where's ours?"

I lean over to them. "Yeah, my friend here ordered his before me and still hasn't gotten his either."

The guy working behind the stand must be at least 6'5" if not taller. He seems to tower over everyone. He looks to be young, probably early twenties, and a bit clueless.

"Hey dude," I say with a mouth full of food. "This guy ordered before me. Where is it?"

The hotdog man looks at me and doesn't even respond.

"Hey, dickbag! Seriously, what the fuck. You ever heard of first come first served?"

He finally responds, pointing tongs at me. "You got a problem?"

"Yeah, my friend here ordered before me and hasn't gotten his food. Is there any kind of order to how you do things?"

He walks around the stand, looking down at me with his tongs jabbing my chest.

"You should watch your mouth. Before I shut it for you," he threatens.

"Fuck you, man!" I bat away the tongs, about ready to start swinging.

He shakes his head, turns, and begins to walk back to the other side of the stand.

Maybe it's the combination of drugs and alcohol in my system, maybe it's something in the atmosphere, or it could be the anger issues that have been mentioned to me on occasion. Regardless of the reason, in a fit of rage, I throw my hotdog, hitting him squarely in the back. As food does when hitting a solid object, the partially-consumed hotdog and condiments splatter over him, then drop to the ground.

He quickly pivots, taking a couple steps towards me, as I tense up and raise my fists, ready for a fight. Suddenly, I'm on the ground, and Sophie is laying over me, shielding me. The hotdog vender is pulling at my foot, trying to get me out from under her. As I struggle to move, my shoe comes off, which he throws towards the street.

"Someone call the cops!" I hear from somewhere.

Sophie is pulling on me to get up. "Let's go," she says.

Everything still looks a bit hazy and black, like I just dived into the deep end of a dark lake and I'm trying to swim my way to the top.

I stand up on shaky legs and she pulls me away, across the street. Walking is a struggle. Kai grabs my other arm, and together they half carry, half drag me along. I try to turn to get my shoe, but they won't let me. We hurry in the direction of Sophie's apartment. I turn to look and can see the crowd watching us, but it doesn't seem like anyone is following. My head is heavy as I find it difficult to look up from the blur of the pavement. Small rocks and other bits of street debris poke into my socked foot as I limp along.

It isn't long before we get to her apartment. "I can take him from here?" she tells Kai.

"Okay. Call me." He says, looking me straight in the eyes, only a few inches from my face.

I blink a couple of times in response, and we get into the elevator. The blue light in the elevator is blinding and I have to close my eyes, listening for the ring of each floor as we pass it. The doors open and I can open my eyes again. We're in her apartment now. She sets me down on the sofa, goes into the kitchen, and comes back with a dishtowel wrapped around some ice.

"Here."

She hands me the towel. I take it in my hand and she guides it up to my eye that hurts like hell right now. I can feel it swelling and slightly closed.

"What happened?" I manage to get out.

"You got in a fight?"

"I know that," I mutter. "But what happened. I hit the guy with my hotdog and that's the last thing I remember."

She pauses, deciding what to say. "Another man hit you from the side, then they both started beating you. I had to jump on you to get them to stop."

I wonder if she is making up the part about the guy hitting me to make me feel better about getting my ass kicked by a late-night hotdog vender.

"Really?"

"Yes."

"What about Kai?"

"Kai didn't do anything. He just stood there."

I close my eyes, wishing I could just fall asleep. However, the throbbing pain in my head won't let me. I keep trying to piece together what happened. And why was I so mad? It wasn't even my hotdog. It belonged to Kai, the guy who didn't even come to my defense in a fight. What an asshole. The night was going so well, and now I'm lying on Sophie's sofa with an ice pack on my face, a brutal headache, one shoe, and wondering if one or two guys beat my ass.

23

I contemplate calling in sick because of the massive black eye from Friday night on my face. There would be no point in wearing sunglasses as that would be blatantly obvious. Sophie tried to cover it with makeup this morning, so that now it just looks like I have a massive black eye that I tried to cover up with makeup.

When I arrive, I keep my head down. I walk through the building, silently hoping to avoid drawing any attention to myself. Entering my office, I close the door so that people will assume I am busy and not bother me. Checking my calendar, I only have one meeting with one of the dev guys. This means in-depth tech-speak, and I really don't think my brain can handle that today. I check his calendar and send out an update, moving it to tomorrow and changing it to a conference call instead of an in-person meeting. He will be happy with that, since it means he won't have to leave his darkened cave. Now, I will block off the rest of my day, making it look like I'm fully booked.

With that done, I lay my forehead on my desk and attempt to relax, praying the world around me doesn't decide to interfere with my bubble of silence. For a little while, the world leaves me alone.

Until there is a knock, followed by the door opening with both Jeff and Heather standing there. I curse myself for not locking the door. Damn my concussion brain.

"Hey bro, we are heading to lunch, you want to go?"

I look up in time to see their reactions.

"Shit dude, what happened?"

Heather follows with, "Are you okay?"

"Yes, I'm fine," I sigh.

They both come into the office, closing the door behind them.

Heather repeats the question. "What happened?"

"Well," I hesitate, trying to decide if I should make up a story or tell them the truth.

"From what I've been told, I got the shit kicked out of me."

"I just thought you were hiding out because you had a hangover," Jeff replies.

"Well, that too."

"Do you want us to get you something?" Heather offers.

"Where are you going?"

"Jimmy John's," Jeff answers.

A sub sounds good, actually. I ask them to pick me up a Country Club and do a quick check on my computer to see if there is anything I need to reply to immediately, which there isn't. Instead of laying back down, I stare blankly at my computer screen.

They return with the sandwiches, and bring me a Coke. The smell of freshly baked bread fills the office as the three of us sit around my desk to eat. The food offers a bit of relief from the nausea and headache that multiple ibuprofens haven't helped. However, it also contributes to my desire to crawl under my desk and take a nap. We chat as we eat. Or, they chat, while I force myself to focus on the conversation, occasionally smiling at points that seem appropriate. As the sandwiches are consumed, the empty paper tossed in the garbage, they excuse themselves to return to work.

I have spent most of the day holed up in my office, only leaving for brief visits to the men's room. Somehow, I've managed to avoid running into anyone that would require an interaction. That is until I get a message from Chris, proving that bad things always seem to find me.

"Hi, Matt. Do you have a second?"

"Sure, what's up?" I type back.

"Can you swing by my office?"

Damn it! I should have said that I was busy, that I was in a meeting, which he would have seen by my status in Outlook. But no, I thought he wanted to message me something or ask me a question about something or have me do some menial tasks he doesn't want to do himself. Instead, he wants me to come to his office – the number one thing on my list of things I don't want to do.

I contemplate messaging him back that I can't while coming up with some excuse. Unfortunately, my fog-filled brain isn't working quickly enough. So, instead, I get up and walk to his office, dreading what he will say about the black eye.

His eyes open wide as he leans back in his chair deciding what to say. "What happened?"

"What happens in fight club, stays in fight club," I say with a smile.

He doesn't look amused.

"Are you okay?"

Why do people keep asking that? Yes, I'm alright. Why wouldn't I be? As if throughout history people have never been punched in the face before. I would imagine a hundred years ago, bruises, scrapes, and black eyes were pretty common. Back in the day, if someone pissed you off, you could deck them with no repercussions other than getting hit back. Now, people get arrested for stuff like that. Fortunately, the cops weren't called, considering that – even though I was the one who lost the fight – I was the one who started it. Wouldn't that have made for an even better evening? On the plus side, sitting in jail today would be better than sitting across from Chris's condescending face.

I could explain that the fight wasn't my fault, that I did nothing to cause it. But that would be a lie and he probably wouldn't believe me anyway. At this point, to him this is just another example of me doing something that resulted in someone else being angry at me.

"Okay. Well, let me know if you need anything, okay?" he says while scratching the back of his head with one hand.

Thanks for the fake concern, except if I did need something, you are not the person I would talk to about it. The warm embrace of a soft-skinned sensuous girl is a nice place to go, the office of a man with a poster on his wall that says 'Let your failures inspire you' is not.

"Sit down," he nods towards the chair opposite his desk, "I have something I want to tell you."

Shit, what did I do now?

"I am informing everyone individually before it is announced at the next team meeting. I've made the decision to accept a position at another company, and my final day here will be the Friday after next."

Maybe this isn't such a bad day after all. Maybe karma is paying me back for the bitch slap in the face I am currently wearing.

"Oh, congratulations, I guess. Where are you going?"

"Well. Don't tell anyone, I've been offered a position at Expedia."

"Okay." As if I really care. "I didn't know they were based in Seattle."

"They have an office in Bellevue. Also," he informs me, "until Kerry can find a replacement, Joline will be taking over my role."

The air is forced out of my lungs, as if the punch to the face was followed up with a punch to the gut. Because in life you can't just have one bad thing happen to you, you need to have multiple bad things happen all at once.

"Joline! Really?"

"Yes, we feel with her experience that she is the most suitable candidate for the interim position. As such, you and the rest of the team will report directly to her for the time being."

"Most suitable? Really. You realize she is a moron, right?"

"Hey, that's not appropriate."

"Not appropriate? I don't think that woman has ever once been on time for anything. Having a conversation with her is like getting punched in the face. Pun intended. The woman is a functional moron. She spends more time talking about her pugs than work. And honestly trying to explain something to her is kind of like explaining something to a dog, with the exception that the dog is actually capable of learning."

He lets out an exacerbated breath. "Your opinion has been noted," he says sternly. "Now, regardless of if it aligns with your opinions, she is the person you'll be reporting to. Which means she will be made aware of the fact that you are currently on disciplinary action."

"Of course," I mumble.

"So, my advice to you would be, use this as an opportunity for a new beginning."

The throbbing in my head increases.

"Yes, I will. Sorry. Anything else?"

"No, that is all."

Leaving his office all I want to do is get in my car and go home, but I should probably give it a couple more hours before I do that. Instead, I head to Jeff's office.

"Smoke break?"

Down in the alley between the buildings, I replay my conversation and my dilemma. Do I quit during a recession with high unemployment, or do I stay on, smile and take it in the ass with the short stubby fingers of a baboon?

Two strands of smoke exit his nostrils before replying, "Umm, you can't just leave, that's for sure. It might take a while to find something new. Plus, I'd miss you, bro. There's no one else I can take smoke breaks with and gripe about our colleagues."

"Hmm, well then of course I'll stay here. Wouldn't want you to be lonely."

"You know what I mean."

"Sure."

There's a moment of silence.

"Maybe you should talk to a recruiter. I know a girl who works for a recruiting agency, I can forward her your resume if you want."

"Yeah, I guess. It doesn't hurt to start looking now. Though, the way my week is going, a construction crane will probably fall on my head and clear up all my problems, anyway."

"It's not that bad. Look on the bright side. You and Sophie reconciled, so there's that … Umm, and yeah, it sucks working for Joline, but it's just temporary and it's probably easier to get away with stuff with her than it is with Chris."

"Hopefully. And, I guess, since she never arrives to work before ten, it's not like I'll have to rush in to work in the morning."

We stomp out our cigarettes then head back inside where I return to my office, with lights off, to wallow in pity.

24

I haven't been out to visit my mother in a few months, so when my brother called, I did what I usually do, which was to ignore him. But you can only ignore someone for so long. So, after a few voice messages and texts, I gave in. I was even more surprised that Sophie was willing to come with me.

She's wearing blue jeans, cowboy boots, and a red and white checkered button-up shirt tucked into the jeans. The jeans make her ass look fantastic. She has pulled her hair back into a ponytail. Looking over at her in the passenger seat as I drive, her breasts rise and fall under the checkered shirt, she turns and catches me checking her out, as my head turns back to focus on the road and not the tingling sensation that just ran down my spine to my groin.

"You realize we are just going to Snohomish," I say, "not Texas," in an attempt to give the impression that I was looking at her outfit and not her tits.

"I know," she replies with a smile knowing that I am full of shit.

"So, when my family wants to know what you do for a living, what do you want me to tell them?" I ask.

She doesn't pause at all, as if ready for this question.

"You tell me. You could simply introduce me as an accountant without mentioning the dancing bit if you are worried about how your parents might react. I don't mind. Technically, I still do some accounting work. So, you're not lying."

This makes me wonder how often she has had to say that to a guy's family. We've never had the 'how many' talk, because, in all honesty, I don't want to know. I consider myself a pretty liberal person, yet she takes her clothes off for a living; she's bisexual; she met me by randomly making out with me at a party; and we had sex on our first date. Plus, she is fantastic in the sack, so I have to imagine the number to be reasonably high. We have been having unprotected sex since we met. She claims to be on birth control and is STD free. But just because she says it, it doesn't necessarily make it true. Reminding me that I should probably get myself checked, just to be on the safe side.

"I don't care what my family thinks. I just was concerned about you. In case you would feel uncomfortable about it."

"Honey, I'm not uncomfortable with anything."

"I know," I say, "but we aren't talking about that."

She rolls her eyes.

My mother and her husband live in a one-story rambler just north of Snohomish. The claim to fame in Snohomish is that they have the most antique shops within a single block, or square mile, within Washington, or maybe the west coast. I don't know. Something about a lot of antique shops.

"You said your mother is remarried, what about your father? Do you guys get along?" she asks.

"Yeah. And no, he's not. My father is just one of those people who is happier single than in a relationship. I think he only got married because that was what was expected of people."

"Your parents still get along?"

"Yeah," I shrug. "They just grew apart, I guess. My mother did her thing, my father did his thing, and my brother and I did our thing. When we were teenagers, they split. No biggie."

I'm saved from the third degree, as we pull into the driveway where my brother's Ford Explorer is already parked. I don't know why I am uneasy about being here. I get along fine with my brother and his wife. And the kids are fun to visit with. That's the joy of being an uncle: I get to have some fun with them, then give the little rodents back to their parents. Although it does make me feel old at times. Mom's not entirely irritating, and her husband is a decent guy. They got married a few years back at an old farm turned wedding venue here in Snohomish.

Maybe it is the conversation about how my work is going that I am not interested in having. Maybe it is the judgment of dating an exotic dancer. Or maybe the issue is the fact that I haven't indulged in any substances today except for a couple of cigarettes. As we get out of the car, I check my jacket pocket and find my pack with the American Spirits logo on the front. And as expected, there are only two inside.

"I might have to run to the store," I tell Sophie.

"Or you could quit smoking," she retorts.

"There he is!" My mother gushes at opening the door to see us, visibly reacting to my black eye. "Hi honey." She hugs me. "And who is this?"

"This is Sophie." I introduce her. "And this is my mother, Linda."

She leads us inside the house.

Brad comes in from the kitchen and gives Sophie a hug and a once over with his eyes.

"Are you going to tell us what happened to your eye?" my mother asks.

I knew this was going to happen and that I would have to deal with her judgmental tone. Whenever we talk, she asks me when I am going to get married and give her more grandchildren like

Brad. I try to explain that neither of those things will ever happen, especially at seeing how miserable Brad is.

"I was mouthing off to Sophie and she punched me in the face."

"Haha very funny. So, really what happened."

"Nothing. Just got into a little scuffle."

Brad adds, "And apparently lost."

"No," I lie. "And, there were two of them and just one of me. So, of course, one would get a decent shot in."

"What did you say to start the fight?" my mother asks.

"Thanks for assuming it was me that started it. Maybe I wasn't doing anything. A couple of guys just decided to jump me."

"Is that what happened?" she says directly to Sophie.

"Yes," she says, nodding, "a couple of guys were harassing me and one tried to grab my ass, and Matt came to my defense. It was rather heroic of him."

Damn, she's good.

"Is that how you met?" My mother asks.

"No," I say. "We met through a mutual friend. Can we change the subject now?"

"Yes, yes, yes. Sit down. Give me your coats."

We sit down in the living room. The house is the one she and my father bought when we were kids. When they got divorced, she kept the house and my father moved out. She and her new husband have done a decent job of remodeling the place. They ripped out the old carpets and put in some nice wood laminate floors. The coffee table is an old solid oak table with a dark wood stain on it, she has had for years. The furniture is a dark brown leather. Over in the corner, they have a wood stove that is currently heating the room, giving the whole place a nice wood fire smell to it.

"Would you like something to drink?" She offers. "I just brewed some coffee if you want."

"Sure, I'll have a cup," I reply.

"You still take it with cream and sugar."

I nod.

"And you, dear?" She turns to Sophie.

"I'm not a big coffee drinker. Just some water would be nice."

"I have Coke or Diet Coke?"

"No, thank you. Just some water with ice would be great."

While waiting I turn, "Hey Brad. Do you remember that dog we had when we were younger? Humbug?"

He pauses, his eyes squinting as the memory returns to him. "Oh yeah. He was like a collie and shepherd mix, I think. Haven't thought about him in ages." A smile forms on his face at the memory.

"Yeah. His name was Humbug, right? What happened to him? I don't remember him dying or anything. Do you?"

"Umm … Yeah … You don't?"

"No."

He looks to the side as if deciding how to reply, then shrugs and blurts out, "Our bus drove over him."

"What?" I exclaim.

"Oh no," Sophie adds.

"Yeah. He got out after we left for school one day and apparently tried to follow the bus. Remember, it felt like we hit a bump. Then the bus driver got out and was like, 'does anyone own a black, white, and brown dog.'"

"That's so sad," Sophie offers.

"Wow, I don't remember that."

Our mother returns with the drinks.

"Mom," I say, "our dog got ran over by our school bus."

"What honey?" She looks confused.

"Our dog, Humbug got ran over by our bus. Is that true?"

Brad adds, "he doesn't remember."

"Don't talk about that kind of stuff," she says. "Let's talk about something else."

"No. He popped into my head the other day, but I didn't remember him being hit by the bus."

Brad tries to cheer me up by mentioning how we got to skip school that day.

Slight bits of the memory come back to me. Including what she said happened to him.

"You said he went to live at Uncle Gus's house," I say.

"That's what mom and dad told you. Because you were crying. They said he was fine, just needed to go to the vet, and then they sent him to the recovery farm," he adds air quotes to 'recovery farm.'

My mother snaps at him, "Don't say that."

"Well, it's true," he says.

"Look honey," she turns to me. "You were seven, I think, and we didn't think you were ready to deal with his death because you boys left the door open—"

"It wasn't me," Brad interrupts.

We all give him a hard glare.

"So, we told you that story to make you feel better."

"So, you lied to me."

"You were just kids. Sometimes when you love someone, you don't tell them the truth to make them happy. Now let's talk about something else," she says without stopping. "Did Brad tell you that Gareth got laid off from the bank? They closed that branch. Since he had been there so long, it was cheaper for them to lay him off and give him a severance. It's this recession, but thank the lord we don't have that tree hugger in office. I could only imagine what a state the country would be in. Fingers crossed."

Sophie reaches for my hand, holding it as I try to hide my feelings, not sure why I'm so upset by this revelation. I'm an adult. I shouldn't be upset by a white lie and a dog I barely remember.

Following our mothers lead, Brad says, "he probably got a decent severance check out of it. What is he doing now?"

"Oh, I didn't tell you. He is working part-time at the auto parts store in town."

"He doesn't need to work, does he?" Brad says.

"He's okay. He has invested well over the years, plus what I'm getting with social security. The house is paid for. And, we don't have a lot of expenses. He works there mostly just to have something to do. He likes to keep busy. Idle hands are the devil's playground."

"Well, tell him if they have an opening to keep me in mind," I instantly regret saying.

She responds quickly. "Why, are you getting laid off as well?"

"No, or not that I'm aware of anyway." I don't want to listen to her lecture me about having a stable job and all that crap. "Why don't we change the subject. Where are the wife and kids?" I turn to Brad.

"Suzy is sick so Vanessa decided to stay home with her. And Dylan is at a friend's house today …"

I wonder how much Gareth has in the bank? In the few conversations I've had with him, he told me about some investments he made in the stock market over the years, usually with an insinuation that I should open an investment account, and what stocks to buy. He's at retirement age, so he'd be eligible for social security as well as whatever he has saved up with a pension or in a 401k. They live a reasonably frugal life. No car payment or much else in the form of high expenses. They take a vacation each year, often those old people bus tour types through Europe or a cruise, which can't be that much. As for me, I'm practically living paycheck to paycheck.

"—and did I tell you Suzy is walking now."

"They sound adorable. I can't wait to have children," Sophie says.

What! The conversation took a quick change for the worse.

My mother's eyes widen with anticipation. "Oh, more grandchildren. I keep telling Matt he needs settle down. That's wonderful to hear."

"Wow, slow it down people." I need to stop this conversation fast. "Sophie and I haven't been seeing each other that long. So, don't be getting ideas here."

Sophie adds, "True, we haven't had any of those conversations yet."

"Yet? What, is that a conversation or something we are supposed to have?"

Brad interrupts, "Yeah man. Vanessa and I had that discussion on like our third date."

"Well, that's because you are a little bitch, Brad."

"Hey, language," my mother snaps.

"Yeah Matt," adds Sophie, along with a soft slap on my leg and a smile.

"What? I'm just messing with him. But seriously. Every time I talk to Brad, he sounds miserable. Why would anyone want to subject themselves to that? Crying, diapers, snot, never going out to do anything fun, and no money because it all gets spent on them."

"That's not true. I love my children. They are the best thing to ever happen to me."

"Really, because you sound more like you are trying to convince yourself than me."

"Oh, up yours."

"Boys. Be nice," Our mother interrupts.

"We are," I reply.

"Always," adds Brad.

"Enough about us," my mother says, turning to Sophie. "Tell me about you. What do you do dear?"

"I work as an accountant," Sophie replies. "I do the books for a small real estate company that owns a few businesses."

"Oh, that sounds interesting. Would I know any of the businesses?"

That gives me a bit of a smile. My mother and Gareth heading out for a night on the town, a few drinks followed up by lap dances. Even young, I can't imagine her going out and partying. The most she ever drank when we were growing up was an occasional glass of wine, maybe one or two cocktails when they went out. Honestly, I don't think I've ever seen her drunk. Or my father, for that matter. He drank a bit more regularly, however, usually coming home from work and pouring himself a glass of bourbon before sitting in front of the TV for the remainder of the night. Your traditional boring parents compared to some stories I hear about people. Other than the fact that they never seemed to interact with one another or my brother and myself.

That lost love must have happened years before they were divorced.

"Maybe, but we deal mostly with the buildings not the businesses in the buildings. They lease from us. It's not very exciting. A lot of spreadsheets and numbers."

"Pretty *and* smart. I like her," my mother says looking directly at me.

"So, what's for dinner?" I ask.

25

When Sophie mentioned heading down to Portland for a weekend, I was glad to offer my services as a taxicab. After the past few weeks, a weekend out of town, without easy access to narcotics, is exactly what I needed.

We are sitting inside a long narrow restaurant, bar, or strip club, depending on your point of view. A more apt description is probably a *dive bar*. The walls are painted in a burgundy red. The space is no more than twenty feet wide, yet extends far back into the building, into what I assume is the bathrooms, kitchen, and possibly private dance area. If this place offers private dances, that is.

A half-finished plate of hot wings and fries sits on the little round table in front of me, and a Falafel and hummus platter for Sophie. The friend of hers we are here to meet is picking at a chicken Cesar salad. She has bleached blond hair with large curls. Her cheeks have a soft roundness to them that compliment her full lips. Her wardrobe, consisting of a thick tan-colored wool sweater and baggy rolled-up blue jeans, somewhat conceals her figure. Yet, even under the layers, it is evident that her ample bust is part of her allure to those who frequent places like this.

There are seven additional little round tables throughout the bar. The lunch rush hasn't started yet, if one is going to start at all. The only other table in use has two guys sitting at it with burgers and fries in front of them, paying no attention to the woman dancing on a small circular stage, raised a few feet off the ground, towards the center of the room. She is likely in her mid-forties or older, and doing her routine to Def Leppard's "Pour Some Sugar on Me." The walls of the room have dim lighting features evenly spaced throughout, with most of the lights directed towards the stage. Two of the lights are rotating through a series of colors in sync with the music, and a disco ball suspended above the stage center bounces light around the room. The light doesn't do much for the appeal of the dancer, starkly highlighting the lines on her face and the makeup painted on to mask them. She incorporates a chair into her routine, using it as a prop to sit on, bend over, and generally spoil the appetite of anyone who might be watching.

I had heard that you could eat and drink in strip clubs in Portland, but until this little early lunch of ours, it was something I had never experienced. Judging by the food's quality, I have no interest in trying it again. The wings are drenched in a thick layer of cheap sugary sweet sauce, and, according to Sophie, the hummus isn't much better. Trying to cut back on the booze, I ordered a Coke while both girls are sipping on Diet Cokes.

"You are too good for this place," Sophie says to Brooke the voluptuous blond.

"I know. But besides my usual rate, the manager is paying for a room at the Paramount for the weekend. 10% of the door, and my flight to get here," she says enthusiastically.

From what Sophie has explained to me, strippers typically pay a house fee at the places they dance and earn most of their income through lap dances. That's how she describes it at her workplace. So, why is this girl being paid outright? I want to ask but also don't want to sound ignorant.

"He's likely expecting something more from you, you know," Sophie says, gesturing towards the bar on the right. "This place can't make that much in drink sales."

Working the long battered wooden counter is a burly black guy barely paying attention to the customers, instead he appears to be playing a game on his phone. The only other person in the place is the waitress who took our order. She is a bit younger than the dancer, wearing a tight black t-shirt and tight black jeans. Both her arms are covered in beautifully designed sleeve tattoos.

"You might be surprised," Brooke says. "Last night it was packed in here, standing room only."

Is there such a thing as famous strippers? The poster on the outside has a picture of Brooke on it, making her look like a 1920s era screen queen. Her stage name, Amélie, is boldly displayed, announcing that she is 'here for one weekend only.'

Brooke continues, "And honestly, I'll totally let him bone me if he wants. He's hot. Wait till you see him – he's tall, dark skin with a bit of face scruff, and huge arms. He looks like Lenny Kravitz. He can toss me over his shoulders like a caveman all he wants."

She then pounds her chest with her hands making caveman grunt noises.

They both laugh.

"My god, you're the worst," Sophie replies.

I roll my eyes. Yet, to be honest, there is something about Brooke's directness that is a turn on. I bet she is great in the sack, and those tits must be amazing. Assuming they are real, of course. This train of thought leads me to wonder if the two of them have had sex?

After lunch, we swing by some massive book store Sophie says she visits every time she comes to Portland. She purchases a couple of books. I however, find the place a bit too much. It spans multiple floors in a massive building. They must have some system of organization, although I'm not entirely sure what it is. From the bookstore, we head back to our room for a nap. Sophie booked us a room at Lucia for the weekend – a posh establishment. The invite said I had to drive, and she'd take care of the rest. No complaints from me.

Later that same night, we're back at the club, and Brooke was not exaggerating about how busy the place gets. It is wall-to-wall people. There's a ten-dollar cover charge to get in, so between that and drink sales, the place must do pretty well. We haven't seen Brooke yet.

We press through the crowd towards the bar to order drinks. I get a Jack and Coke while Sophie goes for a vodka cranberry. There are two bartenders working, neither of them the same guy from earlier, and it takes forever to get their attention. After that, we slowly edge as close as we can to the stage to watch Brooke's show.

The girl currently on the stage is much more attractive than the one from earlier. With slender, long legs, thin arms, and short blond hair slicked to the side, she is much more appealing to watch. She is wearing thin red lace lingerie. Underneath is matching underwear, and red heals show off her calves nicely.

"Oh, my god," I hear from my left in the flamingest of flaming voices ever.
We turn to see two guys within arm's reach of us. The first, the one who spoke, is wearing a tight

yellow t-shirt. The sleeves are shorter than the typical short-sleeved shirt, outlining his skinny arms. His shirt is tucked into tight blue jeans with dual yellow stripes running down each leg, and white running shoes that look like they were purchased new today. His short hair is heavily gelled up with bleached tips. The other guy is his opposite. Slightly shorter than the first, he's dressed in a black cowboy-style button-up shirt, adorned with white embroidered flowers. The shirt is stylishly tucked into skin-tight leather pants. His hair is black, dyed as well. However, his most distinguishing feature is the thin mustache above his upper lip and a small soul patch beneath the lower lip. He has the same look of confusion on his face as I do. Both of us wonder who his partner just called out to.

It turns out Sophie is the recipient, as she turns, recognizing him.

"Ian," she yells back as the two of them embrace. "What are you doing here?" she asks after they let go of each other.

"The same as you, darling," he says with a wave of his right hand. "We are here to witness the glory of Améliiie."

"Hi Glenn," she says to the other guy picking up the tones of Ian.

The two of them hug.

Sophie then turns to me. "This is Matt."

I lean over to shake hands.

"And this is Glenn," she says, introducing the guy in black. "And this is Ian."

When Ian shakes my hand, he sticks his chest out in a mock manliness. "Nice to meet you," he says, lowering his voice a few octaves.

"You as well," I reply.

"You should have told me you were in town. We could have met up earlier," Sophie says.

"Samsies," Ian replies.

It's obvious who the bottom in this relationship is.

"So," I say to Glenn. "You guys visiting from Seattle as well, then."

"Close. Olympia actually."

"Oh. So how do you know Sophie?"

"Through Amélie. We've all, um, known each other for a while I guess."

There is something in the way he pauses with a knowing grin that I don't appreciate. But before I can ask what that means, the music stops abruptly, replaced by a voice over the speaker system.

"Ladies, gentlemen, and scoundrels. Take your hands off your neighbor's ass and put them together for the queen of fab, the star of starlets, the one and only … Amélie!"

"Lady Marmalade" starts playing at a much higher volume than the previous song. The room erupts in applause and cheers.

A path clears as she works her way through the crowd from the back of the room. In front of her, clearing people out of the way, is a burly man. The guy must be at least 6'2" if not taller. He has a thick, curly black beard that matches his hair. He is wearing a tight black t-shirt that shows off each can in his six-pack abs. The sleeves on the t-shirt look stressed at holding in his biceps, and I imagine if he were to flex, they would give up and split like the Hulk. When the phrase 'brick shithouse' was termed, this is the man they were describing. There was no pushing back as he cleared the crowd for Amélie. His presence moved people out of the way more than any parting with the hands. I wonder if this is the manager that Amélie was describing earlier, or just a bouncer.

"Helllooo big fella," I hear Ian say behind me.

As Amélie passes us, she gives a wink with long eyelashes attached. Her cherub cheeks have a rosy blush on them that is enhanced with the dark red lipstick she is wearing.

At the stage, the previous performer has moved off, leaving the platform empty. Now standing next to the stage, she is replacing the lingerie she had removed.

Brick shithouse leads Amélie with one arm up the stairs, and she waves a hand around her face in a mock faint, then leans down, runs her hand through his hair and gives him a kiss on the cheek.

The crowd shouts and applauds.

Sophie leans into me or I into her as the crowd pushes forward for a better view. The bouncer hasn't moved, just crossing his arms and watching the audience, letting us know that our behavior must stay at a level he deems appropriate.

The music shifts to Chris Isaak's "Wicked Games," an unusual choice for a stripper. Although it seems like more of an upbeat, bass-heavy dance version. Then the bouncer hands Amélie a microphone and instead of Isaak's voice, she begins singing the song while sensually moving to the rhythm. The crowd erupts in applause once more. The room's lighting dims so the colors of the strobes bounce from her dress display a mesmerizing pattern as she continues her performance.

Wow, this is not the show I expected. Sophie moves her hips along with the music and I wrap my arms around her to enjoy the pleasure of her ass in my crotch. Another drink would be nice, but I don't want to get drunk tonight and there is no way I'm moving through this fire hazard of a crowd to get one.

On the stage, Amélie begins to slide down a side zipper on her dress as the lyrics smoothly pass her lips. As the song moves towards the final few lines, she slides the strap from one shoulder, then the other, perfectly timed so that the ensemble hits the floor for her to step out and kick it to the side.

Her breasts are a sight to behold, accentuated by a white and light pink bra and matching panties. The straps have a small bow on each side. Her stockings also feature the same soft champagne pink lace as the rest of her outfit.

I need to move back from Sophie for a second, between the show and her rubbing her ass into me, I don't want to pop a boner.

The people closest to the stage are tossing bills for her, and the girl who has been collecting Amélie's clothing is moving around the stage and scooping them into a pile so that Amélie doesn't step on them.

A song starts playing that sounds familiar, but I don't fully recognize it. She trades the microphone for a chair. The song has a nice beat to it as she sets the chair down, dancing around it, lip-syncing to the music. A song by Beyoncé, I think, with lyrics about feeling sexy and being a naughty girl. Which, I have no doubt, Amélie is.

Working the chair in a much more sensual way than the girl at lunch time, she leans over it, weaves seductively around the chair, and then kneels on it. Turning to one side, accentuating her curves, she smoothly slips off one of her heels and hands it to the girl, then does the same with the other. Which makes me realize, I don't think I have ever seen any of the girls at Sophie's club take their heels or boots off. They always seem to keep them on when dancing.

Amélie then turns, so that she is now sitting on the edge of the chair, a coy smile as she effortlessly glides one stocking down her flawless leg. She doesn't fully remove it, teasingly extending her foot toward the audience, inviting one guy in the crowd to pull it all the way off. He instantly bundles it up and pushes it to his face. The female assistant moves over and takes the stocking from him, placing it with the dress and heels. Amélie repeats the process with the other leg.

As that song ends and another begins, she is handed the microphone, and begins singing, "I know I may be young, but I've got feelings, too." As she does this, she moves towards the crowd, singing it to some guy that has been placing money on the stage from what I can tell. And I doubt they are singles. Once she reaches the chorus, I figure out the song is a Britney Spears song. Sophie wasn't kidding when she said Amélie is too good for this place.

Arriving at the chorus, she reaches around, skillfully unclasping her bra with one hand, while the other holds onto the mic. The straps slide down her arms before slipping off completely, liberating those captivating mounds from their restraints. The audience goes wild with cheers and applause, momentarily drowning out the sound of her voice. Sophie cheers at the top of her lungs and I join her, cheering and clapping as well. If there is only one thing on my list to do before I die, it is to peel those tassels off with my teeth and bury my face between those tits.

As the song continues, she sensually runs her foot through the hair of a guy standing by the stage's edge. He responds as if he were having a religious encounter at a Baptist Church revival, compelling him into a spasm. Foot fetishism was never really my thing, but my opinion on the subject might be changing after this display.

The song ends as one star is removed and tossed to the audience in our direction, clearly intended for us, but caught by some guy with a bald spot on the top of his head in front of us. And as the last lyrics are said, the other is removed and tossed as well. These are left for the audience members who have caught them to enjoy. Personally, I'm enjoying the view of her ample areolas. The crowd has been celebrating the whole time with applause, whistles and cheers.

The music transitions to another song with a heavy dance rhythm I don't recognize. As it does, she slides the chair to the stage's edge, arching her back and emphasizing her alluring figure for the audience to admire. My eyes travel along the graceful curve of her spine, seamlessly flowing into those endlessly captivating legs that exude sensuality and strength. Legs that could give even the most pious man wet dreams.

After doing a few more moves with the chair, it is taken by the assisting woman to be removed from the stage along with the microphone. With the stage clear, she works the platform. Bills are being tossed to the stage as Amélie expertly teases the audience with her choreographed movements. She leans into those close, engaging them by stroking their hair, shaking her backside, and working the crowd into a frenzy. Occasionally someone will reach out and attempt to touch her, prompting brick shithouse to move them back. As the song continues, she sways to the rhythm, teasing the audience who are spellbound by her provocative display. People push towards the stage as a herd to the trough, as her panties slide down and she steps out of them, swiftly sliding them towards the assistant with her foot, avoiding the grasping hands of eager fans who erupt in cheers and applause.

Fully nude, her sinful hips sway to the rhythm of the music as she runs her hands seductively along her curves. As the show comes to an end, the audience presses closer to the stage, leaving no room for anyone to move. Except for brick shithouse, who has no problem parting the mass of people. He hands her a sheer white see-through negligee, which she drapes around herself as he guides her down the steps with one arm, while using the other to create space amidst the thick crowd.

Leaving the audience in a heightened state of sexual excitement, everyone cheers for more. Some applauding, some yelling 'encore', whistles, and other phrase of encouragement. From our location, we are shoved into her path as if the doors were opening at a Walmart on Black Friday. For those near Amélie, they can't help but be pushed into her. Happily, I'm sure. The bouncer, with his arm around her now, is battling to keep people away. Even with his menacing look and size, he seems to struggle a bit to move through the throng of perves angling for a grope. She continues to smile, unoffended as hands reach out to touch her in any way they can. I want to do the same, but as she moves past us, the people around make it difficult, and with Sophie here, I don't think that would be a good idea. The other girl is close behind, carrying the clothing and money tight in her arms, clearly worried that she might get manhandled as well, which seems to happen a bit.

There is an announcement over the PA system, letting us know she will be back and to wait while enjoying a drink from the bar. Wanting to get out of the oppressive heat and mob in this club, and not having any interest in watching the unfortunate woman who has to follow that act on the stage next, I suggest to Sophie we try to find a less busy place.

Ian buys the first round of drinks at some gay bar they suggested, along with a round of Jager Bombs. *So much for my attempt at moderation.*

The bar is less crowded so that we have no problem finding a table against the back wall. The brick walls of the small establishment are worn and covered in a menagerie of paraphernalia: some black and white pictures of people I don't recognize; painted art; and textured art of various designs, including one that looks like it is made from various brass musical instruments fused together. Our table is worn and weathered with drink stains and scratches from years of use. The music is playing standard mindless dance club music, though no one is dancing.

Sophie tells me that they all know each other through the mutual connection of Brooke. Apparently, the girl gets around. She works as a showgirl in Vegas, does burlesque in Seattle, and is a singer. And, of course, does the occasional strip show.

The second round of drinks is on me. The bartender knows how to mix a strong drink – mostly alcohol, with just a splash of mixer. I give him a good tip in response. Amidst loud chatter around us, the three of them take turns sharing stories of their previous encounters, as old friends often do when caught in a haze of alcohol-induced honesty after not seeing each other for some time. Ian tells one about the time they were at a party and Sophie, after a few too many drinks, climbed the fence for some late-night skinny dipping in the neighbor's pool. Sophie acts embarrassed but then adds with a grin that the pool didn't have the heat turned on, so as soon as she jumped in, she was back out. They all laugh, blending into the bar's vibrant atmosphere.

"Did the neighbors wake up," I ask.

"Yes," she says. "I screamed so loudly that they started yelling at me from the window."

"It wasn't the first time that happened," Glenn adds.

Sophie says, "They threated to call the cops on me."

The three of them laugh at the memory.

The final stop of the night features male strippers tea bagging any willing participants near the stage. I position myself at a safe distance to avoid an encounter with a man's sweaty nut sack. With each shot and drink, we become increasingly unsteady. By the time the bar closes for the night, we can barely maintain our balance as we stumble outside with nowhere else to go.

Out in front, as the place clears out, there is a dark-skinned guy in short-shorts and sleeveless t-shirt talking to Ian. I hope he is trying to get us some coke, as I could use the pick-me-up.

The throngs of inebriated are spilling out from the bars and clubs, while taxis are lined up for the last fare of the night, mostly likely crossing their fingers the person doesn't vomit in the back seat. Sophie holds my hand and leads me down the street, past people trying to decide where to go for the rest of the night. Most are in search of an after-hours venue, while others are on their way home to pass out. Glancing back, Glenn and Ian have disappeared.

"Where are we going?" I ask.

"Back to the room," she says.

"Oh, I thought we were going to … umm, an after-hours, or … isn't that guy getting us some coke."

She laughs, "They are going to the bath house."

"Oh."

We head toward the hotel, only to realize that we've taken a wrong turn. Then, after wandering aimlessly for what feels like an excessively long time, we eventually stumble upon the hotel, only to find that locating our room is a bit of a challenge.

"Ummm, which floor is it?" The words fall out of my mouth.

"I don't know." Sophie whispers while running her hands through the back of my hair.

Feeling confident, I pick the correct floor and after a few swipes of the key card on the wrong door, we make it to our room.

Inside the room, our clothes are stripped off as we drunkenly jump on the bed, embracing the other's naked body. Drunken sex is the best reason to drink. The reduced inhibitions, the animal instincts let out of the cage. There isn't a worry about insecurities, as every concern or doubt dissipates into the background, replaced by a singular, all-consuming desire for one another. It is only moments before I am inside her.

"Fuck me from behind," she demands.

"Gladly."

Rolling over, she is up on her hands and knees while I'm firmly grasping each of her hips, pounding her from behind. Her arms stretched tight, allowing for every inch to grind deep inside her. Her black hair falling forward into her face, moving with each rhythmic thrust, her perfectly curved back with muscles tight. The *smack, smack, smack* of each thrust blends with heaving breathing and her passionate moans fill the room.

I begin to slip my finger in her ass.

She screams, kicking her right foot into me, knocking me down, as she also turns around, whipping her right hand, backhanding me in the nose while I fall to the floor.

"Fuck!" I yell after landing.

There is blood running down my face which I try to cover with my hand.

"What the fuck!" she yells back. "You just stuck your finger in my ass!"

"And you punched me in the face. Jesus Christ."

I get up, pinching my nose to the bathroom to look in the mirror and see the blood running down from my nose to lip. I grab some tissues on the counter to wipe my face.

In the other room, she continues. "You can't just stick a finger in someone's ass without telling them. What the fuck is wrong with you!"

"Christ, I thought you'd like it. And it was just the tip."

She is now at the door watching me with my nose pinched, head tilted back, rolling wads of tissue into each nostril.

"That's creepy as fuck! You can't just finger someone's butt during sex without their permission! How would you like it if I did that to you. Just randomly start fisting your butthole when I'm going down on you."

"I didn't stick my fist in there, I was just going to use one finger. Why the fuck are you so mad about this? Come on, don't tell me *you've* never tried anal play before"

"That's not the point asshole. Did I give you permission to do that? No, I didn't."

She turns around and goes back into the other room. I follow with my head held back and tissue in my nostrils.

"Maybe yell that a bit louder why don't you. I'm sure the people in the neighboring room would be happy to call the cops to tell them there is a girl screaming her head off in the next room."

"Maybe they should. Or maybe I should."

She starts putting her underwear on.

"I think you are being a bit dramatic, don't you. After all, you did punch me in the face. Maybe I should call them for assault."

"If you ever do something like that again, I will punch you on purpose, and you'll deserve it!"

"To be clear, are you saying no to all anal play ever, or just randomly sticking things in your butt without letting you know first."

"Eat a bag of dicks and choke to death, you asshole!"

There are those arguments that are valid. Then, there are those arguments that get a bit out of control because two people have had too much to drink. This particular one falls into the latter category. Realizing that this fight is leaning toward being out of control, and not wanting to end up explaining what happened to the hotel manager, the neighbors, or the cops – and thankful to the fact that being smacked in the face sobered me up a little – I try to calm things down.

Taking a long deep breath, I say, "Okay. I'm sorry. I didn't realize that it would be that big of an issue. I didn't really think about it. I just had this urge, thinking that it would be fun and obviously I was wrong. Maybe it would be best if we talk about this tomorrow, okay?"

"Fine."

She doesn't fully calm down but at least the fight stops, giving me a moment to remove the tissues from my nose and get some clothes on. We both get into bed silently, acknowledging that, yes, this is probably not the best time to argue about this.

She places a pillow between us, silently agreeing to save the conversation for our drive back to Seattle tomorrow, when we will have plenty of time to discuss it, while also dealing with throbbing hangovers.

26

"For fuck's sake" I blurt out. "Obviously, you are still mad. You've barely said a word all morning and you haven't said a thing since we got on the road. Again, I'm sorry about last night. We both had a decent amount to drink, and I got a bit caught up in the moment. You've always been pretty GGG about things. *But* that doesn't mean I should just assume that you are open to everything. After all, I have no interest in having anything shoved into my pee hole."

The corner of her mouth moves as if into a smile. She turns her head to the right, looking out the window to hide it from me.

"So, it only makes sense that there are some no-go places on you as well."

"I said, I'm not mad."

I turn the radio off. "Yes, but you clearly still are. You've barely said anything all morning and you've just stared out the window the entire drive."

She turns in my direction, "I appreciate you acknowledging that things got a little out of hand last night."

"Thank you."

"Just so we're clear, I'm not into anal play. I've experimented with it in the past. It's uncomfortable and I don't find it enjoyable. If that's a deal breaker for you, then let me know now."

"Well, not like big stuff, but what about—"

"—No, no what about. If you want me to stick something in your butt, fine. But nothing in mine."

I don't really care all that much that she isn't into it. It's just surprising to hear that someone like her not being into something sexual.

"I guess the thing is, you've done all this cool stuff. You've lived in other countries, you've snuck into pools and skinny dipped, you've done all this cool, interesting, fun stuff, while I live less than an hour away from the place I was born. You …"

I have to catch myself before saying she's had more sex than me. One, it might not be true, although it most likely is. And two, I don't think she would take that well.

"I guess, I just want to … I don't know, I guess I just want to not be boring."

"Honey," she says while patting my leg, "sticking a finger into someone's butt doesn't make you less boring. It makes you an asshole."

"So, you *do* think I'm boring."

"I didn't mean it that way. Actually, the qualities you see as mundane are precisely what I like about you. I've never stayed in one place for more than a couple of years. Even as a kid, we moved around a lot. My parents were always buried in their work, running the business. All they cared about were my grades. I was practically invisible to them. You got to grow up with a brother and the same friends."

We sit in silence for a few moments. The only sound is the steady rhythm of the engine and car's tires on the road.

"I'm thinking, maybe I might cut back on the alcohol a bit," I say.

She smiles and nods her head.

"Not completely, probably, just limit myself to two drinks whenever I go out, you know. I'm tired of waking up with hangovers. And of course, I'd be less inclined to inappropriate behavior when drunk."

She reaches over and starts combing her fingers through the back of my hair, massaging my scalp with a gentle touch. The tension in the car dissolves along with the tension in my shoulders.

27

"Evelyn told me last night she thinks we should split up. Maybe get a divorce," Jeff tells me.

I have to pause for a second at that. Looking at his face, he appears genuinely upset about it, his eyes a little glossy, and he continues to move his jaw as if attempting to dislodge the Cesar salad he's been picking at from his teeth with his tongue. We are having lunch at the Irish bar down the street from the office. The sounds of the lunch crowd add background to the conversation. He seemed a bit out of sorts on the walk here, but I didn't think his wife leaving him was why, figuring maybe he was hungover or had a bad day at work, or maybe they got in a fight, but not this. The thing is, I don't really want to get into his relationship with his wife. It's none of my business.

"Why? What happened?" I ask.

"Remember how I told you about that girl on LustLab?"

"No way. The girl was Heather, and you got caught with her. Dude, how was she?"

"No." He shakes his head with annoyance at my joke. "I didn't do anything."

"Then what?"

"Umm … You can't tell anyone at work about this."

"Seriously? Who the hell would I talk to about your relationship with at work?"

He pauses for a few seconds before speaking, giving me a chance to take another bite of my chicken burger.

"I messaged that girl, and it wasn't Heather."

He takes a bite from his salad, chews it.

"We were chatting online. Nothing happened. Ummm, just messaging for amusement. You know, just for the fun of it and all. Evelyn stumbled upon the conversation while using my computer."

"Dude, that's why you clear your browsing history, and log out of sites. That's 101-stuff man."

"Come on, I'm being serious here."

"Sorry. Go ahead."

"Well, that's essentially it. She came across the messages, and we had a big argument about it last night. Now she wants me to move out."

"Oh, that's not that bad. Give it a few days, she'll calm down I'm sure, especially if it was just some harmless online flirting. Or you could, you know, do some couple's counseling or something. You know how girls are. Buy her some flowers, take her out to dinner, maybe take a weekend out of town or something."

There is a pause while he looks down at his salad – his jaw moves from side to side, continuing the search for something that isn't there. Usually, our conversations comprise of inappropriate talk about the opposite sex or trash-talking our coworkers. I've only been around Evelyn a few times, since she rarely wants to come out with us, and I don't want to go all the way out to their house in the Stepford village.

The first time I went to Issaquah to see them was when I was dating Jennifer. We drove up and down the streets around his neighborhood, only they all looked exactly the same. It was like a freaky Santa village without Santa, just a bunch of creepy cookie-cutter houses lined up in rows next to each other in a bizarre series of interlacing streets. A corn maze of wooden doors, matching lawns, and SUVs.

"I don't know if I really want to," he says, looking back up. "I don't think I love her anymore and I don't think she loves me either."

I hate these types of conversations. Am I supposed to congratulate him since he wants out of the marriage, even though he looks upset about it, or should I express sympathy?

"I envy you being single," he says. "I met Evelyn during my sophomore year at university in a data analytics class. Then our paths kept crossing, in places like the library or cafeteria. I jokingly remarked, 'are you following me?' which she thought was a charming pickup line." He pauses. "I wasted my college years committed to a single relationship.

All those gorgeous single women and I end up with the first girl I meet in a fucking analytics class."

"Some might say that is a good thing," I respond. "Don't tell anyone I said this because I will deny it, but I'm not totally cynical and bitter. In fact, I look at your life as kind of a good thing. I know I come across as this cool laid back studly single guy, which I am, of course, but there are advantages to you getting to go home to a loving wife each night. You have someone to help take care of you if you are sick or don't feel good, you have someone to grow old with. You don't have to worry about dying sad and alone. And, let's be honest, she still looks pretty good for her age."

He turns a forced smile saying, "Marriage sounds great when you talk about it, but if it doesn't make you happy, it makes you depressed, you know. I don't hate Evelyn, but I think if we stay together, I will. I've reached a point where I don't want to be with her anymore. We were too young when we met, but I've evolved since then.… I need a drink."

I can't say no, even though I should, so we order two drams of Glenlivet, which arrive quickly.

"To the future, no matter where it might lead us," I toast.

"Cheers."

We order two more after that.

"You are more than welcome to crash at my place, by the way. I can put an air mattress in the office," I say, referring to the spare room that I've turned into my home office and storage room. "I don't know how thin the walls are, so you might have to listen to Sophie and me having loud, wild sex all the time, and that might depress you even more."

"Thanks, you dick," he chuckles. "But I'll be fine. For now, I am going to stay in the guest room, until we can sort stuff out. Since we own the house, we will have to figure out who gets that."

"You should let her have the house and move into the city where the real people live."

"Whatever, bro, you don't even live in the city."

"Closer than you do."

We finish our meals with one more round of drinks before heading back to work.

Not long after lunch, Joline messages me to come to her office. I wonder what would happen if I just completely ignore her. At some point, she would get mad and come to mine. Then what? So, I get up and go to hers.

"Yes?" I say, standing in the doorway.

"Have a seat," she gestures.

Rolling my eyes, I sit in the chair opposite her desk.

"I used this spec training document you sent Chris with one of our external clients, only to find out the system design you included isn't correct."

"I have no idea what you are talking about."

She turns her monitor around and shows me the presentation I sent to Chris a while back. The one that he had me do last minute and was mostly made up.

"Oh, that. Yeah, well, I have no idea how it is supposed to work. And I told Chris that, but he didn't listen to me," I say with a shrug of the shoulders.

"I used this with a client and it makes us look like we don't know what we are doing."

I laugh a bit at the irony of that statement, not seeing how that would be any different from any other times she meets with clients.

"Well, yep, that sucks, I guess."

"Matt, I know you and I haven't always had the best relationship. But now that I will be your manager, I think we can use this as an opportunity for a new beginning. And I would appreciate it if you didn't speak to me in that tone of voice."

"You do realize that this is only temporary until they find a replacement for Chris?"

"Temporary now, but that might change. I've decided to put my name in for the permanent position."

"Okay. Well … good for you."

"I can tell by your attitude that you are not taking me seriously. I don't know if it is because I am a woman and you have a problem with that, but—"

"Look," I interrupt. "Let me tell you right now, I don't have a problem with you because of your gender. I don't have a problem with you at all. Maybe it is you who has a problem with me and you are just projecting it on to me. Maybe I should be the one who is offended right now?"

"I have always been really nice to you, even though you are constantly rude to me. And I don't want to have to put something on your permanent record beyond what is already there. But if I have to, I will."

I pause for a second, then calmly and politely tell her to "shut the fuck up." Continuing with my calm behavior, I politely get up and leave the room.

I message Jeff on Communicator: *Hey, buddy. Just an FYI, I just told Joline to fuck off, so I'll probably be getting fired pretty soon. So, if you do need to crash at my place, give me a call. Although I might need to charge you rent now.*

I am going through my desk and putting the few personal things I have into my backpack. My coffee cup, portable computer speakers, and a hard drive that has some random crap on it. I am also adding a few pens, and Post-it notes, to the collection. One nice thing about not keeping a lot of stuff at work is not needing to use boxes when being walked out of the building. Also, I clear my browsing history and cache to get rid of any sites and passwords that might be stored on my computer.

What happened? Jeff replies.

She was being irritating, and I lost my patience with her.

Fuck bro, I'm on a conference call. I'll swing by your office when I'm done.

K

It turns out there won't be time for that, because Kerry is in my office with a serious expression on her face.

"Hi, Matt. Joline just came to me, and she is pretty upset about something you said to her. And I just want to get your side of the situation."

I think about making up some story, saying that I didn't swear at her. Play the 'it's her word against mine' argument and see if I can get away with that. But what's the point? Truthfully, I am a terrible employee. I barely do any work as it is, and even when I work, I do the bare minimum. The only reason that no one has noticed, is because everyone is so up their own asses, they pay no attention to me. It is a nice gig for that. I make decent money, and would only need to play the game for a few hours a day to be successful, yet I can't do that.

343

"I'm assuming it has to do with the fact that I told her to fuck off?"

Her eyes pop like a Looney Tunes character, and she takes another step into the office. "What she said is that you told her to shut the fuck up."

"Yeah, that sounds about right. I know it was something like that. The work fuck was definitely used."

"Do you want to explain why?"

Is it worth explaining that the woman is unqualified to bag groceries at a convenience store? Or should I tell her that if someone were to ask her specifics on any of our products that she would respond with a stare as if she were a deer in headlights? Maybe I should tell her that she would be better off hiring one of Joline's pugs to do her job. They would be cheaper labor and do better quality work.

"No, not really," is all I respond with.

"At this point, I'm going to need to have you leave for the day while I consider how to handle this."

"Yeah, I was expecting that."

I grab my coat and throw my backpack over my shoulder. We are now both standing close to the door.

"Is that alcohol on your breath?" she asks.

I respond with, "Scotch to be exact."

"I'll need your badge. At this point, there doesn't need to be any further communication. I will inform HR you have been terminated as of today."

I hand her my badge with a smile and a nod.

"That's fair," is all I can say.

She walks me out of the building.

"Good luck," she says as she sees me out the door, in a way that doesn't make me think she is actually wishing me good luck.

"Thanks."

It is odd being outside at this time of day. Yes, I come out often for a cigarette or lunch or a coffee, only it feels different this time. I have no purpose, no place I'm coming from or going to. I could just go home, but maybe a walk in the park would be in order.

Instead, I end up at the coffee shop.

"Do you ever not work?" I ask Jessie. "It seems like you are always here."

She smiles. "It feels like that sometimes. I think it's just that you usually come in early and I normally work the morning shift."

"It's not morning now." I point out.

"I'm getting off pretty soon. Just cleaning up a bit and closing out my till."

Maybe this is providence finally intervening in my life. Something good to balance out the bad, arriving just as she is getting off work for the day.

Technically, she said no before when I asked her out, but that doesn't mean she will do it again. Plus, if she rejects me a second time, it won't matter, since I will not be coming around anymore. On the other hand, there is Sophie – my girlfriend. Jessie is just some chick at a coffee shop. An attractive bubbly one, yet just some chick. One who works at a coffee shop turning down guys who ask her out, instead of working at a strip club accepting twenties from guys in exchange for a lap dance. The phone in my pocket rings with Jeff's number is on the display.

"Hey what's up?" I answer.

"Where you at?"

"Down at the coffee shop."

I point to the phone at my ear and move away from the counter while Jessie continues to make my drink.

"Come meet me for a smoke?"

"No, I'm good man. I don't really feel like being around that place right now."

"Kerry sent out an email to everyone about you. What happened?"

This intrigues me a little. Jessie sets my coffee on the counter and gives me a goodbye wave as she heads to the backroom of the shop.

"Fine, I'll meet you in the alley in a couple of minutes."

I'll have to go to the parking lot anyway to get my car, as it's still parked there.

On the way to meet them, I swing by the convenience store to pick up a fresh pack of cigarettes. Rounding the corner while juggling my coffee and opening the pack, I see Jeff and Heather standing next to him.

"I heard what happened. I'm so sorry," Heather says as I walk up, offering me a hug.

Jeff mooches one of my smokes, which we finish as I quickly recount the series of events that led to my being escorted out of the building. Including the smart-ass remark that sealed my fate. They cheer me on for saying what everyone secretly wishes to say about Joline.

"After you left," Jeff says, "Kerry sent out an email saying that you were no longer with the company. But that was it. She didn't say why in the email. Just that you have decided to 'pursue other opportunities.'"

"Well," I reply, "at least I can feel good knowing that Joline is now responsible for her job, Chris's job, and my job all at the same time and will totally fuck it up."

"At the end of the email she included a request for us to forward her the resumes of any potential candidates we might know." Jeff says.

"Ha. You should send her mine."

At the end of our conversation Heather gives me a tight hug, saying to keep in touch. Her husband was cool, she's cool, and maybe we could do couple's things. Judging by the night we hung out, she and Sophie got along well. If I am going to be in a serious relationship, we should have couple friends to hang out with and do couple's stuff like wine tastings, barbeques, and other crap like that. Now that Jeff is single, that rules him and Evelyn out. All of this is assuming that I don't end up on the street begging for change. Maybe I could hit the gym, while taking some dancing lessons, so that Sophie and I can do parties as a couple? Something for the boys and the girls to enjoy watching. Saucy!

28

I try calling Sophie, but it goes straight to voicemail. Thinking she might be at work early, I decide to drive up there, curious what she is going to say when she finds out about my lack of steady income.

At the door, the bouncer gives me a nod of recognition as I walk up.

"Hey, Sophie working?"

"Haven't seen her."

He knows me by now so doesn't give me a hard time and lets me in. Inside, I can see that the place is dead. Two girls are sitting talking with one another at a table near the stage. I don't recognize either of them. They look at me as I enter. I don't want to give them any ideas that they will make a quick twenty off of me, so I look over to the DJ booth and see that Henry is working. He gives me a slight chin tilt in greeting as "Love in an Elevator" by Aerosmith starts playing.

"Hey, busy day?" I say, referencing the lack of customers.

He smiles. "It's usually pretty slow this time of day. We sometimes might get a regular but that's about it."

"Have you seen Sophie?"

"Nope. She hasn't been in yet. She usually doesn't come in until later."

"Hm, yeah, I tried calling her but there was no answer so I thought she might be working."

There is a pause while I decide if I should get up and leave or wait for her. I break the silence by asking, "So, let me ask you, since I can't drink here, does anyone sell anything a little more under the table?"

He doesn't even pause with his response. "What you looking for?"

"Honestly, I don't know. I've had a super shitty day and just feel like getting super fucked up."

"Let me see what I can do?"

He pulls out his phone and texts someone. While waiting for a response, I go get a Pepsi from the bar and text Sophie, letting her know I'm at the club. A few minutes later Henry receives a response to his text.

"He's got some shrooms, weed, and Oxy."

"Well, I definitely don't feel like tripping by myself, and I've got some pot in the car, so oxy it is. Unwind, yet remain functional for the rest of the day."

He texts the guy back and it's not long until we are in the parking lot for the introduction. The man is standing next to a pimped out red Honda. The car has been lowered, with low-profile tires wrapped around chromed rims. He looks to be in his early 20s, wearing a worn out black hooded sweatshirt with the Raiders logo. Tall, skinny, with a shaved head, not completely bald, but most likely trimmed with clippers. If I were to pick a dealer from a lineup, I'd pick this guy. I slip him some cash – which I'm sure Henry gets a cut from – and he provides me with a small Ziplock bag that has a few pills in it. Two of which I swallow with my soda once we are back inside. I'm not drinking, so I figure I might as well take both now. Henry's fine with me hanging out in the sound booth with him, so I sit back with my phone and start playing solitaire while waiting for Sophie to show up, as the effects of the oxy begin to kick in.

The strain in my muscles relaxes, my body sinking into the chair as my shoulders drop and the tension in my mind melts away. My breath is slowing down and the gloom that has been smothering me all day fades away. Everything feels better. The bass from the speakers vibrates through my tired bones. I don't care so much about the game on my phone and lay my head back, my body heavy, close my eyes, and let my feet tap to the music.

"Hey baby," a soft velvety voice.

My heart skips a beat, my pulse quickens, as I take in a breath to settle the quiver that just ran down my spine at the sight of a muse capable of inspiring generations of artists. Her dark hair is combed smooth and straight down each side of her shoulders, so that the light from the room dances off of her with an ethereal glow. Her full red lips begging to be kissed, she's dressed business fashionable, with slacks on and a matching jacket, and a white shirt.

"What are you doing here?" she asks.

"I'm here to see you. And you look good. Very professional."

I pull her towards me and give her a long slow kiss. She tastes like cherry or raspberry, or some kind of berry lipstick.

"I know that. I got your text. Do you want to get some food? There's a good Italian place down the street."

My stomach responds with an affirmative at the mention of food. I'm feeling pretty good as we walk outside to find that it must have rained a bit, with a misty haze in the air. It feels nice to get out of the club and the loud music. There's a peacefulness in the city, as the light dims from the setting sun and the clouds give everything a softer, muted look. It's serene and calming. Getting to my car, I find I have to force myself to focus – I might be a bit too relaxed.

Arriving at the restaurant, the parking lot is cracked and warn, with only a few cars scattered in the lot. The building looks as if it was a Denny's, or something similar, at some point that closed down and reopened as an Italian place. Inside is entirely different. The lighting is subdued, tables draped in red tablecloths, and the air carries the aroma of garlic, freshly baked bread, and tomato sauce. Instinctively, my hunger grows, and mouth begins to water. Pavlov would be proud.

"So, I have exciting news," Sophie begins after our wine has been poured. A delicious Syrah.

"Oh"

"I got a new job."

"Really? I didn't know you were looking for something different. I thought you liked your job."

"I do for now, but these babies aren't going to be this perky forever." She cups her breasts. "Plus, it will be nice to work normal hours and have weekends off."

"Well, cool then. Cheers!" We toast. "Where at?"

"Amazon. As a Financial Analyst."

She got a corporate job! A soul-sucking ass-kissing Monday through Friday corporate job. Am I supposed to be happy that she wants to be one of *them*?

Trying to maintain a tone of enthusiasm I say, "Congratulations. Um, you know you won't be able to set your own hours anymore and work when you want."

"I don't mind. I'll have all my weekends off, a set salary, insurance, 401k, and stock options. One of my regulars told me about it. I'll be analyzing data and looking at process improvements, which aligns well with my degree. Plus, it will be easy for me to get to work. I can probably walk or ride a bike to get there. And she pauses, "It's only a few blocks away from where you work, isn't that nice? We could grab lunch together every now and then."

"Wait, what? One of your regulars."

Her smile drops.

A tone of annoyance enters her voice, "Yes, one of my regulars who works there told me about it, and I put him down as a referral. That's just so he can get the referral bonus."

"Oh yes, I'm sure that's all he wants is the referral bonus."

"I knew you were going to do this. I knew that you were going to assume the worst – that the only reason I could get a job is because some guy wants to fuck me. This is so typical of you."

"Holy Christ, relax for a second. For fuck's sake. I didn't say anything."

"You were implying it with your tone."

"Look, I don't care if that's why he gave you the referral or not. I assume most every guy you meet wants to have sex with you. You know what you look like. And besides, that doesn't mean you are going to go through with it. Okay? Chill."

I take a sip of my wine.

"Sorry. It just seemed like you were implying—"

"I wasn't implying anything other than I'm sure he didn't have altruistic motives, that's all. I'm not implying that I don't trust you."

"Okay. Sorry."

We each empty our wine glasses.

I have to excuse myself to the restroom, grateful that it's a single occupancy, and can lock the door. What a nightmare. First, I get fired, which sucks but is totally my fault, so I can't be too upset about it. But I accept it. Now she is going to work at one of those places because she thinks she will be working next to me. It's a good thing I bought more than just two pills from that dealer. Initially I was going to save the others for some other time, but I think a third now is justified. The others must have worn off. I take one out and use water from the bathroom sink to swallow it. As much as I want to take another one, I don't. Passing out face-first into a plate of spaghetti might sound funny, but probably isn't that fun to actually experience.

Back at the table, our food has arrived while Sophie has taken the liberty of ordering another glass of wine for each of us. Sitting down, I take a large swallow before digging into the food. I'm not sure if it is this good normally or I'm just really hungry.

Taking a pause from shoveling pasta into my face, I say, "Anyway, that is great about the new job. I'm very happy for you."

"Also, I get free lunches as well. I didn't ask if I can bring people but if it's allowed you can visit. Not every day, of course, we wouldn't want to tire of each other," she smiles.

Avoiding that subject, I ask, "So, when do you start?"

"The Monday after next. I doubt anyone at the club would freak out if I leave earlier. Girls often ghost out by not showing up. Plus, since I handle some of the books, they would need to find someone to take that over from me. From now on, lap dances are going to be exclusive for you."

"Super." I force a smile. "Are you working tonight?"

"Yes, I'll go in after dinner and start getting ready. Do you want to hang out for a bit or are you heading home?"

"I don't know. I might, or I might head home. We'll see how I'm feeling after we eat."

"Oh, are you not feeling well? I'm sorry, I didn't even ask why you were off work so early. Are you sick? You do look a little pale actually." She leans over the table and feels my forehead with the back of her hand.

"Yeah," I lie, "my head hurt and I was feeling a bit nauseous. But I took some ibuprofen and I think the wine and the food are helping."

"Don't feel like you have to stay. I can come over to your place after I get off work if you want."

"How do you normally get home? I just realized I've never asked that. The buses don't run that late, do they?"

"Taxi. There's a taxi service the owner has a deal with, so we can book in advance and get a discount on the rate. It only costs me fifteen dollars to my place. I'm sure I can get him to drop me off at yours if you want? It's closer."

"No, that's okay. I'll probably be asleep by then."

"Okay, well, if you change your mind, text me."

After dinner, we are walking to my car and I realize that I'm having a hard time walking straight. I feel okay, a little queasy actually.

"Do you want to drive?" I ask Sophie.

"You want me to drive *your* car?" she says with wide eyes.

"Yeah, I'm not feeling super well. You know how to drive a stick?"

"Yes, I can drive a stick."

357

The sexual reference is clear in her smirk, but not being in the mood, I pretend I don't get it and hand her the keys. If I weren't feeling so sickly watching her drive my car would be a bit nerve racking. She gets in and scoots the seat forward, oddly close to the steering wheel. She is taking driving my car real seriously. Shifting into gear, she starts moving slowly out of the parking lot. Looking left, then right, then left again, she pulls out on the street, shifts and almost kills the engine by letting up on the clutch too soon. As the car picks up speed, she grips the steering wheel with both hands – ten and two. Watching her makes my stomach feel a little better. That and the moist air coming in through the passenger side window.

Once we arrive, she gets out and hands me the keys.

"Good job," I tell her.

I start to follow her inside, but as we get to the door, I can hear the music and don't think I can tolerate it at the moment.

"You know, I'm going to go for a bit of a walk to clear my head. And I think I might just head home."

She gives me a goodbye kiss with a reminder to call her if I want her to come over after she gets off.

Dolls is situated near the northern edge of Lake Washington, so there must be a way to walk to the lake from here. The rain is more of a mist, and the chilly air is refreshing. The thought of taking a leisurely stroll by the lake seems like a good idea to clear my head. I walk out of the parking lot onto Lake City Way, followed up by a narrow road to the east, looking for a path leading toward the lake.

I know, because I live here, that Lake Washington is right near where I'm currently standing, yet somehow getting to it from the club is turning out to be a total pain in the ass. I've ended up in a residential area where these roads just circle and don't seem to come out anywhere. There are some nice two-story houses, sitting next door to old run-down single-story homes. And lots of trees. Jesus, between the trees and the lack of light coming from the sky, it is becoming harder and harder to see anything. The sounds of traffic from Lake City way seem to come from behind me, leading me to believe I'm heading in the correct direction. Or perhaps towards my left.

I have to stop for a minute. There is a small area with a cluster of trees and overgrown grass, probably at the edge of someone's neglected yard or a vacant lot. Sitting down, my jeans quickly become saturated with cold water seeping through them. The cool sensation is oddly soothing until suddenly my stomach revolts. No warning, just my stomach saying it is not happy and violently rejects any sustenance I have provided it with throughout the day, forcing it back up through my esophagus to hurl out of my mouth.

I lean forward to let the rest of the contents in my system out, which happens in force. My nostrils burn with putrid bitter remnants of the wine and the pasta. If I didn't know what I ate, I would say I was puking blood with long strands of mucus mixed in. The metallic bitterness of it makes me gag as I spit the lingering strands of bile onto the ground.

Putting a finger to each nostril, I blow out as much as I can. Some gum would be nice right now but since all I have is cigarettes, I get one out and light it, which instantly curls my stomach as well. After taking two drags from it, I smash it out and toss it away.

With effort, I slide my wet ass a little to the side to get away from the lingering stench of the puke. As nasty as it was, I am feeling much better now. Laying back on the cold, damp ground feels surprisingly nice, even though my pants and shoes are soaked with water. I adjust my jacket, pulling the collar up and button it to the top. Then I lay my head down and gaze at the sky through the branches above.

Somewhere in the thick fog, there is an occasional noise that I wish would stop. I'm enjoying the mist, the silence, the stillness blanketing my body. It's a sanctuary, a cloak of tranquility. The noise pauses, returns, pauses, and returns.

The phone ringing wakes me as if I had just been hit with a defibrillator. A massive breath in that I don't want, burning my lungs with ice. My clothes are soaked through and when I move, I find I'm partially frozen to the ground, taking effort to break the connection. I lean forward, instinctively reaching for the phone in my pocket. As I move, the sound of frozen fabric being ripped from the ground follows me. Chunks of ice and blades of grass cling to the back of my head. My fingers burn as if they have been held in buckets of ice water, challenging me to use them.

My body suddenly realizes how cold it is, causing me to shiver uncontrollably. As I stand up, every muscle seems to contract and spasm in a futile attempt to generate warmth.

"Fuck!"

It's completely dark by this point, with no light breaking through the cloud-covered sky. There are, however, lights from some houses in the neighborhood and I use those to navigate in an attempt to move the stiff joints in my legs, which must be how the Tin Man feels after a swim in the ocean.

I turn left, retracing my steps to find my way back to the parking lot where my car is. As I continue walking and turning onto different roads in this dense patch of winding neighborhood, my legs loosen up a bit. However, my body requires more heat than is currently available to revive it. Putting my hands in my pockets only leads to them becoming wet and even colder, as that involves sticking them into the cold wet pockets of my jacket or the cold wet pockets of my jeans. And with each step, ice water oozes through the cloth of my shoes, my socks, through my feet, and seems to settle in the space between my foot and the canvas of my shoes.

I'm walking as fast as I can, still nothing looks familiar to where I entered this mysterious suburban green space that separates Lake City Way and Lake Washington.

Luckily, I have Google Maps and with some effort manage to slip my phone from my pocket. Swiping the display to unlock it, I can see that the call was from my brother and that it is a quarter to midnight. I must have been sleeping for at least two or three hours. Christ, I can't believe that I was able to sleep like that.

"Hey, thanks for calling me back," Brad answers.

"N-n-n-no problem."

"Are you drunk? You sound like you might want to cut back."

"J-j-just freezing my balls off."

"What? What the hell are you doing?" he says with panic and concern in his voice.

"I'll tell you later. I … just need to figure out … where I am first?"

"What the hell is going on man? Are you okay?"

My brain feels like it is attached to the end of a popsicle and the kid who was holding it dropped it in the gutter.

"I seem to have … gotten lost."

"Where are you at?"

"If I knew where I am at, I wouldn't be l-l-lost. Okay, just relax. I'm not lost. I have an idea where I am … I just need to figure it out. Do you know where the … um … strip club is that Sophie works at?"

"Yes."

"And Lake Washington?"

"What the fuck! That is kind of a big area. Don't suppose you can narrow it down a little, could you?"

"The sign says 40th," I tell him, looking at the nearest street sign.

"I'm getting in my car right now, and I'm on my way there. I'm going to start at Dolls and work my way in the streets from there. Okay? If you find your way back, just call me, and I'll meet you there. Okay?"

"Okay."

We hang up and I keep walking. *Remember maps. I was going to look at the map. Which is on my phone.* I think as I keep walking in the direction of car sounds.

Brad pulls up next to my car in the parking lot. He gets out and climbs into the passenger seat.

"Jesus, it's like a sauna in here," he says.

The windows are all fogged over and I have the seats and heater turned on high while enjoying the feeling of my core body temperature rising back to normal.

He continues, "So, what's the deal? You look like shit."

"Want a beer?" I reply.

"Here?" He gestures to the club.

"No, they don't serve alcohol. My place?"

"Sure."

He follows me back to my place, and after I change my clothes into a nice pair of sweats, we sit down to crack open a beer. To be honest, I'm not that interested in drinking except that I offered him one, making me feel obligated to take one as well. The cold bottled brew tastes like crap to me. So, I set it down and start the coffeepot for an Irish coffee instead.

After a moment he says, "So, do we need to have an intervention?"

"No. I ummm"

Hmm, what do I say here? We've always been close but not that kind of close, not the talk-about-our-feelings kind of close. We are the kind of close where, when someone gets emotional, we respond by roughhousing, cracking jokes, and talking shit.

"I've had a pretty shitty day." I eventually say, "I got fired from my job." Not wanting to mention the drugs, I continue, "And, it is slightly possible that I might have consumed just a bit too much alcohol. And passed out under a tree."

He gives me that disappointed headshake that I have seen many times in the past.

"I'm sorry to hear that. What happened?"

"A change in management … and let's just say I don't get along with the person who would be my new manager."

He takes a drink from his bottle, "You know, I mean, the economy is bouncing back and with your degree and experience I'm sure you will find something else."

"Yeah, probably. The thing is, I don't want to do that kind of work anymore. I mean, I don't enjoy it." I pause. "You remember how growing up I was always like 'I'm going to be an entrepreneur,' because I thought that was cool sounding. And the thing is, now that I work in a corporate environment, I've found out, it is not cool at all. It sucks giant harry monkey balls."

"Maybe it's just that place," he says.

"No, it's not that. I just don't enjoy that type of work. I don't think I ever will. It's the people. They're so into themselves and they take the job so seriously, as if it is the only thing that matters."

He takes an exasperated breath before speaking, getting ready to lecture his younger brother.

"None of us enjoy our jobs. Do you think dad went into Boeing every day with a smile on his face? I don't love my job either, but I have a family to pay for, so I suck it up and I go in. Because it is what we do in life. We get up, we go to work, we go home, and we enjoy that little bit of time we have with family outside of work. Besides, what else would you do?"

"I don't know. That's the problem. I'm at that age where I should have already figured that out and haven't."

"What's Sophie think about you losing your job?"

"I haven't told her. She just got some fancy job at Amazon, actually."

He laughs at that, and I have to join in with the laughter.

After a pause, I say, "I think I might break up with her."

"What! You can't break up with her, she is fucking *gorgeous*. I mean *seriously* out of your league."

"Yeah, thanks asshole."

"I'm serious. I've met some of your exes and let's face it, you won't do better. Sophie is smart and beautiful. And you … well look at you, brother, you're a mess."

"That's not cool. What about Jennifer? She's cute."

"Yeah, she's very cute. And Vanessa and mom love her. But from what you've told me, isn't she a bit nutty?" he says, while twirling his finger to the side of his head. "When it comes to women, if you keep breaking up and getting back together, at some point you need to realize there is a reason you keep breaking up."

"I know," I say following with a long breath. "The thing with Sophie is, like, I think she wants me to be someone I don't want to be. She mentioned kids the other night. Remember that? When we were at moms."

The coffee is ready, so I get up and pour myself a cup and add a bit of sugar. I reach for the bottle of Jamison, but then decide against it.

"And I don't want kids, at least not right now. And not to mention the job thing. She was so happy today when she told me we would be working next to each other. And look at you. Every time we talk, you bitch about your family. You want one?" I say, gesturing to the coffee.

He shakes his head and picks up his beer for a swig.

"Well, yes, of course, I bitch about them, but that doesn't mean I don't love Vanessa and the kids."

"I'm not saying you don't. You just seem *sooo* unhappy. You never go out anymore. You suck, is what I'm saying." With a smile.

"Well fuck you too." There is a bit of silence. Before he continues. "Here's the thing. Yes, having a wife and kids sometimes sucks. You don't know what it is like to only have sex with one person for so long. Like, whenever I see a hot girl, I think about what it would be like to fuck her. Correction, whenever I see even a mildly attractive girl, I think about having sex with her. However, I never would because, when it comes down to it, I don't want to, that's just a fantasy. I love my wife and she really is the only one I want to be with."

"Yeah, but that's what I'm saying, maybe I want to have sex with other women."

"Of course, you do, you're a man. The nature of man is to put his penis into as many holes as possible. Being married is about more than that. The reason I don't come out all that often anymore is because I don't want to. I enjoy hanging out at home with Vanessa and the kids. Yeah, you and I had a lot of fun going out and causing trouble when we were younger, but none of that compares to sitting on the floor playing cars with the kids. And I can't wait until they are old enough to take them out camping or to play football—"

"Or mow the lawn," I interject.

"Or mow the lawn," he laughs.

"I don't know. Maybe I'm overthinking it. Sophie and haven't even been seeing each other all that long. Maybe she'll break up with me and it won't be an issue anyway."

"If she were smart, she would already have ditched your sad ass."

29

"So, how upset would you be if we didn't work next to each other?" I ask.

"What do you mean?"

Sophie and I are sitting across from each other in a booth at The Keg Steakhouse. After placing our orders, and having received our drinks, a Coke for me, glass of wine for her, it is time to bring the subject up.

"Well … I don't actually work for Electronix," I tell her.

"You don't. Why? What happened?"

I decided before we came out tonight to be totally honest about everything, so I tell her the story of how I felt about the place, about the various things I did leading up to my firing, and what happened on the day that I was fired.

"I'm so sorry, that's terrible."

She stands up and moves around the table to give me a hug. I hug her back before she returns to the other side of the table.

"Thanks, but I'm fine. Really"

"Um, okay, so what are you going to do now?"

Ah yes, the universal question. What am I going to do now? Because I always need to have a plan for what I am going to do next. How am I going to pay rent? How am I going to make enough money to get married, buy a house, have kids, retire, and die? And according to society's expectations, there can be no deviation. Not for me, and not for anyone else.

"I don't have a plan," I say.

"What are you going to do for money? You know, I'm here for you if you need."

"Don't worry, I'll get a job somewhere. You just found a job. So, clearly places are hiring. The thing is, I don't want to keep doing the same thing. Is any other company going to be different? I don't know. So, I think what I need to do is try to find something that I want to do … It would just be nice to not hate the idea of going into work each day, you know."

We have to pause our conversation while the server delivers our food.

As soon as he is out of earshot, I continue, "I guess I'm just going through a bit of an early midlife crisis, is what I'm saying."

"And us?"

"No, you are not part of my midlife crisis. And I wish you would stop acting like I'm dating you as some kind of lark. You are the thing I'm happiest about when it comes to my life right now."

"Get over yourself, honey. I just want to be clear about where we stand. If I'm going to invest my time in this relationship while you're dealing with this midlife crisis of yours, only for you to change your mind someday, I just don't want to waste my time, you know. So, if this is just a casual fling, let's be honest about it from the start."

We each take a few bites of our meals. I have a nice medium-rare sirloin in front of me, while Sophie ordered the salmon.

"What I am trying to say here is that I don't want to be that person you want me to be. I don't want to do the corporate thing, where I move up the ladder, go golfing with the executives, and perfect the art of ass-kissing all day in some soul-sucking corporation. It seems like that is what you are after."

She half rolls her eyes.

"Why assume that's what I want? I never mentioned wanting that from you."

"I don't know. You kind of said that's what you liked about me and because you left your job for one like mine, right next door to mine. And you knew what I did when we first started dating. So, I figured you want me to be Mr. Stable relationship guy."

"No, I want you to be you. I wasn't interested in you because of your job. I like you because you have never judged me for mine. And, okay, maybe a bit because you're a damn good kisser," she says in a sweet tone.

Leaning in over the table, I move close for a kiss, but our moment is abruptly interrupted as the waiter returns to check on us, forcing a smile on both our faces.

She continues, "I quit stripping because I don't want to do that anymore. It was always meant to be a temporary thing that I did because I could and made good money doing it. But I've seen what some of those girls end up like who do it too long. They become bitter and start hating all men. I don't want to end up like that."

"And children? Um, I don't think I want children. Or if I do, I don't want them for a long time. Not until I'm very, very old."

"Oh god, what makes you think I want children?"

"Because you said you did the other night when we were at my mother's?"

"Oh, I was just saying that because we were out with your family, and I didn't want to have that discussion with them because it is none of their business. Honey, I don't want children either. At least not now. And wow, that's kind of moving a bit fast, don't you think?"

"Yes, it is, but you know, that's what women want. To meet a man, settle down and pop babies out of their va-jay-jays like ping pong balls at a Thai strip club."

She gives me a proper full eye roll, followed with a shaking of her head.

"I'm going to ignore that analogy. Babies are little parasites. Literally, that is how they survive, by sucking the life out of your body. You can tell which girls at the club have babies, all stretch marked and saggy tits. You wouldn't believe some of the conversations we have in the changing room. It sounds awful. For right now, I like the way I look and I want to keep it that way. I told you I took the job because I want a steady paycheck, I want health insurance, and I want to stop living like a vampire sleeping all day."

"Okay," I say taking a bite of my steak before asking, "how's your fish?"

"Good. Um … if you are interested in something that pays minimum wage plus tips and has shitty hours. They are looking for a new bartender at the club."

"Dolls?"

"Yes."

"So, you are saying I should be a bartender at a strip club."

"I'm on good terms with the manager and you said you want to do something different."

"Um, it's not even a bar. The only question asked when someone orders an overpriced soda is, diet or regular?"

She shrugs her shoulder with that smile of hers. The confident, *it's all good* smile that lights up her face.

"And," I continue, "you wouldn't worry about me getting with one of the girls that work there?"

"Honey, I know the people there. If you ever pull a move like that, I'll find out," she says in a tone that implies she might simply break up with me, or possibly cut my nuts off and feed them to me. "And let's be real, we both know I'm quite the catch. I'm not worried."

"You know, I think I love you," is all I can say to that.

"I love you, too, although I'm not entirely sure why," she admits with a smile and a glimmer in her eyes that looks like the light at the end of a long, dark tunnel.

She holds her hand toward me, then with one of her perfectly manicured nails, summons me with a finger. I lean in as she gently places her index finger under my chin, pulling me closer. Our lips meet at the center of the table.

www.ingramcontent.com/pod-product-compliance
Lightning Source LLC
Chambersburg PA
CBHW060152260626
47160CB00001B/237